continued . . .

RED QUEEN

· THE CHRONICLES OF ALICE ·

Christina Henry

ACE

New York

ACE
Published by Berkley
An imprint of Penguin Random House LLC
1745 Broadway, New York, NY 10019

Copyright © 2016 by Tina Raffaele

Library of Congress Cataloging-in-Publication Data

Names: Henry, Christina, 1974– author. | Carroll,
Lewis, 1832–1898. Alice's adventures in Wonderland.
Title: Red Queen : the chronicles of Alice / Christina Henry.
Description: New York, NY : Ace, [2016]
Identifiers: LCCN 2015049583 (print) | LCCN 2016003021 (ebook) |
ISBN 9780425266809 (softcover) | ISBN 9781101618196 (ebook)
Subjects: LCSH: Alice (Fictitious character from Carroll)—Fiction. |
Imaginary places—Fiction. | BISAC: FICTION / Fantasy / Historical. |
FICTION / Fantasy / General. | GSAFD: Fantasy fiction.
Classification: LCC PS3608.E568 R43 2016 (print) | LCC PS3608.E568 (ebook) |
DDC 813/.6—dc23
LC record available at http://lccn.loc.gov/2015049583

First edition / July 2016

Printed in the United States of America
3 5 7 9 10 8 6 4

Cover illustration © Pep Monserrat; border © hoverfly/iStock/Thinkstock;
lace trim © antipathique/Shutterstock
Cover design by Judith Lagerman
Book design by Kristin del Rosario

For Lucienne Diver,
writer's cheerleader and agent extraordinaire,
because you loved this book first

An Interlude in the Old City

In a City where everything was grey and fog-covered and monsters lurked behind every echoing footfall, there was a little man who collected stories. He sat in a parlor covered in roses and this little man was small and neat, his head covered in golden-brown ringlets and his eyes bright and green like a rose's leaves. He wore a velvet suit of rose red and he urged a cup of tea on his visitor, a wide-eyed girl who looked about her in wonder. She was not certain how she'd gotten here, only that this strange little man had helped her when she thought she was lost.

"Do you like stories?" the little man asked.

He was called Cheshire, and the girl thought that was a very odd name, though this room and his cottage were very pretty.

"Yes," she said. She was very young still, and did not know yet what Cheshire had saved her from when he came upon her wandering in the streets near his cottage. She was lucky, more than lucky, that it was he who found her.

"I like stories too," Cheshire said. "I collect them. I like this story because I have a part to play in it—a small part, to be sure, but a part nonetheless.

"Once, there was a girl called Alice, and she lived in the New City, where everything is shining and beautiful and fair. But Alice was a curious girl with a curious talent. She was a Magician. Do you know what a Magician is?"

The girl shook her head. "But I have heard of them. They could do wonders but the ministers drove all the Magicians out of the City long ago."

"Well," Cheshire said, and winked. "They thought they did, but a few Magicians remained. And Alice was one of them, though she did not know it yet.

"She had magic, and because of that she was vulnerable, and a girl who was supposed to be Alice's friend sold her for money to a very bad man called the Rabbit."

"He was a rabbit?" the girl asked, confused.

"Not really, though he had rabbit ears on a man's body," Cheshire said. "The Rabbit hurt Alice, and wanted to hurt her more, wanted to sell her to a man called the Walrus who ate girls for their magic."

The wide-eyed girl put her cup of tea on Cheshire's rose-covered table and stared. "Ate? Like *really* eat?"

"Oh, yes, my dear," Cheshire said. "He ate them all up in his belly. But Alice was quick and clever and she got away from the

Rabbit before he could feed her to the Walrus. The Rabbit marked Alice, though, marked her with a long scar on her face to say she was his. My resourceful Alice marked him too—she took his eye out.

"But little Alice, she was broken and sad and confused, and her parents locked her away in a hospital for confused people. There she met a madman with an axe named Hatcher, a madman who grew to love her.

"Hatcher and Alice escaped from the hospital, and traveled through the Old City in search of their pasts and in search of a monster called the Jabberwocky who made the streets run with blood and corpses."

The girl shuddered. "I know about him."

"Then I should tell you that Alice, clever Alice, turned him into a butterfly with her magic so that he could never hurt anyone again, and she put that butterfly in a jar in her pocket and there he is till this day—unless he is dead, which is entirely possible."

"And what of the Rabbit and the Walrus?" the girl asked. "What became of them?"

"Nothing good, my dear," Cheshire said. "Nothing good at all, for they were bad men and bad men meet bad ends."

"As they should," the girl said firmly. "What about Alice? Did she have a happy ending?"

"I don't know," Cheshire said.

PART ONE

. . .

The
Forest

Alice was a Magician, albeit one who did not know very much about her own magic. She was escaping a City that hated and feared Magicians, which was one of the reasons why she didn't know so very much about it. Alice was tall and blue-eyed and a little broken inside, but her companion didn't mind because his insides were more jumbled than hers could ever be.

Hatcher was a murderer, and he knew quite a lot about it. Alice thought that Hatcher knew so much about it that he ought to be capitalized too—a Magician and her Murderer. He was tall and grey-eyed and mad and dangerous but he loved her too, and so they stayed together, both stumbling toward a future that would let them leave their past in the past.

She wished she could do something magical like in a fairy story—make a carpet to fly on, or summon up a handy unicorn

to ride. It seemed very useless to be a Magician without spec-
tacular tricks at hand.

At the very least she would have liked to be able to summon
a bicycle, though the thought of Hatcher balancing on two
wheels while holding his axe made her giggle. Anything would
be better than this tunnel, an endless, narrow semidarkness with
no relief in sight. She never would have entered it had she known
it would take so long to get out again—three days at least, by her
reckoning.

Alice thought it must be close to that long, although they
had no true way to determine the passage of time.

They slept when they were tired, ate what little provisions
they had left in the sack Hatcher carried. Soon enough they were
hungry and thirsty, though it had become a familiar feeling and
therefore just another discomfort. Food and water never seemed
to be a regular occurrence since their escape from the hospital
and its regular delivery of porridge morning and night.

During the long walk Alice dreamed of the open fields and
trees that she would find at the end, a beautiful verdant land
described by Pipkin, the rabbit they rescued from the Walrus'
fight ring. Anything, she thought, would be better than the
crushing fog and darkness of the Old City.

Hatcher, in his own Hatcher way, alternated between moody
silence and fits of mania. When not brooding he would run
ahead of Alice and then back again over and over until he was
white and breathless. Sometimes he stopped to box with the
walls until his hands were bloody, or take chunks out of the wall

with his axe. It seemed to Alice that there was more brooding and less running about than usual, though to be fair he had more to brood on.

He'd just remembered he had a daughter, more than ten years after she'd been sold to a trader far to the East. It wasn't really his fault that he'd forgotten her, because the events of that day had turned him from Nicholas into the mad Hatcher he was now. Alice suspected that there was guilt and anger and helplessness all churned up inside him, and these feelings mixed with his dreams of blood and sometimes she saw all of this running over his face but he never spoke of it.

And, Alice thought, *he's probably a bit angry with me for putting him to sleep when it was time to face the Jabberwocky.*

Alice didn't regret the decision, though she knew it didn't suit Hatcher's notion of himself as her protector. Hatcher had a tendency to swing his axe first and think later, and as it happened, no blood-spilling had been required to defeat the ancient Magician.

She felt the reassuring weight of the little jar in her pants pocket, deliberately turned her mind away from it. Soon enough the Jabberwocky inside would be dead, if he were not already.

The tunnel, which proceeded along level ground since the initial entry into the Old City, sloped abruptly upward. It was then that Alice noticed the lanterns set at intervals had disappeared and that the interior of the cave was lightening.

Hatcher trotted up the steep incline while Alice labored after him, tripping several times and clawing in the dirt to push her body upright. Everything always seemed much harder for Alice, who was not as strong nor as graceful as Hatcher. Occasionally it seemed that her body was actively working against her progress.

When they finally emerged, blinking in the sunlight, Alice decided her disposition was not well suited to a life underground.

She crawled over the lip of the cave entrance, half blind after days underground and squinting through slitted eyes, expecting the soft brush of grass beneath her fingers. Instead there was something that felt like very fine ash, and a few scrubby grey plants poking brave faces toward the sun.

Alice forced her eyes to open wide. It took much more effort than it ought to; her eyes did not want all that glaring light and kept stubbornly closing against her will.

Hatcher ran ahead, already adjusted and seemingly glorying in the freedom after the constraint of the tunnel. She was aware of him as a half-formed shadow through her partially closed lids. He stopped suddenly, and his stillness made Alice struggle to her feet and take a proper look around. Once she had she almost wished she hadn't, for this wasn't an improvement over their recent tunnel life.

They had emerged on the side of a hill that faced what must have once been an open meadow, perhaps dotted with wildflowers and trees and filled with tall grasses. Now there was nothing before them but a blackened waste stretching for miles, broken only by the occasional mound or hill.

"This isn't what we expected," Hatcher said.

"No," Alice said, her voice faint. "What happened here?"

Hatcher shrugged. "There's no one around to ask."

Alice fought down the tears that threatened as she looked at the blight all around them. There was nothing to cry about here—no criminals kidnapping women, no streets lined with blood and corpses, no Rabbit to steal her away.

It's only a wasteland. There's no one here to hurt you or Hatcher. You can survive this. This is nothing.

Perhaps if she repeated this to herself often enough she could make it true. *This is nothing, nothing at all.*

But the promise of paradise beyond the walls of the City had sustained her, the dream of a mountain valley and a lake and a sky that was actually blue instead of grey. To have been through so much and discovered only this burned-out land seemed such a poor reward that crying seemed the only reasonable option. She let a few disappointed tears fall, saw them drop into the ash beneath her feet and immediately disappear. Then she scrubbed her face and told herself that was enough of that, thank you very kindly.

Alice walked around the hill to see what lay in the other direction. The New City sparkled in the distance, its high walls and tall white buildings shimmering on the horizon. Caught within the ring of the New City was the blackened sore of the Old City, completely encircled by its neighbor.

"I never realized it was so big," Alice said as Hatcher joined her. His burst of energy had passed and he was subdued again, though by his troubles or by the landscape Alice did not know.

The combined Cities were a vast blot upon the landscape, stretching into the horizon. *Of course it must be tremendous,* Alice thought. It took them many days to cross from the hospital to the Rabbit's lair, and still they had seen only a fraction of the Old City. The close-packed structures of the Old City had, somehow, made it seem smaller.

"Now what to do?" Alice muttered, returning to the cave entrance. Hatcher trailed behind her, silent, his mind obviously elsewhere.

They had counted upon being able to forage for food and water once they escaped the tunnel, but that seemed impossible now.

"There must be a village or town somewhere," she said to Hatcher. "Not everyone in the world comes from the City. And there must be something beyond this blight, else Cheshire and the other Magicians would not have been interested in maintaining the tunnel."

Hatcher crouched and ran his fingers through the dark substance that covered the ground. "It was all burned."

"Yes," Alice agreed. "But burned unnaturally, somehow. That doesn't seem like ordinary fire ash."

"Magic?" Hatcher asked.

"I suppose," she said. "But why would a Magician want to burn all the land in sight? And how recently has all this occurred? It seems the burning goes right up to the edge of the New City. How was it that the City was not burned too?"

"Whatever happened, you can be certain that no one in the City was told of it," Hatcher said.

"But the residents of the New City," Alice said. "How could such a thing occur without their notice?"

"You once lived in the New City," Hatcher said. "Did you notice anything that you weren't told to notice by the ministers?"

"No," Alice admitted. "But then, I was a child when I lived there. I didn't notice much beyond my own garden, and my governess, and my family."

And Dor, she thought, but she didn't say it aloud. Little Dor-a-mouse, scuttling for the Rabbit. Dor, who had sold Alice to a man who'd raped her, who'd tried to break her. Dor, her best friend in all the world.

Thinking of Dor made Alice remember their tea party with the Rabbit and the Walrus, and the enormous plate of cakes, beautiful cakes with high crowns of brightly colored frosting. She'd give anything for a cake right now, although not one of the Rabbit's cakes, which had been filled with powders to make her sick and compliant.

For a moment she wished for one of Cheshire's magic parcels filled with food, but then remembered that such a thing would require a connection to Cheshire that she didn't want.

She might be able to summon up food for them. Her only excuse for not doing such a thing before was that she wasn't yet accustomed to the idea of being a Magician. Perhaps, when they were far from the City, she could search for another Magician, one who might teach her. They couldn't all be terrible, couldn't all be like the Caterpillar and the Rabbit and Cheshire and the Jabberwocky.

She must stop thinking of the Jabberwocky. The wish had said she would forget him, and he would die because of that. So she needed to forget, because she never again wanted to see the results of the Jabberwocky's rage. The streets of the Old City lined with bodies and rivers of blood, those streets utterly silent, nothing living remaining except her and Hatcher.

Much like this, really, Alice thought. Just her and Hatcher and the burned land.

Sitting in the ruins of what was probably magical fire, remembering the horrors committed by those men in the Old City, the belief of the existence of a good Magician seemed naïve.

"Maybe power corrupts them," Alice said.

It was a frightening thought, one that made her suddenly reluctant to try any magic at all. She'd spent years under the influence of drugs that made her think she was insane. She was only just learning who Alice was, what it was like to be her own self. She would rather use no magic at all than become someone unrecognizable.

"Power corrupts who?" Hatcher asked.

"Hm?"

"You said, 'Maybe power corrupts them.'"

"The Magicians," she said. "We've yet to meet a decent one."

"Yes," Hatcher agreed. "That doesn't mean they don't exist. In the story Cheshire told us, a good Magician saved the world from the Jabberwocky. At least for a while."

"Of course," Alice said. "I'd forgotten."

"It's easy to forget the good things," Hatcher said, and this statement seemed to set off another fit of brooding. He sat back in the ash and began idly drawing with the point of one of the many knives he carried.

Alice decided to leave him to it. Hatcher wasn't voluble at the best of times, and forcing him to talk would only leave them both irritated.

It couldn't hurt to try a little magic. They obviously weren't going any farther at the moment, and Alice was hungry.

The only magic she had performed thus far—on purpose, anyway—had been in the form of wishing. She'd wished the Jabberwocky into a butterfly; she'd wished the connection between herself and Cheshire broken. A delicious meal should only be a wish away, then.

Alice sat a few feet away from Hatcher and his drawings. She noted that he wasn't merely idly tracing shapes in the dirt. There appeared to be a pattern to his work, and the pattern was growing larger and more complex. He was on the balls of his feet now, crouched like a monkey, darting to and fro as he added to the design on the ground.

"What are you doing?" she asked, curious.

He grunted at her, and Alice frowned. *Well, if he is going to be that way about it.* She deliberately turned her back on his activity and concentrated on her own task.

First, she thought with a thrill of anticipation, *what to wish for?*

Alice had a terrible sweet tooth, one that had not been suppressed in the least by ten years of bland oat porridge. Her first instinct was to wish for plates of cookies and cakes, and a large pot of steaming tea and pretty china cups to pour the tea into. But that was not a practical wish. Even Alice knew that they could not walk for miles on nothing but frosting and butter.

What, then? Something that would pack up easily in Hatcher's bag, and not spoil in this bleak, hot landscape. It was very hot, Alice realized. Beads of sweat had formed on her forehead and upper lip and trickled down her chest. The tunnel they'd left was cool and dark. Now the full scorch of the sun made the shirt and jacket and heavy trousers Alice wore cling to her skin, which resulted in her being more cross and more uncomfortable than she already was.

She took the jacket off, transferring the little knife she always carried to the belt of her trousers. She put her hands in front of her, palms down, though it felt a little foolish to do so. Alice had an odd idea that the magic would come out of her hands. She closed her eyes and focused hard on what she wanted.

"I wish for . . . six meat pies," she decided. "And a dozen apples. And a jug of fresh milk."

She opened her eyes and peered under her hands. Nothing. Only fine grey ash, and the hot wind lazily blowing it in little swirls and eddies.

Alice frowned. Now, why hadn't that worked? She kept her hands in her lap this time, and repeated the words, staring at the blank space in front of her intently.

Again, nothing. She realized Hatcher had ceased his frenzy of activity and peered over her shoulder.

"I don't think it works like that," Hatcher said. He sounded almost normal, like the fever that seized him had passed.

"What do you know about it?" Alice snapped. She felt a little embarrassed, like she'd been caught being naughty.

Hatcher shrugged. "As much as you, I suppose. Or probably less."

"Then why do you think it wouldn't work?" Alice asked.

"You're trying to make something out of nothing," Hatcher said. "When you wished the Jabberwock into the jar as a butterfly, you were using the Jabberwock himself to start with. When you broke the connection between you and Cheshire, you were breaking something already in place. You didn't start with nothing."

Alice frowned. "And what about when I pushed the Jabberwocky away from you? I made something out of nothing then."

Hatcher shook his head. "No. You used your own fear, your own love, and you pushed it toward the Jabberwock."

"I'm hungry and thirsty," Alice said. "Why can't that make food, then, if love and fear can chase away a monster?"

"You're the Magician," Hatcher said, and he waited to see what she would do.

"Something from something," Alice muttered. "So many rules, always, no matter where we go. What's the good of being a Magician if you can't help yourself now and then?"

"I'd say all the Magicians we've known have done nothing but help themselves," Hatcher said. He cocked his head to one side. "Do you hear that?"

"What?" Alice asked. She was busy scooping ash and piling it into little mounds, each about the size of the meat pies she wished for.

Hatcher stood, gazing off in the direction of the City, his hand shielding his eyes from the sun. "Something buzzing."

Alice heard it then—a low, whiny sort of buzz, not the kind an animal would make, but a machine. She abandoned her ash project and stood next to Hatcher, mirroring his posture. There was a black blot in the air just above the City.

"What is that?" Alice asked, trying to make sense of the shape and the noise.

Hatcher shook his head slowly. "I don't know, but it isn't natural. No insect makes that kind of noise."

"No insect should be that large either," Alice said. "Unless it's magical."

"Cheshire?" Hatcher wondered aloud. "But why such an obvious display?"

"Yes, it seemed he preferred to keep his power under wraps," Alice said. "He likes to operate in secret."

Perhaps there was another, unknown Magician in the City. This was certainly possible, even probable. The very existence of the Magicians that they had already encountered proved the City government had been unable to drive them all out.

The buzzing grew in volume despite the distance of the object. As Alice and Hatcher watched, the black blot broke into several smaller blots.

"A flying machine?" Alice asked.

"I've never known of one so small," Hatcher said. "You saw them from the window in the hospital."

"Yes," Alice said.

The airships were always large and silver and slow-moving, and the passing of one had seemed as thrilling as a parade, given how infrequently they flew over the skies of the City and the lack of excitement generally in the hospital. Entertainment, as such, was limited to the days when the workers would try to take Hatcher out for a bath. Alice amused herself some days by counting the number of noses and fingers Hatcher managed to break before they gave in and left him in his cell.

There was a flash of metal from the approaching objects, and the buzzing that preceded them ground in Alice's skull. She covered her ears just as Hatcher tugged her toward the tunnel entrance. She gave him a puzzled look and removed one hand long enough to hear his answer.

"Whatever it is, we don't want to be out in the open," Hatcher said.

Hatcher ducked inside the tunnel, pulling Alice after him. She would have rolled down the incline again if he wasn't gripping her upper arm with a strength that bruised. Alice dug her elbows and toes into the packed dirt, pressing her hands hard against her ears. Beside her, Hatcher had the eye-rolling look he got when he was agitated. The noise had set him off again. He was shaking all over, a fine trembling like clenched muscles about to release.

And just when he'd settled down, too, Alice thought. She

didn't mind his fits as much as she probably ought to, but he could be very impulsive when he was in this state. Part of her feared that he would leap out of the hole in the ground and attract the attention of whatever approached.

The noise penetrated the mouth of the tunnel, seemed to seep into the earth and through the flimsy cover of Alice's fingers. She felt like a worm, returning to the earth for safe haven.

"My jacket," she said, remembering she had left it out in the open on the side of the hill. And she also remembered the complicated pattern Hatcher had carved in the ash. Whatever creature approached, Alice hoped it would not notice the signs of their presence.

The sound reached its crescendo long before the objects passed overhead. Alice actually thought for a moment that the blots had gone by and she had somehow missed them.

Then there was a flash of silver, followed by another, and another. They seemed like a weird school of fish in a stream, miraculously lifted to the clouds. Alice realized what she was seeing were flying machines, as she'd initially thought, but not like any flying machine she had seen before.

Instead of the huge, stately airships with their giant balloons and large propellers, these were slim pods, perhaps the length of a tall man. Each pod had a small propeller at one end, though Alice could not see how the tiny things made the pods move or how they would have managed to get off the ground without the assistance of magic. Each pod was ridden astride by a man in strange black clothing—clothes that clung tightly to their bodies and covered their head and faces.

Mother would call those clothes indecent, Alice thought.

She glanced at Hatcher and noticed his lips moving. He silently counted all the ships until they disappeared, sweat running down both sides of his face as he fought for some measure of control. The fliers had not appeared to notice the hole in the side of the hill, the pattern carved in the ground or Alice's jacket.

They clambered out of the tunnel again, peering after the pods that gradually shrunk and disappeared into the horizon.

"I don't like this," Alice said. "I thought that once we'd escaped the City, we would also escape the reach of the City."

"Why would you think that?" Hatcher asked. "Cheshire and the others went out of the boundaries. It only stands to reason that those in power would too."

"Yes, of course," Alice said, but she was troubled. Troubled by these machines that she had never seen before, and by the mysterious figures that rode them. Troubled by the thought that they might be pursuing something or someone beyond the borders of the City. Could someone—a minister, a Magician, a doctor—have discovered that Alice and Hatcher survived the fire? Were they being hunted?

She said nothing of this to Hatcher. He would scoff and say that they weren't that interesting to the doctors or her family. Or else he would tell her that of course they were being pursued, and make her feel silly and naïve for not considering it in the first place.

Alice realized she stood before the pattern Hatcher had so carefully carved in the ash. She squatted on her heels to get a better look.

It was a five-pointed star, encircled by six smaller stars. Five of the stars were of equal size, but the top one shone very large and bright. As Alice stared at the star it seemed to shift in the sand, to glow in a way that could not be possible without magic.

Alice stood up quickly, and the star returned to its original state.

"What's all this?" she asked Hatcher, gesturing toward the drawing.

"It's the sign of the Lost Ones," Hatcher said.

"Who are the Lost Ones?" Alice asked, glancing at him.

Hatcher seemed surprised. "I haven't a clue."

Alice sighed. "A vision, then. Something else we will have to see or do later."

She bit back the comment that his Seeing might be more useful if it were more specific. She wasn't exactly a competent Magician, and therefore not in a position to criticize Hatcher's abilities.

"It might have something to do with Jenny," Hatcher said, and he could not disguise the hope in his voice. He'd forgotten his daughter and remembered her again, and now he was clutching for any hint or hope of her.

Alice put her hand on his shoulder. He gripped her fingers

with his opposite hand so that his arm crossed his body, like he was holding tight to keep from flying apart.

"Let's see if I can't make some pies out of ash," Alice said gently, pulling her hand away. "It seems we have a very long way to go."

After several attempts Alice managed to produce two small pies (though the pies were inclined to be greasy and the gravy was not very good), four pitiful-looking apples, and some milk that was so curdled they immediately dumped it onto the ground.

"At least you were able to make food," Hatcher said philosophically as he chewed on his pie. Something crunched between his teeth and he fished out a small bone.

Alice tried telling herself that something was better than nothing, but the pie was barely edible.

"I wonder if it doesn't taste good because I made it from ash," Alice said, and again thought longingly of frosted cakes and hot tea. It would be lovely to even have plain water to wash away the gritty taste of the pies.

They packed away the apples, not knowing whether any decent food would be in the offing, and began to trudge in the direction the pods had flown. The only clue they had to Jenny's location was that she was in the East. The City was to the west, so they went the opposite way.

Alice tried not to worry about the men who had flown out of the City on the strange machines. She tried not to worry about the fact that they were horribly exposed in this landscape, and that they had no way of knowing what types of weapons those men carried. She tried not to think about the gun that Hatcher had hidden in his coat, the gun with one bullet for him and one for her, just in case anyone tried to capture and return them to the hospital.

She tried, and failed.

In the distance were a few features, small hills like the ones that they had emerged from. Alice wondered if they also had tunnels within, and if so, where those tunnels might lead.

"Look," Hatcher said suddenly, and pointed at the ground.

Imprinted in the ash was the distinct paw print of a rabbit. A very, very large rabbit.

"Pipkin!" Alice said. She'd half forgotten the rabbit they'd saved from the Walrus, and the band of girls who'd joined him in escaping the City.

How disappointed they must have been, Alice thought sadly, *when they left the tunnel and discovered this blight instead of the green land they were promised.*

Alice knew her own disappointment could have been nothing to those girls, those girls who had been locked away in bedrooms with men they did not know, and some of them locked in cages to be eaten by the monster who'd captured them.

"I wonder how far ahead they are," Alice said.

"Can't be that far, if the print is still clear in the ground," Hatcher said. "It's not so windy."

Alice peered ahead, hoping to see figures moving on the horizon. There was nothing but blank sameness, and they themselves were the only living creatures in sight.

She resigned herself to another long and tedious walk, and let her mind drift away as they trudged through the ash.

"How did you do that, Alice?"

A little girl's voice. Dor's voice. It was full of wonder and, Alice knew now but had not known then, jealousy.

"I don't know!" Alice said as they both peered at the little blue jewels that had appeared on Alice's palm.

She had been holding a blue forget-me-not, plucked illicitly from her mother's carefully tended garden, and thinking that the petals were like little jewels in the sun, and suddenly they were jewels.

Not very useful, Alice thought, *making jewels out of flowers.* Too bad she had never made bread out of dirt. She might have a better clue how to fill their bellies then.

Alice had spent the majority of the last ten years feeling hungry, but it had never bothered her so much in the hospital. Mostly that was because they kept her drugged all day, so that everything seemed to drift around her like a dream.

Since they'd escaped she'd been aware of an almost constant low-level gnawing in her belly, a feeling that she might never be full enough, and that feeling was only exacerbated by the constant threat they'd been under—threat of capture, torture, death.

What Alice really wanted was to sit right down and have a nice meal, and then a long sleep, and she also wanted to take a really good bath, a proper bath in a copper tub with hot water poured from kettles and sweet-smelling bubbles everywhere. The closest thing she'd had to a bath in recent days was when she'd swum through the lake in the center of Cheshire's maze to save Hatcher from . . . whatever that creature had been.

There had been quite a lot more blood and fighting and scrabbling through the dirt since then, and Alice was uncomfortably aware of the scent of her own body after these exertions.

The sun went down, and the moon came up, and the wasteland around them seemed suddenly alive with things that skittered and crawled and shifted through the sand, shadows that made Alice creep closer to Hatcher.

Hatcher's grey eyes shone in the moonlight like a cat's, and so did the blade of his axe. This was Hatcher's time, his element, the place where he could show the hunters that he was not to be hunted.

Alice took out her own knife, ashamed of her fear. She'd faced down men and animals more dangerous than any small scuttling thing that might be out here. All these creatures were small, barely recognizable as live things and not simply tricks of the eye. They couldn't possibly pose the same threat as, say, the Walrus.

Then suddenly the sky was filled with a bursting light so bright that it seemed the sun had risen again and launched straight to the top of the sky, impatient with the moon's stay.

Alice fancied that it was the flare of a torch, for it flickered like fire, though no fire she'd ever known could be so large.

Save the fire that burned this land, you nit, she thought.

The light revealed what the darkness had concealed. Dozens of small creatures dotted the landscape around Alice and Hatcher, their eyes gleaming in the flare of yellow that illuminated the night. At first Alice thought they were stoats, but a closer look told her that the animals weren't quite right. No stoat Alice had ever seen had long curving fangs like that, or mad red eyes.

"Alice," Hatcher said, and his voice was very calm as he stared into the distance, at the place where the light emerged from the horizon. "What if Jenny hates me?"

This was the reason for all the brooding, then, although Alice felt it would have been better if Hatcher had waited until they were not in potentially mortal danger to discuss it.

"She likely will," Alice said, inching around behind Hatcher so that they stood back-to-back. She felt it was best not to lie generally, and found she was incapable of lying to Hatcher in any case. "Little girls think their fathers can do anything, save them from any danger. Your father is the strongest person in the world."

Alice remembered the wonder she'd felt when she'd learned her father had killed a rat that had gotten into the house when she was young. She'd thought her papa was the greatest hero who ever lived.

Alice was sure that Jenny had cried every night for her father. And when he didn't come she would have learned to despise him for not saving her.

"That's what I would have done, if I could have remembered her," Hatcher said as the light began to fade. "I would have killed anyone who ever touched her, ever harmed her. I would have mangled them to pieces like I slaughtered the men who killed her mother. But I don't expect that intentions will count for much now."

"No," Alice said. "I don't expect that they will."

The stoats, or whatever they were, moved closer. They made low hissing noises in the backs of their throats. It was not the sibilant song of a snake, but a rough, threatening sound that was harsh in the silence.

Alice had a brief vision of being swarmed, overwhelmed by these tiny vicious animals, her flesh stripped from her bones even as she screamed out her death wail.

"No," she said.

The animals stopped. She could barely see their faces now as the blaze of light faded to a faint glow. Their heads tipped to one side in unison, suddenly doglike, curious.

"No," she repeated, and this time she put force behind it, and the air shimmered with magic. "Let us pass."

The last droplet of light disappeared, leaving them in a dark that seemed closer than before. But Alice did not need her eyes.

There was still so much about magic Alice did not understand. There was power in her words, and the creatures responded to it, though she did not know why. The night was as it should be again, dark and full of stars.

All about them the stoat-like animals kept still as Alice and Hatcher passed, their silence somehow respectful.

Hatcher sighed, and Alice felt rather than saw the relaxing of his axe at his side. He was disappointed, she knew. In his heart Hatcher was a killer, and he longed to exercise his best skill, to feel the crunch of bone and muscle beneath the blade, to be baptized by the hot splatter of blood. He would regret any missed opportunity for wild death and mayhem.

Alice knew all this, knew that his heart wanted this release. She also knew that, somewhat inexplicably, he was a good man, and that the latter impulse kept Hatcher's murderous tendencies in check—mostly.

She did not know how far they walked that first night, but the notion of sleep never entered her mind. The thought of placing her body against that slippery ash, vulnerable and insensate to all around her, did not seem even a little bit wise. Just because the stoats did not attack now didn't mean they wouldn't take their chance if it were offered.

A persistent worry troubled her too, keeping her thoughts so busy she couldn't imagine quieting them to sleep. She'd been convinced (somewhat naïvely, it now seemed) that if they left the City they would also leave the City's influence. The strange flying machines and their mysterious mission seemed to indicate that would not be the case, that the City's tentacles stretched away from its bloated body like a living monster. How far could those tentacles reach?

Alice wished to shed her life in the City as a snake shed its skin. She feared being snatched back into that life, plucked from her freedom. And she wished to be as far as possible from Cheshire. He might decide that she was too valuable to let escape.

She must have dozed off, for one moment she watched the slightly darker shadows that were her feet moving against the black ash, and the next moment the sun was shining and she was tucked against Hatcher's chest like a child.

He moved steadily through the strange desert, seemingly untroubled by her weight in his arms. Alice blinked in the glare and noticed several large birds circling overhead.

"Best put me down, Hatch," Alice said. "Those birds are looking for a meal."

"They are, but not us," Hatcher said, placing her on her feet. He ran his hand over her short hair and down over her cheek, lingering for a moment. Then he pointed straight ahead. "Whatever they're after is up there."

There were several black shapes disfiguring the flat landscape ahead. It was difficult to tell, owing to the utter sameness in all directions, how far away those shapes might be.

Alice didn't want to see what was there. It couldn't be anything good, and she'd had enough of what wasn't good. But they were heading east, and the dark shapes were right in their path.

When they reached the place where the vultures collected, Hatcher spent a few enjoyable moments chasing the birds away with his axe. Alice stared at the bodies in confusion. They were all piled together in a charred heap, and there was barely enough flesh remaining for the scavengers to bother with.

"What caused the burning?" Alice wondered aloud, approaching the corpses. Then she stopped, her heart in her throat, choking her.

"Whatever's burned these fields to nothing, I expect," Hatcher said. "The same something that made the sky light up last night."

Hatcher hefted his axe from one hand to the other and eyed a truculent vulture who'd refused to leave with the rest of his fellows.

"Hatcher," Alice said.

He appeared not to hear her as he stalked toward the bird. It had its back turned to Hatcher and was busily grooming one wing.

"Hatcher," she repeated, and this time she pierced the fog.

"What is it?" he asked, straightening.

The vulture glanced behind, noted Hatcher's proximity and flew away.

"Pipkin," she said, and pointed.

Now that she knew what was there, Alice could make out the charred shape of a rabbit's ear, a blackened shoe, the delicate rib cage of a girl.

"This wasn't how it was supposed to end for them," Alice said. Her grief threatened to bubble over, to explode out into the desert, to cover the corpses of those who were supposed to have found a better life. "They were supposed to be happy in green fields."

It had all been for nothing, Alice thought. Their suffering, their escape. She didn't feel, suddenly, that there was much hope for her or Hatcher.

"The world gobbles us and chews us and swallows us," Hatcher said, in that uncanny way he had of reading her thoughts. "I think happy endings must be accidents."

"But we hope for them all the same," Alice said. She looked sadly at the remains of those hopeful faces. *Above all, we hope not to die in terror.*

They walked on, leaving the remains of the giant rabbit and the girls behind them, as they must. Alice tried to leave her sadness behind, but it clung to her heart like a wraith.

By the dawn of the third day Alice was heartily sick of the desert, for that was what this surely was, whether created by man or nature. It was hot and dry and the sun was unrelenting. She would have been thrilled beyond imagining to see a ray of sunshine in the Old City; now she wished for even a single cloud to relieve the constant glare.

They slept each afternoon, when the sun was at its zenith and any creature with sense hid from it. The long-fanged stoats did not trouble them, although a few occasionally followed Alice and Hatcher's footsteps, sniffing curiously.

Each night Alice observed the same flare of light from the sky, although it came from a different direction each time. As they moved farther east the light tended behind them. The mysterious men on flying machines did not reappear. Alice wondered if they were the cause of the strange light in the sky, or if they were seeking it.

Alice crested a rise, one of the few they'd encountered, and stopped beside Hatcher.

He gestured in front of them at what he obviously thought might be a hallucination.

"Is that real?" he asked.

Alice blinked, and when she looked the hallucination was still there.

The rise they stood upon overlooked a little valley. About halfway down the slope, the fields of ash abruptly terminated, as if stopped by an invisible wall. Beyond were green grass, and fragrant pines, and an expanse of rolling hills that gradually stretched into snowcapped mountains, far in the distance.

A silver-blue stream wound through the little valley, and beside it was a series of small neat buildings, almost like a doll's village. Smoke wisped from chimneys, carrying the scent of breakfast cooking.

"Do you see it?" Hatcher asked.

"Yes," Alice said, and relief broke over her.

She'd half thought they would never see water again or sleep without a cradle of ash. She'd forgotten what it was like to see without grit clogging her eyes or to breathe without inhaling fine particles of dust. She was too exhausted and hungry to run down the hill—and she would likely fall flat on her face if she tried—but her pace quickened as much as she was able.

Hatcher scampered ahead, as always seemingly unaffected by fatigue and lack of food. When he reached the stream he dropped his pack on the bank and waded right in, dipping his head beneath the water and splashing like a happy dog.

Alice was uncomfortably aware of just how dirty she was, but at the same time she glanced uneasily at the little village just a short distance away. Its citizens might not appreciate two strangers swimming in their local waters.

She knelt by the bank and cupped her hand in the stream, drawing it to her mouth. It was clear and cool and delicious. Alice had never tasted water like this before, not even when she lived in the New City. It was like melted snow and sweet honey and summer flowers and an autumn breeze all in one, and she was so thirsty. She wanted to gobble it all down, plunge her face into the stream and drink until she was a spider bloated with the juice of too many flies.

But Alice knew that would give her a stomachache, especially after so many days without proper food or drink. So she contented herself with a few careful sips, enough to relieve the parched withering feeling in her throat. Then she washed her face and hands and neck and splashed a little water in her hair, and hoped that her scent would not offend any villagers they met.

Hatcher's odor, she noticed as he climbed out of the stream and flopped on the bank, had not improved by the dunking of his whole self in the water. Steam rose from his clothes and carried with it a sour stink that reminded Alice of a dog that just rolled in the streams of refuse that ran along the curbs in the Old City.

They lay in the sun for a time, content to let the breeze touch their faces and hair, to breathe in warm green smells and, underneath, the hominess of black earth, an earth that let things grow instead of killing them. Then Hatcher sat up, his nostrils flared, and a moment later Alice smelled it too.

"Bread," she said, breathing the word out like a prayer.

She could already taste it on her tongue, slathered in fresh sweet butter and berry jam, filling up all the aching, gnawing places under her ribs. Perhaps there would also be tea, or milk, or soft creamy cheese. Perhaps there would even be cake.

Without awareness of her actions she rose and followed the wafting smell of baking bread. Hatcher was a few paces ahead of her, his nose in the air like a hunting animal sniffing out prey. They found a little worn track from the riverbank and followed it to the edge of town.

All of the houses were small and well kept, porches swept, pretty little flowers in boxes at the windows, blue and pink and yellow. Two rows of homes faced one another over the main road, which led to a small village square and a fountain spouting the same beautifully clear water as the spring. Each building in the square could be identified, not by a written sign indicating ownership or the type of business, but by a small picture painted on a board. A hat for the milliner, a horseshoe for the farrier, a loaf of bread for the baker.

These little icons only emphasized the sense of a doll's village instead of a real one, and that sensation was reinforced by the lack of people. Hatcher paused as he reached the fountain and Alice noted his stance had changed. He'd lost the aspect of a sniffing dog. His axe was in his hand, the knuckles tight around the handle.

The scent of bread was stronger here, as the baker was directly opposite. Alice reached for her own little knife, resolutely ignoring her rumbling stomach.

"It's not right," Hatcher said. "Where are they?"

"What if we look inside?" Alice asked. "Maybe they are only wary of strangers. They *are* alone here in a valley on the edge of a desert. New folk likely don't pass this way often."

"I suppose," Hatcher said, and he sounded very grumbly, "this means you want me to put away my axe again."

Alice laughed, a short laugh that surprised the tension out of her. She tucked her knife away. "Wouldn't you prefer to meet some slightly suspicious but otherwise kindhearted villagers rather than be forced to hack your way through a population of enemies?"

Hatcher only grunted at this, which Alice took to mean that either option would be welcome. She wondered how he'd subdued his impulses when in the hospital, then realized with a shock that he had not suppressed them at all. Many a night Alice fell asleep to the sound of Hatcher punching the padded wall, punching so steadily and determinedly that she'd been certain one day his hand would emerge on her side like a sprouted fungus.

Alice's first inclination was to explore the bakery, where she hoped to both meet a friendly baker and fill her stomach. She and Hatcher climbed the steps and peered through the window. Rows of cakes and breads were arrayed on shelves, but no one was visible through the glass. By silent and mutual consent they tried the door. It gave easily under Alice's hand. Hatcher had put his axe away but he had a tense, coiled look, ready to spring.

"Hello?" Alice called.

There was no movement to be heard from the room beyond, no indication whatever that anyone was present. Yet the goods all appeared freshly baked, and they certainly smelled that way. Alice staggered a little, her hunger overwhelming her.

"Hello?" she called again.

She had a strange thought, that perhaps the people of this village didn't speak her language and couldn't understand what she was saying. *But they still should have responded to my call,* she thought. *They would hardly cower under a table simply because they did not understand "hello."*

Alice and Hatcher looked at each other, the same thought in their eyes.

"I suppose it would be all right to take some food if we left money," Alice said hopefully.

"I still have some of the trader's gold," Hatcher said.

Alice spotted an enormous slice of yellow cake with a thick layer of lavender frosting atop it. A little moan escaped her lips. Yellow cake and colored frosting, her favorite.

The cake was crammed in her mouth before she even realized

she'd crossed the room. Sweetness exploded on her tongue—the soft moist crumble of cake, the thick, melty butteriness of frosting. A moment later the entire slice was gone and Alice's head was rushing, swimming in sugar and ecstasy. She sank to the floor and waited for the dizzy spell to pass.

She soon felt herself again, and glanced at Hatcher, embarrassed at her behavior. She needn't have bothered worrying, as Hatcher was on the floor opposite her, surrounded by things he'd pulled from the shelves. He was busy stuffing his face and took no notice of her whatsoever.

Alice stood slowly and chose two loaves of bread and some paper to cover them. She wrapped one loaf in its entirety, then broke the other in two, saving half for later. She ate the other half carefully, chewing and savoring.

No person appeared in all the time Hatcher and Alice were in the baker's—not the shopkeeper nor any customer from the village. When Hatcher finally had eaten his fill they swept out the crumbs (*evidence of guilt*, Alice thought), left a generous quantity of gold in exchange for the goods they'd eaten, tucked some extra supplies in Hatcher's bag and left the shop.

Outside in the square everything was just as it had been before, silent and still, though the silence seemed less ominous somehow. A full belly, Alice reflected, went a long way toward improving one's outlook.

The sun was almost at its zenith, but the little valley felt cool and shaded. Hatcher and Alice went around the square, entering every shop, calling out for any resident.

In each case they discovered the same scene—goods laid out, everything fresh and clean and dustless, but no people. It was as if all the village had woken that day and walked away, leaving everything behind.

Given the state of their clothes and their meager supplies Alice and Hatcher took the time to collect things they needed—cheese and fruit to accompany the bread, an extra sack for Alice to carry, ropes and blankets.

Alice swapped her ill-fitting trousers for a new pair and a clean shirt, though there were pretty dress patterns on display, just like in a City shop. She fingered one, a light cotton patterned all over with blue flowers.

"You would look very fine in that," Hatcher said.

Alice dropped her hand from the cloth, color rising in her cheeks. "It's not practical," she said. "Anyway, I'm too tall to fit in it, and I've grown used to trousers in any case."

It's much easier to run in trousers, she thought. She hadn't forgotten all peril behind them, nor what might be ahead.

She chose two of each item, carefully rolling up her old trousers and placing them in the bottom of her sack, mindful of the presence of the bottle in her pocket, the one she had not yet disposed of.

Alice dressed in a clean shirt and pants, wishing now that she'd bathed in the river with Hatcher. The crispness of her new clothes only seemed to emphasize the layers of grit on her skin.

In all the empty shops they left behind what they thought was fair payment for their goods. "After all," Alice reasoned, "what if they are all simply away for a festival or some such thing? How would they feel upon returning to find they'd been looted?"

"What if someone comes along after us and takes our gold and their goods?" Hatcher countered.

"At least we'll know we did the proper thing," Alice said. "And besides, who would come along after us? We never saw another soul crossing that blight."

Besides the men from the City, Alice thought, though she did not say it.

"There is more than one way to approach the village," Hatcher said, pointing toward the mountains. But he left the money, because Alice wished it.

Once they'd purchased everything they needed, Alice and Hatcher returned to the fountain at the center of town. Hatcher peered up at the sky.

"The sun is going down. We may as well stay here tonight instead of taking our chance with the mountains."

"I hate to sleep inside someone's house uninvited," Alice said. "What if the owner returned and found you sleeping in his bed?"

She remembered a story one of her governesses told her, about a little girl who went into a house that wasn't hers. She sat in three chairs and tasted three bowls of porridge and rolled in three beds. And for being too curious (and, Alice thought, very rude) the little girl was eaten up by the bears who lived there. She repeated this story to Hatcher, who gave her a curious look.

"Are you worried about bears?" he asked.

"Well, no," Alice admitted. "But the moral remains. Considering the type of person we've encountered since we escaped, I wouldn't want to make assumptions about the owner of any of these houses. We might go to sleep and wake up to discover a madman with a knife leaning over us."

"*I'm* the madman with the knife," Hatcher said. "And you are not exactly scrupulous with a blade yourself."

Alice rather resented this remark, as she felt she had killed only in defense or out of necessity. She wasn't like Hatcher, who if left unchecked would instigate a bloodbath for the fun of it.

"Still, we can sleep here in the square if you prefer," Hatcher said.

"I do," Alice said. "But first I want a bath."

They returned to the stream. Hatcher watched in open frankness as Alice undressed. She knew she ought not allow him to do so, that it wasn't a proper thing for an unmarried girl. But he'd already seen her whole body, had embraced her while she stood naked in Bess' spare room. And while Hatcher had never pressed his attentions on her, there was an intimacy between them much stronger than any man and wife. That was what happened when you killed for each other, to keep the other person safe.

Alice waded into the clear, cold stream and scrubbed the days of grit and sweat from her skin and hair. Hatcher never took his eyes from her. Then she climbed out and shook off the water and put her new clothes on again.

Hatcher stayed her hands as they moved toward the buttons of her shirt, performing the task himself. His fingers brushed against her damp skin. When he finished she was breathless. Then he smiled, and turned away toward the village. Alice followed, feeling out of sorts and not certain why.

The sun disappeared behind the desert. They rolled their blankets close together beneath the fountain in the village, Alice nestled in the curve of Hatcher's body. She was certain she would not be able to sleep, that the strange atmosphere of the village would make her restless. But there was something to be said for a full belly and clean clothes, and if the ground was hard it was at least better than sand, which had a perverse way of getting between one's clothes and skin and itching you awake.

Alice dropped off immediately, her breath and Hatcher's rising and falling in the same rhythm. As she slept, she dreamed.

She dreamed of a giant shadow looming over her, and as she looked on, one shadow split into three. There was a sound of something heavy scraping across the ground, like it was being dragged behind the shadow. Then the darkness began to speak in three voices.

"We can't," said number one.

"What do you mean, we can't? They're right here," said number two.

"We can't; they haven't broken the rules," a third cut in.

"Not a single one," the first voice said mournfully, and Alice could see the shadow shaking "no" from side to side.

"There's gold in every shop," said number three. "They didn't even drink from the fountain."

"But I'm hungry," number two said. "There haven't been any travelers for ages."

Number one grunted. "Well, that's *his* doing, isn't it? Burning up everything in sight."

"There isn't much to them anyway," number three said. "Hardly worth the effort it would take to chew and swallow them."

"Well, that one is scrawny," number two said, and Alice had the strangest feeling he was pointing at her. "But the other looks right healthy, lots of good meat on him."

"We can't," said number one, and this time there was a finality to his voice that brooked no disagreement. "There are rules, and we must follow them. Unless you want her to get angry."

"No," said number two, and his voice was both sullen and slightly afraid.

The shadows moved away then, only to be replaced by another, a gigantic black specter with wings that covered the sky. The night was colder than it had ever been, and then it was abruptly filled with flames, flames that lit the sky so that the moon was brighter than the sun. The fire seemed to have a voice of its own, a growl and hiss that opened into a howl of delight as it burned and burned and burned.

Underneath that howl was something else, full of dark and dangerous glee. "Alice. Don't forget me now."

Her eyes flew open. The sun streamed over the mountains,

and all was quiet. There was no one about except Hatcher and her, and the echo of the Jabberwocky inside her head.

"I'm going to forget you," Alice said, her voice low and fierce. "I will."

There might have been a small dark chuckle from deep inside her pack, where the bottle was inside her old trousers and her old trousers were rolled tight and buried beneath all their new supplies. But then, there might have been no noise at all, only the clinging edges of a nightmare burned away by the dawn.

Hatcher woke at the same moment Alice did. She recognized the quality of tension in his body that told her he was alert even if he had not moved. She shifted, moving to rise, and he unwrapped his arm from her waist.

They silently rolled their blankets and slung their packs over their shoulders. When all the tasks were complete Alice asked, "Hatch, did you hear them last night?"

"No," he said. "But I see their footsteps."

He pointed to the place where the grass was trampled by large feet, and something else. Something that dragged behind those large feet and left a long track. Something that might be a hammer, or a club.

The flattened grass was very near to where Alice and Hatcher had lain, as if the creatures leaned over them in the night.

"What are they?" Alice asked.

Hatcher shrugged, though Alice could tell he was not as nonchalant as he wished to appear. "Nothing we want to run into. Best get on. The mountains will take some days to cross."

He reached toward the fountain with a cupped hand, to take a drink or splash his face with water. Alice threw out her own hand in alarm, knocking his back.

"No!" She did not know whether the conversation in the night was real or imagined, but Alice would take no chances. "Let's take water from the river."

Hatcher's fingers were a whisper from the flowing spout. "Why?"

"Can't you take my word?" Alice asked, grabbing his elbow and leading him away. Under her breath she added, "I'll tell you when we are beyond the borders of the town."

Alice's neck itched, like someone stared at it. Like someone was thinking of grabbing and twisting it and crunching on bones. Yesterday the village seemed eerie, but not actually dangerous. Today danger seemed to be all around them, making the air thick and Alice's breath fearful.

The village ended as abruptly as it began. There were no outlying houses or sheds or—and this only just occurred to Alice— signs of animals or farming.

Who had baked the goods in the bakery, and where had the eggs and flour come from if there were no pecking chickens to feed, no golden fields to tend? This isolated place could hardly gather resources from a nearby town.

"Why, oh, why didn't we see it right away?" Alice said.

"See what?" Hatcher asked.

He allowed Alice to lead him to the stream that ran alongside the village. Here the water tumbled merrily over grey-and-white rocks before widening into the pool where Alice had bathed the previous day.

"It's magic," Alice said, and as she said this she could smell the enchantment on the air, and see the faint shimmer of mist around the village.

Hatcher washed his face and drank from the river before filling a skin with water. He twisted around to stare at the buildings as he did so. "It's not real?"

Alice shook her head. "It's real. But it was put there by magic, not by human hands."

She could hardly credit her stupidity, although if she were fair to herself she would remember that when they arrived they were parched, exhausted and half-starved. Alice supposed under those circumstances she might be forgiven for not recognizing the enchantment.

Still, they would need to be more watchful in the future. There was much more magic out here than inside the walls of the City. Magicians had been driven from the City, and that meant the wide world held even more peril for Alice and Hatcher.

"Why plant a pretend village?" Hatcher asked.

"As a trap," Alice said, and repeated the conversation she'd heard (or possibly dreamed) the night before.

"I suppose it's lucky you're so honest," Hatcher said. "If we hadn't left payment for the things we took, we would be in no end of trouble."

"I may have imagined it all," Alice admitted. "Because I felt

I was right in leaving the money and my dream-self wished to congratulate me."

Hatcher grinned. "Feeling very clever?"

"If it saved our lives I suppose I have a right to, at least in a dream."

His grin faded. "You didn't dream those tracks. Some creature was near us last night for certain. For reasons of its own it did not harm us, whether because it had no need or wish to or because it was restrained by some outside force. 'Her.' I wonder who 'her' is."

"If everything follows, then she is the one who made this place, and that means she is very powerful."

For the second time Alice wished to speak with Cheshire, an impulse that irritated her greatly. The little Magician was hardly a friend and probably a dangerous ally, but at least he had experience and knowledge. And for some reason unknown to her, he liked Alice.

It was possible she'd been foolish to break the connection between them. She'd like some advice from someone who had experience and knowledge. She'd like to know how to recognize magic before it was used against her.

"I suppose it was safe to eat those cakes and things?" Alice said. She could hear the doubt in her voice.

"If it wasn't, there's nothing to be done about it now," Hatcher said.

That's true, Alice thought. And it was also true that not for the first time in her life did she wish she could go back and undo her actions, make a different decision. How many times had she dreamed that her sixteen-year-old self was not so curious, not wishing for a little thrill of danger, not so silly as to follow Dor into the Old City, a place nice girls should never go?

But if she had not followed Dor, had not been through everything an innocent young girl should not have experienced, then she would never have known Hatcher, and she couldn't be sorry for that.

No man in the New City could love her as Hatcher did—of that Alice was certain. It was deep and all-consuming but somehow never suffocating. It was unselfish. It did not ask for anything and yet he made no secret of his need. There was no one in the world like Hatcher, and if she hadn't been mad, there would be no Hatcher for her.

So she should not wish to undo the past but learn to accept its consequences, and remember that not all consequences were evil.

They had eaten food from the enchanted village. They must now accept what came next.

Although, Alice reflected, *it would be lovely if a village were just a village.* She would like it if for once things were exactly as they seemed.

They followed the stream until about midday, as it led toward the mountains and there was no obvious footpath to follow. Occasionally they saw the flashing silver of fish in the water. Around lunchtime Hatcher decided to try his luck catching a fish.

"But you don't know a thing about fishing," Alice protested. "You've lived in the City your entire life."

"It can't be that difficult," Hatcher said as he stripped off his shirt, jacket and boots.

He rolled his pants to his knees, revealing pale white bony feet and legs so lacking in fat that Alice could see the veins and muscles pressing against his skin. His naked torso was covered in scars, the product of his life before the asylum.

"There's fish and chips on offer every day in the City, so someone must be able to catch fish," he said.

"Those fish are brought on boats," Alice said. "Boats that come from the sea, and the fish are caught in nets."

Alice recalled a young nurserymaid had once taken her on an outing to the docks, but only after obtaining Alice's solemn promise that she would not speak of the incident to her parents. Alice was very small at the time, perhaps three or four, and was so excited by the prospect that she promised immediately, would have promised anything to be allowed to go.

Her mother always scrupulously avoided that part of the New City, sniffing that it was "full of common people." Alice's nurserymaid dragged the gawping child through the masses of burly, sweaty men, reeking of salt and fish and whiskey and tobacco smoke, their teeth and clothes stained, their arms and faces so brown from the sun that they looked like visitors from some exotic Eastern land.

Everywhere there was noise and movement—men shouting,

carrying barrels of goods, old sailors mending nets or sails, docks being scrubbed and supplies carted aboard for the next sailing.

There were a few people like Alice's father, dressed in suits, speaking intently to captains. There were men who invested in ships' concerns and kept scrupulous track of those investments.

There were others from the upper echelons of the New City, wrinkling their noses as they were led to ships' quarters for a sea voyage. *It would be lovely,* she thought, *to sail on a ship to a far-away country.*

Her nursemaid halted before one of the smaller fishing boats, where she was hailed by a grinning young man with hair so pale it could not be called yellow and eyes of startling blue.

His name was Mathias, and he had a strange accent. He told Alice he was from a country of ice and snow, a place where there was barely anything green and the land was filled with white bears twice the size of a man.

Alice could hardly credit this, but Mathias said it was true. Then he put her on his knee and fed her some very strange dried fish that tasted mostly of salt and told her a story of a woman who fell in love with one of these great white bears, who was actually a prince in disguise.

This story so thrilled Alice that she wanted to go with Mathias back to his home, so that she too might marry a bear and live in a palace made of ice. He laughed and kissed her cheek and set her down. Then he and the nurserymaid (*Why can I not recall her name? I remember his but not hers*) had sat close on overturned barrels, holding hands and murmuring to each other while Alice played a game collecting odd things she found on the dock. A ripped bit of netting, an interesting rock, a tarnished coin from someplace far from the City. She ran to and fro, gathering things in a pile at their feet.

After a time she'd found everything within easy reach and strayed farther and farther in search of something interesting. Suddenly she looked up, and realized she could not see Mathias' boat, and all around were the dizzying tall masts of ships and a busy crush of people who did not notice her.

She wanted to burst into tears but instead took one or two hesitant steps, hoping the movement would reveal the fishing boat nearby. But there was nothing familiar.

Alice felt her insides shrinking and all she wanted then was to be at home. It was nearly teatime, she was sure, and her stomach growled and her hands shook and she wanted her mother, wanted the sweet scent of roses to envelop her.

Then there was a man before her, a man clothed in the respectable suit and top hat of the New City, a man with a kind voice and hard, hungry eyes, offering to help her and pulling a sweet from his pocket.

She reached for it, forgetting her fear, forgetting the need to find her nurserymaid, and the man's other hand reached out for her, to close around her.

Then she heard, "Alice! Alice!"—a frantic cry—and she turned about and saw the white face of the nurse just behind her.

She scooped Alice into her arms, her face wet with tears, and scolded her for wandering. As she carried Alice away, Alice saw that the man with the top hat had disappeared.

They never went on another outing to the docks. A few weeks later, the nurserymaid left in the middle of the night and never returned, which of course made Alice's mother very cross until she could find a suitable replacement. But Alice hoped she had run away to the land of ice and snow, and that when she arrived she found Mathias as a great white bear, a prince in disguise.

Alice blinked suddenly, for her face was splashed by water, and found Hatcher standing before her looking proud and holding a struggling speckled fish in both hands.

Alice blinked again. "Where did that come from?"

"I caught it. Didn't you see?" Hatcher said, his face falling. "Were you not watching?"

"I'm sorry. I was remembering . . . something."

Only now did she recognize that hard, hungry look of wanting in the man's eyes and realize how close she had been to danger. What would have happened to her if she had been too young to fight and run away, as she had with the Rabbit?

She pushed the memory away, returning her attention to Hatcher, who now appeared sulky that she had not properly appreciated his efforts.

"I'm sorry," she said again, eyeing the fish as its flapping slowed. "What are you supposed to do with it now?"

"Cut it open and cook it," Hatcher said.

"I don't know anything about cooking fish," Alice said. She

had never eaten a meal that wasn't prepared by somebody else. "Don't you need a butcher or a fishmonger or something?"

"I *am* a butcher," Hatcher said, and he proceeded to skin and gut the fish as though he'd been doing it all his life.

While he did this, Alice collected dry sticks and managed, after several tries and much repeated instruction from Hatcher, to start a fire. Soon enough the fish was roasting on sticks, and they made a lovely picnic of it with some bread from the village and water from the stream.

Alice hesitated over the bread, not wishing to eat more enchanted food, but Hatcher felt it was of no consequence now. They'd already eaten some, and more would not make a difference, was his reasoning. Alice paused, dithering, suspicious now that she knew the bread was made by magic.

Which is silly, really. You would be thrilled to eat this bread if you made it with your own magic, she thought.

Hatcher noticed her uncertainty and snatched a large chunk off the loaf, shoving it in his mouth and remarking, "If you don't want it, I'll eat it."

Alice ate the bread.

She was still inclined to worry that it might somehow be used against them. In a fairy tale the food would have led them to a witch's cottage, where the witch in question would imprison them until they were fat enough for eating.

Or else the bread would not be bread at all, only something enspelled to appear as bread. Alice half expected to find not a freshly baked loaf wrapped in a towel in her bag, but a worm-ridden lump of dirt or something equally repulsive. However, the bread had still been bread, and she didn't know if she was relieved or disappointed.

All the elements of a story are here, Alice thought. The enchanted village, the mysterious creatures in the night. Yet there was something not quite right, some element that didn't result in the usually expected end.

Alice and Hatcher had escaped without a struggle, without a confrontation of any kind. If Alice's dream were true, then the reason for this was because she'd insisted they pay for anything they took from the shops.

Somehow, though, she didn't think it was that simple. Why place a trap—Alice was fairly certain now that was the purpose of the village—and then allow fish to swim out of the net instead of closing it?

"And why did we never see what was causing that light in the desert?" Alice muttered as they packed up their things and started again.

"What was that?" Hatcher asked.

"Nothing," Alice said. No need to trouble Hatcher with her unsubstantiated worries.

The trees were thicker ahead, and the stream veered away from the easterly course Alice and Hatcher followed.

Hatcher paused as they entered the woods, peering at the ground. "There's a deer track here. We can follow this for a while."

"How do you know so much about these things?" Alice asked

suspiciously. "About deer trails and fishing and so on. You've never left the City in your life."

Hatcher shrugged. "I don't know. I just know. The knowledge is there when I need it, like when we escaped the hospital and were trying to find Bess."

"That, at least, made sense," Alice said. "You'd been there before. You were only following your nose, so to speak. But this . . ."

"Maybe there's more to being a Seer than just seeing the future," Hatcher said. "Maybe I can call on some other power."

Or maybe, Alice thought, her eyes narrowed, *someone is helping you. Someone who was forced out of my head but made no promise to stay out of yours.*

She did not say this aloud. She had no proof of Cheshire's interference, although the relative ease with which they had passed through the desert only increased her suspicion. Cheshire liked to set and clear the chessboard according to his own whims. If it suited him to steer them away from the mysterious light in the desert, then Cheshire would not be above using Hatcher as his tool to do so.

And Hatcher had so much noise in his head that he wouldn't necessarily notice the presence of another. She would watch him carefully and see whether she could find any trace of Cheshire in his manner.

Hatcher moved along, confident and sure-footed, into the forest, seeming to know precisely where he was going. As for Alice, her unease grew as the trees thickened.

She'd never spent any real time in the woods. The avenues in the City were lined with carefully trimmed branches and rigidly spaced trunks providing the exact amount of shade for strolling nursemaids that pushed prams at midday.

There was a large open park near Alice's childhood home, but even there the trees were scant, planted here and there in a field of well-kept grass. There was nowhere in the City where the trees pushed close, snagging one's clothes, thickening the air with the scent of bark and leaves decomposing underfoot. It seemed a wholly alien world to Alice, and not one she was certain she liked.

"It's so quiet," she said, and though her voice was barely above a whisper it seemed to fill in the empty space left between the breathing of the trees.

The quiet was oppressive. It gave her a sense that the forest lurked, waiting for its chance to do . . . Well, Alice wasn't certain what a forest *could* do, but it didn't give her a pleasant feeling. She felt she might never see the sky or the sun again. The only roof visible was the arcing canopy of trees twining their arms about one another in an eternal embrace above their heads.

"Yes," Hatcher said, and his voice was even lower than hers, so faint it was barely distinguishable from the exhalation of his breath. "No birds, no squirrels, not a sign of the deer whose trail we follow."

Of course now that it was mentioned, Alice noted the lack of twittering and scampering and scurrying, the sorts of sounds you might expect in a forest even if you had never been in one before. But nothing moved except themselves.

"What does it mean?" Alice asked.

"It means," Hatcher said, and suddenly his axe was in his hand, "that there is a hunter about, and the hunted things have tucked out of sight."

"But not us," Alice said, looking around. The shadows were thicker, more sinister, shifting into shapes that may or may not actually be there. "What if we're what it's hunting?"

"I'm certain we are," Hatcher said, his eyes gleaming.

She knew he longed for this, the tension of the hunt, the aching silence before the thrill of blood and mayhem. Alice might understand Hatcher, but she would never understand that need. She fought only when necessary, only when she had to defend her life—or his. She would never revel in the melting of flesh beneath her blade. *(Except the Caterpillar's flesh.)*

Well, that was different, wasn't it? He was keeping those girls captive for his own amusement.

It was sort of funny, Alice mused. She'd thought when she left the City behind she would also leave all the horrors, shed them like that snake sliding out of its old skin that she longed to be. Instead they returned to her over and over, sleeping and waking—the Caterpillar, the Walrus, Cheshire, the Rabbit, and the girls they used and broke, the girls taken screaming from their streets and homes. Girls like Alice was, once.

"Alice," Hatcher said.

It was only then she noticed that he'd kept going while she'd stopped, gazing into the hole of her past instead of looking for peril in the present. She hurried to his side.

"You'll be in someone's stew pot before long if you don't keep a sharp eye about," Hatcher said.

Alice nodded, knowing it was true, but also knowing it was as hard for her to stop it as Hatcher's bloodlust. Sometimes the lure of thought and memory was too much for her, a tug that compelled her away from the world and into her own head. It came, she supposed, from all the years in the hospital, with only her own brain for company aside from Hatcher's voice through the mouse hole.

Though she did have a vague memory of her mother's voice, sharp and impatient: "Straighten up and stop dreaming, Alice!"

Yes, she'd been a dreamy child, and the experience of her life had not removed that impulse. Despite the danger that unraveled before them at every turn, Alice seemed unable to keep her mind on what she was doing.

Several minutes passed as Alice and Hatcher walked shoulder to shoulder in the woods. Alice felt the coiled tension pouring off Hatcher. The woods, however, kept their secrets, and she wondered if this was simply a quiet place with no animals. It didn't have to mean anything sinister because they didn't see any scampering rodents. *(But no birds? Not even the buzz of insects? Nothing?)*

Then she heard it.

It was such a small noise it could almost be dismissed as the rustle of leaves in the wind. Except there was no wind. The air was heavy and still, and Hatcher stopped moving, holding up his hand so Alice would do the same.

His grey eyes were hard and alert, and his facial muscles moved ever so slightly, just enough for Alice to receive the message. *Behind us.*

She'd always been dreamy, but she'd also always been curious, which was why she turned around to look before Hatcher was ready to strike. She gasped, her scream of horror swallowed in shock. There was a thing, a thing she could never have imagined, and it was much nearer than it should have been.

It was directly behind her, long fingers extended and about to brush the place where her nape had been a moment before. Its face was hideously distended, as if the whole skull had been pressed between two blocks and then a child had pulled the nose out long and the chin down to the chest.

Its limbs, too, were unnaturally elongated, though its whole body was drawn into a crouch that put its face at Alice's eyes. The skin was a mottled green, covered all over by some shiny yellowish substance that oozed. It wore a kind of jerkin composed of patches of skin sewn together, and Alice thought some of those patches looked like human skin.

All this she registered in an instant, and then the smell of it, the reek of decay and death, reached her nostrils and she choked, staggering out of the reach of those long, grasping fingers.

It hissed at her, took a step forward on its oversized feet and reached again. Hatcher spun, swinging the axe so hard and fast

Alice felt the brush of air as the blade whistled past her. She squeezed her eyes shut, anticipating the hot splatter of blood splashing over her, the final agonized cry of the thing that had stalked them through the woods.

It did not come.

Alice opened her eyes again to find Hatcher staring in bewilderment at the empty space where the creature had been.

"Where did it go?" She could not disguise her astonishment.

Hatcher never missed. It was a truth as reliable as the rising of the sun and the blue of her eyes. Hatcher never missed once he'd unsheathed his axe and moved with intention. And yet, somehow, he had.

"It disappeared," he said, then shook his head. "No, that's not exactly right. It sort of . . . stuttered, I suppose, in front of me and then I didn't see it anymore."

The image of the creature was burned in Alice's eyes, so that it was almost as if the thing stood before her still, fingers grasping for her face now instead of her neck.

"Was it real, do you think?" Her heart pounded in her chest, and she could hear how breathless and fluttery her voice was.

The encounter disturbed her greatly, much more than she would have thought possible given all the horror she had already seen. It would have been a comfort to have the bloodied corpse of the monster at their feet. Then at least Alice would know for certain that it *had* happened.

Hatcher sniffed the air. "It smelled real enough. I can still smell it."

"If it was real, what is it? What does it want with us?" Again she was surprised by the intensity of her fear. It looked like something from a childhood tale, a thing that crept out from under the bed in the darkness, a thing that reached its thin, creeping arms over the bed to snatch little girls from their blankets before they had a chance to scream. It looked like a—

"Goblin," Alice said, remembering a maid called Liesl who'd come from the forest in the high mountains, a long way from the City.

She'd told Alice stories of goblins and of witches with candy houses that lured children, of girls who chopped their feet in two to fit inside a glass slipper.

They were not, Alice reflected, very nice stories, although Liesl claimed they were told to children.

"What's a goblin?" Hatcher asked.

"Something that's not supposed to exist," Alice murmured.

The thing that had been there a moment before still did not seem real. It was easy to accept the presence of magic in the world, and that animals could talk if you knew how to listen to them, and even the idea of a mermaid. It was easy to accept the pleasant and nice things (*although magic isn't always used for pleasant and nice things, is it?*), but monsters, especially ones from children's stories, were somehow more difficult to grasp.

Her mind wanted to slide away from the reality of the goblin, to deny that her eyes had seen what they had seen, to pretend her nose had not smelled what it smelled, to forget the almost-touch of long fingers reaching for her neck.

Alice shook her head, telling herself to stop being foolish. She'd faced and defeated the Jabberwocky—

(Alice)

—and surely this hob would be nothing compared to that.

(I'm still here, Alice.)

There might have been a dark laugh emerging from the roll of dirty clothing at the very bottom of her pack, but Alice refused to hear it.

Hatcher crouched to the ground, inspecting the place where the creature had stood. Alice saw no obvious sign of its presence, nor of the way it had retreated. She remembered her brief glimpse of its long, oversized feet and the protruding blackened toenails. There ought to be footprints or some other kind of mark in the ground from those appendages. But there was nothing. Alice saw Hatcher glance around, then stand and scrub his face in frustration.

"I don't know what a goblin is, but it sure disappeared bloody quick," Hatcher said. "If both of us hadn't seen it I would say we hadn't seen it."

He slapped the blunt end of his axe in the palm of his left hand, his eyes searching around the forest. Alice could see the longing in his eyes, the desire to hunt the thing that had slipped away from his blade.

"Come on, Hatch," she said, with a certainty she did not feel. "If it appears again you can have another go."

She knew he wouldn't move unless she did, because he

wouldn't let her walk through the woods unprotected. So she did the thing she did not want to do. She held her chin high and pretended she didn't feel like a scurrying mouse, like she didn't want to find the nearest hole and dive into it. She pretended that her heart wasn't a faint little flutter in her chest, trying to make itself small and unnoticeable. She pretended she wasn't terrified to look back over her shoulder and see not the carved bones of Hatcher's face but the distorted ones of the goblin. She pretended, and she led the way.

A moment later Hatcher fell in step beside her and patted her shoulder. "I'll get it next time. You don't have to worry."

"I'm not worried," Alice said. But she was. Because Hatcher never missed, and this time he had.

They trudged along, both of them lost in their own thoughts. Alice noted the return of birds and chipmunks and little noises from the brush. She even saw a flash of antlers through the trees. Another time she might have pointed in amazement at the sight of a wild deer, but not now.

The fear had suffused her, like a poison that spread from the place where the goblin had almost touched. She felt cold all over, cold in her bones, and her hands shook so hard she closed them in fists in her pockets so that Hatcher would not see.

Alice could not have explained why the goblin scared her so, scared her more than anything else she had seen—more than Cheshire, more than the Walrus, more than even the thing that she was not supposed to think about because she was going to forget it. All she knew was that as the shadows lengthened and the faint sunlight disappeared, she wanted to hide under her cloak until the sun rose again.

Hatcher, however, had a different idea. The darkness drew out the predator in him, and as the creatures of the forest settled into their nests and burrows, his teeth gleamed like a wolf's.

Alice heard Liesl's voice in her head, that nurserymaid from long ago who came from the high forests. *Grandmother, what big teeth you have.*

Hatcher was no wolf in an innocent's clothing. He was a wolf in a man's form, a killer forced to pretend that he was civilized. And now, in this raw and uncivilized place, his nature could finally find its full bloom.

She sensed the shift, felt the expectation that built in him. And then she saw the goblin, and felt her heart stutter and her blood halt.

It was just ahead of them, on the path, a silhouette that did not quite fit into the shape of the trees. Alice was faintly surprised she could recognize anything at all with the sun gone. She realized the night was not entirely black, that there were differing qualities of darkness that made monsters loom where once had been only forest.

She squinted, not certain that the goblin was there after all. Perhaps it was only her imagination, and the crooking of a tree branch, for it wasn't before them now.

Hatcher was muttering beneath his breath as he stalked, a

single phrase repeated over and over that grew louder with every step. Alice leaned closer to hear.

"The night is alive and so am I," he said, and his voice came from somewhere that was not his throat, but deep in his belly. "The night is alive and so am I. The night is alive and so am I."

Alice felt chill all over at the sound of that voice. *I can't lose him,* she thought. *Hatcher, stay with me.*

She reached for him, not knowing what she would do, not knowing the words to keep him with her, to keep him human.

And then the night was alive.

All around were the sounds of trees expanding against their bark, the flexing of branches, the brushing of leaves against one another. A hissing sound rose, the singing of a thousand snakes. Far behind them was the crashing of something huge, something moving through the wood with dangerous intent. A wolf howled, and then another, and another.

Alice stared around, unsure which threat was most dire. Were the trees about to snatch her from the ground? Would a wolf pack descend on them and tear them to pieces? Or would the goblin arrive to finish its business?

Then a wolf howled very close to her ear. She turned slowly, full of dread, expecting the glint of yellow eyes and sharp white fangs. The only eyes she saw were grey ones, full of blood and mischief, and teeth bared in a murderer's smile.

"The night is alive, Alice," Hatcher said. "And so am I."

She felt a thrill of fear, a fear that surprised her. First, she'd been in a heightened state since the goblin appeared. She didn't think she could be more scared, but there she was. And second—well, Hatcher had never frightened her before. Not directly. Alice was secure in her certainty that he would never hurt her. Or at least, she had been secure.

Now he looked like the wolf she'd imagined him to be, a wolf once trapped and now free.

"The night is alive, Alice," he repeated, and he drew his face close to her still one.

She did not move, barely daring to breathe. Her body was still but her mind was moving rapidly through a series of horrifying images, things that might happen to her if Hatcher snapped. Things that involved leaving her on the forest floor in many small and bloodied pieces.

He would regret it tomorrow; of that she was certain. But whatever happened would be done, and Alice would not be there to reprimand him.

The huge crashing thing continued in their direction. Alice heard it approaching, brush and branches giving way before it, the rush of small creatures as they squealed away from its tread. It would crush them in a moment, and it wouldn't matter if Hatcher had gone mad—or, rather, madder than he was before.

Hatcher seemed not to hear the giant thing. He was listening to something else, something that spoke only to him.

Alice saw movement out of the corner of her eye as the forest broke in pieces before the marauding creature. Several small animals with long tails ran over her feet. It amazed her that even in this moment, when she was fairly certain that she would either have her throat cut or be squashed by a giant, she could think how much she hated rats, and shudder inwardly at the feeling of their tails dragging over the toes of her boots.

Then Hatcher leaned into her face, bit her nose—but gently, very gently—and ran away into the woods.

Alice wanted to be astonished (*he left me*) but the giant monster was upon her, and now she needed to run too.

She couldn't possibly follow Hatcher. The darkness had swallowed him too quickly. Away from the path she would get lost; there was no doubt of that. But the other creature, the roaring, crashing monster, was coming straight down the path.

Up, you silly nit.

Alice reached blindly toward the nearest tree, scraped her boots against the bark and pulled herself up, and up, and up. Even a short time ago she wouldn't have had the strength to do this, but a full belly went a long way, and their adventures had made Alice much fitter than she'd been in the hospital. And fright was a powerful motivator.

All she could think was that she needed to get out of the giant's reach. She didn't know how tall it might be—it sounded huge—so she kept going up, ignoring the angry squirrels that chittered at her and the birds that flew off, squawking in irritation. She climbed, sweat beading on her face and making her hands slippery, until her head spun and she knew she could not go any farther.

Alice glanced down, and only then did she realize she was

much, much higher than she intended to be. The forest floor was not visible, and the darkness below her seemed an abyss ready to swallow her in its maw.

And the creature, whatever it had been, was gone. The crashing, banging, breaking noise had passed on, fading away from her, and Alice had been so consumed by her terror and shock that she hadn't noticed.

She was so high her stomach turned sickeningly. What on earth had she been thinking? How was she to get down from this great height? Where had Hatcher run off to, and how would she find him? And what was she to do if she *couldn't* find him again? Should she go on without him? Or back to the City?

No, there was no future for her in the City. She knew that. Her family would not be pleased to discover she was alive. And if she did not return to her family, what then? There was only Cheshire, and Alice had no wish to be a cat's-paw for Cheshire.

She squinted below her, trying to find a safe foothold down. Everything was soft and blurry and impossible to distinguish. Now she realized that there was some faint star and moonlight trickling in through the canopy above, which had allowed her to climb upward with a surety she did not have going down.

Her hands were wrapped around a particularly thick branch, and she thought she might be able to sit on it. Staying in one place seemed the smartest notion. Alice could not see clearly below her, Hatcher was missing and the goblin could be anywhere. Blundering through the wood was about the most foolish thing she could do.

She struggled to pull her whole body up, and once she was there she realized the branch, while thicker than many of the others, was hardly wide enough to accommodate her narrow seat. Her hands trembled as she gripped the branch with her legs like she was astride a horse and tried to find a comfortable resting place against the trunk. It was not comfortable at all, especially with her pack in the way.

Alice twisted her pack so that the straps still went over her shoulders but the pack itself nestled in front of her, like a mother's pregnant belly. She was taking no chances that she might accidentally drop the pack below, where a certain something she was supposed to forget might fall into strange hands.

Moving the pack only made her uncomfortably aware of the bark scratching the back of her neck, and the fact that she was perched in a tree like some demented bird. She wanted very much for her feet to be on solid ground, where they belonged. She wanted very much for Hatcher to return to her, preferably in a calmer state. She wanted, and she was slightly ashamed to admit it to herself, for their quest to be over.

They were traveling east in search of a vague rumor. Hatcher's daughter might not be where they thought she was. Jenny might not be alive at all. And if she were alive, who was to say she would remember him, or care? What if Alice and Hatcher were crossing this forest and the mountains and the desert for nothing?

And there was something else too—that conversation that Alice might have heard, or might have dreamed. The conversation of three enormous shadows in the night, who talked of "her," and the source of the light that Alice and Hatcher had seen as they passed through the scorched land.

Alice found there were too many worries, too many unknowns that may or may not affect their journey. Her sharp fear (of both the goblin and Hatcher) had faded, leaving her drained and exhausted. Her head nodded forward on her chest and she jolted upright, terrified of falling from her insecure perch. She could not drift off to sleep here. It was not safe.

She listened to the settling forest, all the animals and birds and trees quieting down for the night. Her own heart quieted as she peered up at the stars, the few little specks of light that she could see through the leaves. The breeze was cold, and though she was slightly disoriented by their time on the path, she thought it came from the mountains.

It will be cold there, she thought. *There is snow on the peaks.*

Alice had never seen snow like they got in the northern countries. In the City a few flakes would fall occasionally, hardly enough to blanket the street before turning into a grey, slushy mess. She wondered what it would be like to walk through thick carpets of snow, and perhaps see a snow bear, like in the stories.

A bear that would turn into a prince, she thought, and then smiled sadly to herself. Her prince was not a bear, but a madman. Alice had learned that you could not choose whom to love. If royalty appeared out of nowhere and offered her a future, she would have to turn away from it, because Alice could never love any other but the one with grey eyes and bloodstained hands. Was he thinking of her right now, wondering why she had not followed him? Or was he lost in the thrill of the hunt, not to remember her until morning and regret set in?

She shivered as the wind blew again, and wrapped her arms together, hunching her shoulders.

Cold. So cold.

Her eyelids drifted downward; her breathing was smooth and even. Her eyes snapped open again, and she adjusted herself on the branch. *I can't fall. I can't fall. I must stay awake.*

But it was cold, and the cold made her sleepier than she already was.

Cold. So cold.

Alice stood before a palace made of glass, perched on the highest peak of the highest mountain. Her hands shook so hard she could barely feel them and when she glanced down she saw her fingertips were blue. She could not feel her feet inside her boots, and her teeth clattered together.

The palace glittered in the sunlight, more beautiful than any building Alice had ever seen. But it was a cold beauty, and something was wrong here. Something very wrong. She cocked her head to one side, listening. The wind blew shards into her ear that sang an icy song, but underneath that sound there was something more. A long, high laugh, a woman's laugh that held no joy.

And there was screaming. The children were screaming.

The sound was so terrible, so full of heartbreak, that Alice grabbed her ears and covered them, trying to block it out, trying to pretend she had never heard such a noise.

The screaming wound inside her ear and up into Alice's brain, lodging itself there, deep inside so that it permeated her bones and blood and flesh so that she would always hear it, sleeping and waking, as long as the children were screaming.

They were screaming for her.

No, she thought. *No.*

And she ran, and was heedless of where her steps carried her, and her boots skidded on the ice and she went over the edge of the peak, the highest peak of the highest mountain, and felt herself falling away into nothing, but the screaming followed her all the way down, so that even in death she would not escape those terrible cries.

Her eyes opened, and she was falling, really falling. Despite all her precautions she had drifted off to sleep while perched on the branch and now she would pay for it. She could still hear the screaming from her dream, an echo that followed her into wakefulness.

The wind whistled in her ears. Her back arced toward the ground as her limbs curved upward, grasping for the sky. She had only a moment to brace herself for the hard crash of ground beneath her, for the blossoming of pain as her bones shattered.

But that did not happen. Instead she hit something leathery and tough and very, *very* smelly, like a sulfurous swamp. She had a glimpse of an enormous face—bulbous green eyes, hairy nostrils under a giant potato nose—and then everything went dark as fingers closed over her and a rumbling voice shouted in triumph, "Got you!"

Her body was breaking now, though not the way she'd expected it to when she was falling. The creature's grip was crushing her, but more than that she couldn't breathe. The hideous stink of its skin was overwhelming. She was choking, gagging, and in a moment the hand that held her would snap her ribs and the splintered pieces would pierce her heart and she would be dead.

Hatcher.

It was a thought or a wish or possibly a cry, and she was certain it would be her last.

Then she was able to breathe again, the unbearable pressure gone, but it was hardly reassuring as the monster had opened its hand, grasped her by the ankle, and lifted her to its eye level. Her pack knocked against the back of her head as all the blood rushed from the bottom of her body to the top.

The giant's eyes narrowed slightly as it observed her. "Well, you are hardly more than a mouthful," he said. "But you'll do until I can find your friend."

The creature's maw opened, revealing cracked yellow teeth and a large grey tongue. An astonishingly foul odor emitted from its throat, like the inside of the creature's body was populated with dead things.

This is the last thing I will see in this life, Alice thought, and reflected that death by Jabberwocky would have at least been less disgusting than this.

The bottle with that monster (*butterfly*) was still in her pack, so at least it would also be digested and Alice could go to her death with a clear heart. She closed her eyes, not wanting to see the inside of the monster's throat as she slid down, not wanting to know anything else. She hoped it would be quick. She hoped it wouldn't hurt.

Then, yet again, something unexpected happened, as it always seemed to do to Alice.

As the giant released her and she fell toward its wet grey mouth, she was snatched from her fall by another enormous hand.

"Cod, no!" shouted the second giant, who held Alice by her ankle and shook his hand as he spoke. "You know the rules. You know her law. They've done no harm and we are to do no harm in return."

The giant's gesticulating made Alice feel that all her organs would soon shake loose and fall out of her mouth, and then where would she be?

Dead, she thought sourly, whether by the will of one giant or the accident of another.

"I'm huuuungry, Pen," whined the first giant, whom the second giant had called "Cod." He sounded exactly like a child begging for a lemon ice at the zoo. "It's been ever so long since we've had any human flesh. Not since *he* started burning everything out of spite. That one and her friend were the only two to pass through in ages. No one wants to cross the plains anymore."

"No one left to cross the plains anymore," said the second fellow, who appeared to be called "Pen."

What curious names these giants have, Alice thought. It was something to think about besides the fact that she was upside down and rocking to and fro with every motion of Pen's hand.

"But that don't give you the right to break her laws. She said she'd punish us and you know right well she can and will," Pen said.

"Don't see how she could punish us worse than she already has," Cod muttered.

"I'm sure the Queen has more imagination than you," Pen said. "A maggot would."

"What's that supposed to mean?" Cod roared.

"It means you're a selfish cur without the brains of a dog!" Pen shouted back, and Alice was once more subjected to a violent shaking.

All of a sudden she decided she'd had quite enough, *thank you*. She opened her mouth and emitted a scream so bloodcurdlingly shrill it stopped both the giants dead.

Pen lifted her to his eyes. They were like tremendous boulders in his face; Alice thought she might be only half the height of his nose, and that it might take seven or eight Alices to reach from the bottom of his chin to the top of his head. His face was an almost perfect duplicate of the first giant's.

"Here, now, what's all this?" he asked, and he had the temerity to sound insulted.

The constant hanging and shaking and screaming and the threat of imminent death had quite taken Alice's breath away, but she managed to gasp out, "Turn . . . me . . . over."

Only then did Pen seem to grasp the distress Alice was in and right her in his palm, his expression somewhat abashed. "Sorry about that, miss. It's just I was angry at my brother here and forgot I was holding you."

"Yes, I gathered," Alice said, attempting to look as though she witnessed arguments between giants all the time and certainly failing as she staggered across Pen's hand and was forced to sit. She could have stretched out flat with her arms wide and not covered the whole breadth of his palm. "Do you think you would let me down now? I'd feel much better with the ground beneath my feet. Not that your hand isn't lovely."

She added this last bit hastily, not wishing to offend the giant and have him decide she was better off in his brother's gullet after all.

"Of course, of course, miss," Pen said, lowering his hand toward the ground.

As he did, Alice caught a glimpse of both giants' faces looming above her—and the gleam of malice in Cod's eye. Pen appeared to have noticed the same light, for he hesitated when Alice was still several feet from the ground.

Then he said, "What if I were to accompany you for a short way? Perhaps until you rejoin your companion?"

The creature's formal language was so at odds with its monstrous appearance and the behavior of his brother that Alice nearly laughed aloud. But she didn't dare. The giant hadn't released her yet, and his hand was just as large and bruising as the other's.

"I thank you very much for your kindness, sir," Alice said, matching her tone to his. "But I would not wish to inconvenience you. If you would point me back to the path, I would be very grateful."

"Oh, no, it's no inconvenience at all, miss," the giant said, and instead of lowering her to the ground he lifted her again, higher and higher—

(And I've had quite enough of heights as well.)

—until his palm was level with his shoulder. It was quite clear what he expected Alice to do. She sighed, a very small and almost inaudible sigh, and clambered over his palm to the giant's rather horny shoulder, gripping one of the protrusions so as not to fall off.

"Right," said Pen. "You go back to the village now, Cod. Gil's waiting there for you."

He showed Cod his fist as he spoke, making it clear what his brother could expect if he didn't obey.

"What about you?" Cod asked, an ugly grimace twisting his mouth. "Where do you think you're off to with her?"

"I'll be along directly, as soon as I assist this lady."

"I don't think you are," Cod said. "I think you're just keeping her for yourself."

This thought had already occurred to Alice, and that perhaps Pen would use her to find Hatcher and have two scrumptious mouthfuls for himself, his brothers none the wiser. She'd already resolved to escape the giant as soon as a plan presented itself, although from this height her only real option was to perhaps stand upon the backs of a couple of sturdy crows—always presuming she could get them to cooperate.

Cod lunged for Alice then, his hand swiping out and just missing the tips of her short hair. Pen slugged his brother in the face, a furious crash of knuckle to cheekbone while Alice held on for dear life.

Alice thought that Cod would retaliate for certain, but instead the other giant's great green eyes filled with tears.

"Whatja do that for?" he sobbed, holding one hand to his injured cheek. "Whyja do that?"

"Now, now," Pen said soothingly, patting Cod's shoulder. "There's no need for all this fuss. You brought it on yourself, you know. Go on back to Gil now."

Alice thought he seemed a bit embarrassed by his brother's outburst. He peeked at Alice out of the corners of his eyes, as if checking to see how much attention she was paying.

"You didn't have to hit me," Cod said.

"Well, you weren't listening. Go on. I'll be along soon enough."

Cod moved away, shoulders hunched, sniffling and sobbing. Even though he had just tried to eat her, Alice felt suddenly sorry for him. He looked small and pathetic for all that his head nearly reached the tops of the trees, and while Alice had no wish to be a meal herself, she could well understand the desperate hunger that had driven Cod to act as he had.

"I'm sorry you had to witness that, miss," Pen said, peering down his nose at Alice perched on his shoulder. His breath was just as foul as his brother's. Alice fought the impulse to cover her nose as he spoke.

"That's quite all right," Alice said, trying and failing to speak without inhaling. "And there is no need to call me 'miss.' My name is Alice."

"It's a pleasure to meet you, Miss Alice," Pen said, and held up one giant finger for her to shake.

Alice did so, thinking that she had been in many extraordinary situations since she and Hatcher had broken free from the hospital but this, somehow, was the most extraordinary of all— nearly eaten by one giant and saved by another with better manners than most people in the City.

"Now," Pen said, and he thankfully turned his head away from Alice (who took great lungfuls of air as surreptitiously as possible). "You wanted to return to the path, is that right?"

"Yes," Alice said. "I need to find Hatcher again."

The giant moved forward in great lumbering steps, and Alice felt the bottom drop out of her stomach. It was not a very pleasant way to travel, she reflected as she wrapped both arms around one of the giant's horns and prayed fervently not to fall off. She would be crushed by one of Pen's feet before he realized what happened.

"You got yourself far afield," Pen said.

"Your brother was chasing me," Alice said drily.

"Ah," Pen said. "Yes, of course. That would happen."

He fell silent, seemingly brooding on something. Now that the threat of immediate death had passed, Alice found herself fretting about Hatcher. It wasn't like him to leave her behind. His behavior had been so strange last night, far stranger than usual. It was as if he'd been seized by some power not his own, some temptation too powerful to overcome.

Indeed, for a moment Alice had the odd thought that she'd seen a wolf's yellow eyes in his face rather than Hatcher's grey ones. But that was silly, and probably a trick of the moonlight. Probably.

Whatever the reason, he had left her. And while she could comprehend a brief madness overcoming him, she couldn't understand Hatcher not returning once that madness had passed. Which meant that something must have happened to him, something that would prevent his return.

Alice remembered the goblin, its long fingers reaching for her hair, and shivered. What if the goblin had gotten Hatcher? "Gotten" was all she could allow herself to think, because a world in which Hatcher was dead was not a world she wanted to live in. There was no future for Alice if Hatcher wasn't in it, and so she must extricate herself from the admittedly polite and helpful clutches of this giant and find him.

Even if it means facing the goblin again?

She deliberately moved away from thoughts of that creature and seized on something the giants had said.

"Pen," Alice said. "Who is the Queen?"

Pen shuddered all over when Alice said "Queen," an involuntary spasm.

"The White Queen," he said, and his voice was low, almost furtive, as if he feared being overheard. "This is all her land hereabouts, from the village at the edge of the plain to the top of the mountain."

"And at the top of the mountain," Alice said, almost as if she were in a dream, "there is a palace made of ice, and the walls echo with the sound of children screaming."

The giant gave Alice a startled glance. "I don't know anything about that, Miss Alice. I've never been to her palace. Me and my brothers stay here in the forest, for that's where she told us to stay."

"Or she will punish you. More than she already has," Alice said, and the question in her voice was an invitation.

Pen was silent for a moment. Alice dearly hoped he was not about to grab her and smash her against a tree for being impertinent. Then the giant sighed, a long sigh of such misery and exhaustion that Alice wished, somehow, that she could relieve his burden.

"My brothers and I," Pen began, studiously looking ahead and not at Alice, "we were not always as we seem to you now. We were human once, just like you. Nothing but boys, really, though we had the appearance of men. We all shared the work of a farm at the edge of the plain, quite near the place where the village is now. Our mother passed on when Cod was born, and our father followed when he was twelve, so you really must forgive him."

Pen turned earnest eyes toward Alice and she received a blast of horrid breath again. "For he never had a mother, and Gil and me could only do our best after Da passed on. I'm afraid we let him run a bit wild."

This, of course, was a completely inadequate reason for trying to eat a person whole, but Alice took it in the spirit of apology that it was given and nodded for Pen to continue (and to return his attention to the path before she passed out from breathing his fetid air).

"Well, for a few years after Da died we kept the farm as best we could. Gil and me worked side by side with Da since we could walk, but we didn't really understand about getting a fair price for our crops and all—Da had always gone to the market on his own while we stayed home to tend the animals and Cod. You likely know what happened next. It's a common enough story. When we brought our crops to market the folk there saw we didn't know what we were about and took advantage. And every year we had less money than the one before, less feed for the animals, less wood to repair the roof and the barns. Finally, there were no animals at all, for we sold them, and then the furniture, and finally the land. If our da was alive he would have wept in shame, for that land had been part of our family more generations than you could count."

Then your da ought to have taught you better how to keep it, Alice thought tartly, *instead of keeping all that knowledge to himself.*

She felt desperately sorry for those three boys, parentless, starving, only doing the best they could and failing at that. And still she knew the worst was yet to come, for she rode the shoulder of a malformed giant instead of walking alongside a man.

"When we lost the farm I went out looking for work, but since I had no trade there was no work for me, though I was more than willing to learn and to put my back into the day. But time and again I was turned away.

"Then, one day, I'd had enough of begging and pleading and was ready to go back to my brothers and propose we cross the plains and try to find work in the City. My da always said the City was no fit place for a human, but we were already living like dogs, sleeping out in the open, begging for scraps from the kindhearted. Just when I'd made the decision to tell my brothers we'd go to the City, a man tapped at my shoulder.

"He told me he'd heard me asking for work and said he might have a job for me. Well, Miss Alice, this fellow looked too good to be true, and what he offered was too good to be true too, though I was too foolish to see it at the time. I thought him a heaven-sent angel, though you'd never seen anyone who looked less like an angel.

"He was tall and thin, though a crook in his back made him appear shorter, and his face was just as long and bony as the rest of him. He was dressed like a lord in silks and velvets, and in one of his hands he had a bag of gold—a bag of gold for me if I only agreed to what he asked. I should have turned and run from him soon as I saw his hands. Unnatural, they were, the fingers twice as long as they ought to be."

Long fingers reaching for her hair, almost brushing through it.

"The goblin," Alice said. It burst from her mouth without warning.

"So you know him, then," Pen said. "I'm not surprised, though I am surprised he didn't stuff you in a sack and take you to the Queen. You're just the sort he likes, with that golden hair, even as short as it is."

Alice did not ask what the goblin did with "the sort he likes." She had seen enough in the City of what men—and monsters— did with girls they took away.

"At any account," Pen continued, "he was in disguise then, though he couldn't hide those hands no matter how much glamour *she* put over him. He offered me the gold, and a cottage to live in here in the forest, and all my brothers and I could wish to eat."

"And what did you have to do?" Alice asked.

"Patrol the wood and make sure no one poached from the Queen's herd of white deer. It seemed easy enough. Not many hunted here, and few ever saw a white deer. I'd killed an ordinary deer or two myself in my time, when one had wandered onto our farm. We would eat well then," Pen said, and his voice faded away into a place of pleasant reminiscence.

Alice imagined him remembering sitting around the table with his brothers, back when their hands and teeth were small, a platter of meat piled high between them.

She was reluctant to interrupt those memories, partly out of politeness and partly because she thought she knew how the story would end. *It seems too sad that one small mistake could change the course of one's future,* she thought and then realized she might easily be thinking of herself. One different choice, a choice to stay home like a good girl instead of following Dor to a place where she was not supposed to go, and her life would have been something entirely different.

She might be married now to someone respectable and approved, someone whose eyes never gleamed like a wolf's but who never made her blood race, either. She might live on a clean little lane where cherry blossoms bloomed on the trees and golden-haired children played in the garden, turning blooms into butterflies and terrifying their mother.

"As you may guess, Miss Alice," Pen said, his rumbling voice bringing her back to the here and now, "I took that goblin's gold and his cottage and promised to keep the poachers away from the Queen's white herd. My brothers came to live with me and for a time we were happy and content.

"Content, that is, until Cod saw the white stag drinking from the stream that runs down from the mountain. He was out on a walk one day, not hunting or doing anything in particular, and he saw the king of the herd. He told us the stag's hide gleamed like the moon in winter, and that it had looked on him without fear, such as no other animal ever had.

"From that day forth he spoke of nothing but the animal he'd seen, how such a creature was suffused with enchantment and how anyone who ate the flesh of the stag would gain its power. He'd never spoken like that before, about enchantments and magic and such, and his talking frightened us. Nothing Gil or I said or did turned his mind from the stag. He started to waste away in his obsession, wanting no food unless it was the meat of the white stag, and no drink unless it was that animal's blood.

"Still, we thought the madness would pass. It seemed impossible that it would not, for you have to understand, Miss Alice, that none of us had ever seen real magic before.

"Of the three of us, Cod was the only one who had seen even one member of the herd. I walked these woods from dawn to dusk and never saw so much as a sliver of white in the trees. So we thought he would forget, for how could it be that he was so cursed as to see the animal twice?

"One night, as Gil and I snored away on our mats, Cod rose up and went out into the forest. I would hardly have thought he'd have the strength for such exertions, for no morsel of food had passed his lips for seven days, and the only water was that which we'd forced him to drink. We had not anticipated, though, the strength his obsession gave him, the way his need drove him out to fill the hole in his heart.

"Me and Gil woke only when Cod returned at dawn, the white stag slung over his shoulders, his hands and mouth soaked in blood.

"'What have you done?' I cried, but it was too late. *She* appeared, her horrible creature beside her, and I tell you, Miss Alice, it was almost as though they expected it to happen—or worse, had hoped for it, though I don't know what purpose it would serve other than her own cruel amusement.

"She cursed Cod into a deformed giant for the crime of killing her stag, and she cursed Gil and me for not stopping him."

"That hardly seems fair," Alice said. "You were asleep when he left, and anyway had warned him many times before."

"I don't think fair comes into it. The White Queen, she wanted three giants in her wood, and she was going to make certain she got them."

"Then why not turn three snails into giants and be done with it? Why all of these machinations?" But even as Alice asked she knew the answer. Why did any Magician do such things? For their own pleasure, as when Cheshire had set her and Hatcher against his maze, or to fulfill some ancient and unknowable law of magic. Or simply because the Queen had wanted to see what would happen if she tricked three farmers into breaking her rules.

"The worst of the curse isn't even looking like this," said Pen, gesturing at his body. "It's the craving."

Alice shifted a little, her hand automatically reaching for the little knife Bess had given her so long ago, in the heart of the City. It wasn't there.

A little spurt of panic jolted through her. It must have fallen from her pocket when Cod or Pen dangled her upside down. She was fortunate, really, she hadn't lost the pack (*and the Jabberwocky*) too, but without the knife she felt vulnerable. That little blade had done more than its fair share of work defending Alice's life, and what magic she knew how to use was hardly adequate for a dangerous situation.

Pen grunted, and Alice realized he'd been silent for a long time, almost as if he'd been waiting for her to ask about the "craving" he mentioned.

As soon as he'd said that, though, Alice had thought of her knife. She'd thought of the knife because she didn't need Pen to tell her what he craved. Cod had nearly eaten her, after all.

"It never goes away," Pen said. "It doesn't matter how many sheep or deer or fish I stuff in my gullet. I never feel properly full unless I've eaten some travelers."

Alice looked at the nearest tree branches, tried to gauge whether she could leap from Pen's shoulder to a tree without plummeting to the ground.

Pen, correctly interpreting Alice's movements, held out his hands in reassurance. "But you have nothing to fear from me, nothing at all. For the White Queen's laws say we can only have the wicked—murderers and poachers and thieves. And you and your man, you were the first folk to pass through the village who paid for what you took. So we weren't allowed to eat you and Cod knew that. He's just never been able to help himself, when he sees something he wants."

Pen trailed off, seemingly aware that this explanation hardly sufficed.

"And the Queen will punish you all if one of you breaks her laws again," Alice said.

"Cod says he doesn't know what she could do worse than she's already done, but I'm sure she could think of something."

"She might kill you next time," Alice said.

"Death would be a relief, Miss Alice, and that's the truth," Pen said. "I've been alive for about eight hundred years, I'd say. In all that time I tried throwing myself off high cliffs and sinking to the bottom of the lake and even slashing my own throat."

He pointed to a thick scar Alice hadn't noticed. It ran like a giant ridge from the top of one collarbone to the other.

The wound must have been fearsome, Alice thought. *Or he tried more than once.*

"It doesn't matter how much I bleed or break," Pen said. "She'll never let me—let any of us—die until she's done with us."

Alice felt anger, quick and hot, in her veins. This White Queen was no different from the Caterpillar or the Rabbit or Cheshire, using people for sport. *And she is certainly a Magician, as is the goblin.*

Alice's path was leading her to the Queen just as it had led her to the Jabberwocky. Hatcher had seen a vision of what he called "Lost Ones," and Alice dreamed of a palace filled with children's screams. Yes. She was going to the Queen.

She was going to the Queen and she would try to free the children, and perhaps, too, she could free Pen and Gil and Cod. Though how she was to do such things, she did not know. She didn't have her knife or her Hatcher, and she had some magic but no notion of how to use it.

Still, Alice knew she must try. Just as she must find Hatcher and they must find Jenny and then, at long last, perhaps they could find peace and a quiet place to live a quiet life.

"Pen, where are you going? Are we back to the path now?"

Alice thought they must be, for though she had run ziggetty-zaggetty through the wood, she didn't think she'd run this far, and a giant's steps were much longer than her own.

Pen paused, scratching his head. "Well, Miss Alice, to tell the truth, I've been following my nose. I caught the scent of your friend and thought I would deliver you to him with a bow on, so to speak, but now . . ."

He trailed off, sniffing the air and shaking his head. "I've lost it."

"He disappeared?" Alice asked.

"No," Pen said slowly. "More like his smell got mixed up with something else, but I can't tell what."

"Well," Alice said, still feeling slightly like a meal-in-waiting despite Pen's assurance otherwise. "I appreciate all you have done, and tried to do, for me. Perhaps it's best if you leave me here. I'm certain I can find him on my own."

In truth, Alice felt no such certainty, but she wished to be about walking on her own two feet again and to feel once more like her own mistress. Besides, while Pen seemed kind enough and proba-bly would not eat her, there was no guarantee he wouldn't hand her over to the goblin or the White Queen if ordered to do so.

Alice knew she would have to face the Queen, but she wished to face her as an equal, not a prisoner.

"Oh, I couldn't do that, Miss Alice," Pen said. "This forest is much larger than you think. You could wander for hours without finding your friend. But me, I know these trees backward and forward. I'll get you to him, right enough."

And that, Alice reflected, *was that.* She couldn't get off Pen's shoulder without assistance, and the only assistance he seemed willing to provide was the kind she didn't want.

Still, she supposed she could let him help for a time. Sooner or later he would wish to return to his brothers and then he would leave her alone. She hoped. Everything here looked the same to Alice anyway. She'd no idea how Pen could tell one part of the forest from another.

After a while the gentle rocking side to side lulled Alice into sleep. For once, she did not dream, so when she awoke she was quite startled to discover it was dark, and she was no longer on Pen's shoulder but cradled in his hand.

"You nearly fell to your death, Miss Alice," Pen said. "Lucky thing I caught you in time. I've never seen anyone sleep so soundly."

"I was tired," Alice said, stretching her arms overhead.

She ought to feel alarmed, she supposed, by her brush with death, but mostly she felt refreshed. Alice couldn't recall when she'd last slept without dreams. It was a lovely feeling to wake up without the tangled edges of clinging nightmares.

"Where are we now?" Alice asked.

"Near the place where the forest ends and the mountain begins. There is a village at the foot of the mountain, about a day's walk. But I can go no farther," Pen said.

"Because of the Queen?" Alice asked.

"No," he said, and some quality in his voice made Alice sit up straighter in alarm. "My brothers are calling me."

She peered closely at his face, trying to make out whether he was thinking of eating her or not, but all she could see was the gleam of starlight reflected in his enormous eyes.

"I wanted to get you back to your man, but I walked all over these woods and couldn't catch the smell of him again. I've never known someone to disappear like that here. I've never lost a man under my own nose."

"You said yourself the forest is larger than one expects."

"Yes, but it's *my* forest," Pen said. "No one knows these trees like me, every root and leaf and branch. If he was here, I'd have found him. That means he's not here."

Alice shook her head. "You don't know Hatcher. He's . . . not like other people."

"Not talking about his manner. Talking about his *smell*. He had a smell, and then he didn't. So unless he changed into something else, he isn't here."

Alice deemed it wiser not to argue, and wiser still not to pursue the thought that Hatcher "changed into something else." She'd wanted the giant to let her go, and now that he would finally comply she shouldn't hold him here quarrelling about Hatcher.

"Well," Alice said rather pointedly. "I thank you, very kindly, for all you have done for me, Pen."

She waited, but Pen did not lower her to the ground as she expected. He seemed to have fallen into a kind of fit, seeing and hearing nothing. "Pen?"

"My brothers are calling me," he said, and his voice was low and singsongy and his eyes were very far away. "The night is alive and so am I."

There is something very wrong with these woods. Alice thought she must be the only creature to pass through them without falling under their influence, quite possibly because she found nothing enchanting in rows of trees that crouched over one, almost as if their branches might reach down and grasp you by the neck.

"Pen, you can put me down now," Alice said, very quietly. She didn't want to startle him out of his trance. Her gentle tone seemed to pierce the fog, and he lowered his hand to the ground.

For a moment Alice felt the ground was rising up to snatch her from the air, just as she'd felt about the trees, and when the ground touched her feet she would discover it wasn't solid at all. She would slip into it like sand, like water, and the earth would cover her head and draw her deep into its heart, never to let go.

Pen's fingers touched the ground with a soft thump. Alice put her feet on the forest floor for the first time in more than a day, and as her boot touched the solid firmness of the ground she shook away her odd little visions of being swallowed into the earth.

Really, Alice, and you were just thinking with some pride that this place wouldn't affect you. It was best not to let strange fancies take hold. The real world was quite frightening enough without adding her imagination to it.

Alice glanced about and found that Pen had deposited her practically on the doorstep of a crumbling stone cottage.

"It isn't much," Pen said. "But you'll have a roof above your

head and four walls around you, and that will keep you safe
from most things here."

Alice thanked him once more. Pen nodded, just the movement of a darker shadow against the black cloak of night, and
then disappeared into the woods, the tremendous form making
hardly a sound.

*And here I am again. Alone in the woods, in the dark, no
Hatcher, no knife, no notion of where to go from here.*

She surveyed the cottage with chagrin. "There's probably a
nest of vermin in there."

Pen had doubtless meant it kindly, but the tumbledown struc-
ture hardly qualified as "four walls." The only other option, however, seemed to be another night spent perched in a tree branch,
and Alice had experienced quite enough of falling toward certain
death.

So with much trepidation and certainty of discomfort if not
danger, Alice pushed open the door of the cottage. And blinked.

Inside, the floor was washed, the fire crackled merrily in the
hearth and the table was set with covered dishes. The smell of
roast chicken and potatoes wafted toward her as she stood frozen
in the doorway.

Alice stepped back, on to the small stoop, and surveyed the
building again. It still appeared to be a run-down and apparently
uninhabited fieldstone cottage. The door swung shut, hiding the
vision inside.

The forest has got inside your brain, Alice. When you open the

*door, it will all be just as you expected, some broken furniture and
an empty hearth and a dirty mat inhabited by mice and flies.*

Alice closed her eyes, pushed open the door and looked again.
The fire hungrily devoured wood. The aroma of chicken and potatoes was tinged with fresh baked bread and something . . . Alice
sniffed the air, like Pen, like Hatcher, like a dog that's caught hold
of something good. *Cake.* She walked toward the platters, hand
outstretched, abruptly aware of the gnawing deep in her belly, and
the only food that could stop it was under those covers.

Her hand grasped the lid and lifted it partway, revealing just
a hint of pink and blue and yellow, layers of frosting twice the
thickness of her wrist.

She let the lid drop with a clatter.

Only a fool wouldn't notice the enchantment on this cottage.
Thanks to Pen she knew for certain a Magician ruled here, one
who called herself a queen and kept a goblin at her beck and call
and turned human men into man-eating giants for some secret
reason of her own. If the Queen had not set this enchantment,
then some creature of hers had.

Alice and Hatcher had wriggled out of her trap once. Had
Pen brought Alice here on the Queen's orders? Or had he simply
thought he was doing her a good turn by finding her shelter from
the night, and he knew nothing of the spell on the cottage?

It didn't matter, really, Alice supposed. She was not a mouse
to be tempted by a piece of cheese. There was plenty of food in
her pack. She did not need the Queen's cake.

Nor did she need the crisp white sheets and down quilt made up on the bed in the corner. Alice had her own (*scratchy wool*) blanket and had slept in places worse than a clean stone floor.

As long as she didn't accept hospitality, she thought she would be safe enough. Pen had invited her to use the four walls and a roof and so she would, and it was probably all right to sleep by the fire, as it was already set.

The bread from her pack was dry and stale. Alice tried to work up some enthusiasm for it, the same enthusiasm she'd had when she and Hatcher had entered the baker's in the village on the edge of the plain. But the chicken and the potatoes, and yes, the cake—Alice had always loved cake too much—had lodged inside her nose and wouldn't leave.

You don't need any cake. It was cake that got you in trouble with the Rabbit. You were too young then but you know better now.

"Just because something is there and you want it doesn't mean you have to take it," Alice said aloud. Her voice was not nearly as strong and sure as she would have liked.

She took a sip of warm, musty water from the small skin in her pack. Somehow her throat felt drier than before, but Alice determinedly turned away from the offerings at the table.

She walked about the cottage, blowing out all the candles, careful not to touch anything, careful not to give even the momentary impression that she was using any object other than wood for the fire.

And I'll collect more in the morning to replace it. That'll put a bee in her bonnet.

She was quite certain all of this was the Queen's doing, and equally certain that her pleasure came from cruelty. Nothing good would come of letting such a person have her own way.

Alice wondered briefly what the Queen's interest was in her, and then decided it probably had nothing to do with Alice specifically. The White Queen seemed to keep a close eye on her forest. Alice and Hatcher had passed into it, and through the village trap unscathed. The Queen's interest was roused; that was all.

(or the goblin's)

No, Alice would not think of the goblin. For reasons she did not fully understand, the goblin terrified her. She spread her blanket before the fire, put her pack under her head and wrapped the ends of the blanket around herself.

Alice was not even a little bit tired, having just had a very refreshing sleep in Pen's hand. She stared at the shadows flickering on the ceiling, not wanting to move around the cabin and do something she did not mean to do, like eat the meal set at the table.

Now that there were no giants and no goblins and no immediate danger for a change, she realized something startling. This was the first moment that Alice had been alone—really, completely alone—for the first time in ten years. It was entirely possible that it was the first time she'd been alone in her entire life. She strained for a single childhood memory that didn't include at least one other person—a governess, a maid, her parents, her sister, Dor—

(the Rabbit the Walrus the Caterpillar Cheshire)

(a goblin in the woods)

(Hatcher)

A lump formed in her throat and she determinedly turned to one side. She would not cry just because Hatcher was gone. She wasn't a little girl anymore—

(little girl lost in the woods)

—and she would just have to find him and there was no need to cry about it, no need to cry—

(Hatcher was always with me. Always)

—because he had run away and left her alone in the woods.

The tears ran over her cheeks and nose and she did not wipe them away, because to do that would be to acknowledge that she was crying in the first place.

She would not think about the tears or Hatcher or the creeping, creaking noise outside the cottage. She would not think that it sounded like the trees were curling down to the roof, that their branches would break the panes of glass on the window or sneak under the door where the wind whistled.

Tomorrow she would find Hatcher, never mind what Pen said about knowing the whole forest and still not sniffing out a trace of Alice's beloved,

(Yes, my beloved, but that's my secret.)

She would find Hatcher. She would, and that was all. And after that they would continue to the desert to the East, to finish what they'd set out to do, to find Jenny. But in between them and Jenny was that mountain, and on top of the mountain was the Queen, and the Queen would not, could not, let them pass without paying a price. Alice knew that must be true, for she'd yet to meet a Magician who didn't extract his price in blood or gold or power from everyone they met.

Worry about what's coming when it comes, she thought, and found the shape of a spiky-leafed flower in the fire, a flower she'd noticed growing in the undergrowth outside. The flower became one star, then two. The points of the stars turned into teeth, the teeth of a bear's open maw; then the teeth became the clawed paw, slashing toward her face. She felt strangely apart from this, that the claws would tear her eyes from her head but it was all right. It wouldn't hurt.

"Alice?"

Alice struggled up, her eyes seemingly stuck shut.

(Or maybe gone altogether, taken by a bear and his claws.)

She thought she'd heard someone calling her name.

"Alice?"

A little voice, followed by a scrabbling sound like fingernails scratching at a windowpane.

"Alice? I'm scared."

Alice rubbed her face, forced her pasted eyes open. The cottage was dark, the fire nothing more than a few yellow-grey coals. The room was cold, colder than ice and snow and a winter Alice had never known except in her dreams.

She pulled the blanket tighter around her shoulders and peered into the darkness. She squinted at the fogged window, trying to make out any shape outside but half afraid that she might actually see one. Nothing that was at your window in the dead of night could be a good thing.

"Alice?"

The voice again, a little girl's, so small and frightened. This time it sounded from under the door.

"Alice? Let me in. It's so cold out here."

Alice could see her breath, crystals of frost making a dark cloud in a room of shadows, and felt the ice forming on her eyelashes.

"Alice!" the girl called again, insistent, compelling Alice to come to the door, to let her in.

She was on her feet before she knew what she was doing, stepping tentatively toward the door, her hand outstretched and her mind not quite present. She was nearly there when her bootlaces, half undone, seemed to reach for each other, tangling together, running under her soles, making her fall to the floor and slam her forehead painfully against the perfectly smooth planks. She raised her head, felt an ugly lump forming, but knew she wouldn't open the door now, no matter what sounded outside.

"ALICE!" the girl said, and she was screaming now, the sound of fingernails at the door frantic, her voice desperate, and it sounded exactly like Dor's.

Exactly like Dor's voice when they were small. Alice's wonderful friend Dor, who became a woman who sold her best friend away to a monster. And of course it couldn't be Dor, because Alice and Dor were not little friends in pinafores skipping and singing and holding hands anymore. They were all grown-up, and Dor was dead. Hatcher had cut off her head and Alice had watched it roll away and felt nothing.

But now there was this noise at the door, this scrabbling and scratching and screaming, this nonsense meant to draw Alice from the cottage where she was safe and out into the night where she would be scooped up or cut up or changed into something horrible to make the White Queen happy.

"You'll have to do better than that," she muttered, and turned her back to the door.

The scratching stopped.

The creaking of trees had also ceased, and so had the wind whistling under the door. There was nothing now except a blanket of silence, terrifying in its completeness. All things in these woods obeyed the Queen. They bent to her will. Alice knew then that the trap was not the village, but the whole forest. Once in the Queen's land there would be no escape except by that lady's leave.

And yet there was no fear in Alice, only a sense of waiting. She wanted to see what the Queen would do next.

"Alice?"

That voice, that dear voice. Hatcher.

Fists pounded at the door. "Alice, I know you're in there. Let me in."

It was as if the Queen had reached inside Alice's body and was squeezing her heart, tighter and tighter in her cold white fist.

It couldn't be Hatcher. How would he find her? How could he know she was within these four enchanted walls? She hadn't walked here, but been carried. He couldn't have tracked her footsteps, and if Hatcher had seen her being carried by a giant, he certainly would have done something about it.

No, it wasn't Hatcher. She was sure it wasn't Hatcher. It was another trick.

A wolf howled out in the forest, and then another.

"Alice? Enough of this—let me in," Hatcher-Not-Hatcher said. "There are wolves."

"Hatcher isn't afraid of wolves," Alice said, and now her voice sounded small, as small as Dor's had, like she was a little girl in a pinafore hiding from the monster under the bed. "Hatcher isn't afraid of anything."

She said this because it was true, and because she needed to believe it. Because otherwise she was standing on this side of the door while the one person in this world who cared about her was on the other side with the howling, barking, snarling wolves that were getting closer every moment.

"Alice, open this door. They're coming," Hatcher-Not-Hatcher said, and now he sounded scared, and that was when Alice was sure, just absolutely sure that it wasn't him, because Hatcher never sounded scared, not ever.

(But he might if there were wolves. If he thought he was going to be eaten by wolves.)

"It's not him," she said. "It's not."

The wolves and their screaming drew closer, and Hatcher-Not-Hatcher's pounding continued. He kicked with his boots and he banged with his fists and he shouted and shouted and then suddenly there was a yelp, and the sounds of Alice's beloved crying out her name as wolves rent his flesh from his bones, as their canine teeth tore him limb from limb.

She covered her ears and crouched down to the floor and put the blanket over her head, rocking to and fro and whispering, "It's not him, it's not him, it's not him."

Outside the wolves barked and growled and tore and ate, and Alice pressed her fists into her ears and wouldn't hear them.

After a long time it seemed like the noise had stopped but she didn't want to look; she didn't want to hear; she didn't want to know. She stayed under the blanket all night long, and hoped that it wasn't because she was a coward.

When she saw the first shafts of sunlight through the thin weave of the blanket, she lifted the cloth from her head. Her pack was still by the fire, imprinted with the shape of her head. The food on the trays no longer gave off its tempting smells. As Alice looked, one of the tray covers seemed to move, almost as if something alive was beneath it.

She would not look. It was another trick, another kind of temptation. Alice knew well, better than anyone, the dangers of curiosity. If she lifted that tray, there would be a plate of squirming maggots instead of a roast chicken and a nest of spiders instead of bread. She would not look.

And she thought, with just a touch of contempt, that the White Queen was really quite predictable. Or perhaps it was simply that Alice herself was no longer helpless, and that she had become better at negotiating the dangers of this world.

She slowly repacked her bag, then glanced at the charred wood in the fire. She'd promised herself she would replace it, but Alice didn't think she would want to reenter this cottage once she'd left it.

Her own magical ability was something she hadn't spent very much time thinking about since her rather pathetic attempt at making food out of sand. But she didn't want to change one thing to another here, just turn the wood from burned back to unburned.

She knelt before the fire, and touched the scrap of wood there. "Make a wish, Alice," she whispered.

(I wish that you would come back to me, Hatcher.)

(Come back to me.)

(Come back to me.)

"Come back to me," she said aloud, and to her wonder and surprise the charred bits in the fireplace seemed to grow before her very eyes, to become something they had not been a moment before—whole, and untouched. As they grew, the air inside the cottage seemed briefly to grow as well, to puff up like a balloon, to fill all the space more than it had before. Then it abruptly stopped, like it had been popped by a needle, and there was a sound like an angry exhale.

The trays on the table rattled in earnest for one moment, and then were silent.

Alice placed the tip of one finger on one of the logs, just to be certain it wasn't an illusion. A splinter slid beneath her skin, quick like the strike of a snake, and she yanked her finger back, sucking at the sore place.

"I suppose it's real enough, then," she said, and felt a little glow of pride.

She had done a spell, real magic like a real Magician, and she had outlasted the Queen and her horrors in the night.

A drop of blood from Alice's finger stained the splinter protruding from the wood.

Don't leave that.

It wasn't her own thought but a voice that wasn't quite there, floating in the room, a whisper that should not be.

Alice felt a flash of anger, anger that Cheshire was still following her somehow despite the connection she'd snapped between them, anger that he was still trying to interfere. She stood, shouldering her pack, determined not to do anything *he* wanted her to do.

Don't LEAVE that!

The whisper was now annoyed. The voice clearly said it was annoyed at her behavior, at her stupidity, and this was her last chance not to be a silly nit, as far as the voice was concerned.

I'm not stupid. Alice stared at the bloodstained splinter, wavering between an admittedly childish desire to deny the voice what it wanted and a sudden understanding of why it was dangerous to leave some of her blood behind.

Blood was a little bit of yourself, a little piece that someone with magical powers might be able to take and use. After spending a long night resisting the assorted enchantments on this place, it would be very foolish indeed for Alice to walk through the door without the splinter.

She carefully tore a small strip of cloth from the bottom of her shirt and wrapped it around her fingers. Then she pulled off the bit of wood. It grew much larger than the initial splinter as Alice peeled it off until she had something more like a wooden dagger than a splinter. Still, there was none of her blood left in the fireplace. She shoved the piece of wood into her pack and finally left the cottage.

She'd half expected to discover the ragged bones of a person torn apart by wolves, but of course there was nothing. The sun filtered weakly through the trees, never seeming to really brighten the forest floor.

It always seems to be almost-night here, Alice thought. She longed to feel the sun full on her face—though not the way she had while crossing the burned plains, she considered. There must be some step in between scorching and shadow.

As she pulled the cottage door closed behind her, Alice noticed deep scratches on the wood, as if made by long fingers scrabbling all night long.

The goblin, she thought. He'd been the one outside while she huddled inside. He'd been the one pretending to be Dor and Hatcher and a pack of wolves. The goblin, with his long, long fingers reaching for her hair. She shuddered and moved away from the little building, tumbling down again now that she was no longer in it.

But why, Alice wondered, *was he not able to enter the cottage? Why try to draw me out?*

There were so many things Alice didn't understand about this forest. In the City there had been guides and guideposts, Bess and Cheshire and the other Magicians. There had been a clear beginning and a clear end to their journey. Now she and Hatcher were supposed to be looking for Jenny, but they'd both gotten lost in the woods. All she wished was to find Hatcher and to be free of this place, and sometimes in her very secret heart she wished not to look for Jenny anymore, either. She wanted to rest, to find a place where terror was not always at their heels.

Alice struck out east—at least she hoped it was east—toward the mountain. She didn't want to spend one more moment than necessary in this forest, where she felt the goblin and his grasping hands might appear at any moment. If she found Hatcher on the way, all the better. If she didn't . . .

You will find him, she told herself, although her thoughts didn't seem very sure of themselves.

Once Alice had passed out of sight of the strange little cottage, she felt her heart lighten. All around her the scampering of the small animals and the tweets of birds filled in the silence, making the place seem more friendly than it had ever appeared to her before.

She walked for perhaps an hour, and was just thinking she might take the rest of her bread out and eat when she heard someone crying. Someone very, very large and rumbly, crying like his heart was broken.

Alice frowned. "Pen?"

She hurried toward the noise, hoping it was in fact Pen and not Cod or the other one (*Gil?*), hoping that she wasn't running toward another trick.

That thought made her slow just a bit, made her cautiously consider. The goblin could pretend to be anyone, it seemed, so why not pretend to be a distressed giant? Why not try to attract Alice's attention this way?

Soon enough you won't trust anything, Alice, not your own ears or your own eyes or your own heart.

As she thought this, there was another huge wail from somewhere ahead. The sound was in her path. Wandering around it would only make her lost, and perhaps that was the intention? To have Alice stray from the path, and straight into the hands of the goblin?

"You can't be afraid of everything, Alice," she said, and went toward the sound of weeping.

She didn't see any sign of the giant, and then suddenly he was just *there*, crouched beside the path, his face covered by his tremendous hands.

Alice was fairly certain it was Pen, but she didn't want to approach him until she was *completely* certain, so she paused several feet away and called, "Pen?"

The giant didn't seem to hear her, too consumed by his weeping. Alice repeated his name more loudly, then again, then once more. Finally Pen sniffled and looked over the tips of his fingers.

"Miss Alice? You're alive?" he asked, and dropped his hands to his sides. His eyes went wide in astonishment.

It was then that Alice noticed his face and body were covered in soot. His great green eyes looked like freshly watered leaves in a mass of blackened skin.

"Yes, of course I'm alive. Why wouldn't I be?" she said briskly, though she didn't feel brisk. She remembered how her governesses would force her out of a crying fit by being firm and practical, and she thought that tack might work on Pen.

Except it didn't. The very fact of Alice standing before him, whole and somewhat hearty, seemed to set him off again.

Alice blew out one frustrated breath. What to do? Continue on her way and leave the giant crying here? That might be the best course. After all, what could she do for the fellow?

And yet . . . it seemed cruel to ignore a creature in so much distress.

Really, Alice thought, *you have quite enough to get on with, don't you? You don't need the troubles of a weeping giant.*

Alice edged around Pen, moving down the path, feeling more than a little heartless. After all, the giant had saved Alice from being eaten by his brother.

She paused, and blew out a hard breath, and went back to Pen. Standing beside him made her realize just how enormous he was, something she'd not really been aware of when being held in his hand because she couldn't see all of him then.

Alice's head only just cleared the top of the giant's foot, and she was an exceptionally tall girl. Unfortunately, standing this close also brought Alice into contact with the revolting reek that wafted from his skin. There was also the smell of ash and smoke to go with Pen's soot-covered face, and Alice had an idea what might have happened, and if she was correct, then it was very dreadful indeed.

"Pen," Alice said, placing a hand on Pen's horny foot. "Were your brothers hurt? What happened?"

"*Him. He* happened," Pen said, lifting his face from his hands. "He burned the village, the one you stopped in. And Cod and Gil, too, just like he's burned everything else from the forest to the City. And all because of her."

Alice was startled by the venom in his voice. Yesterday, when Pen told Alice of the Queen's curse on him, there had been resentment and fear, but no heat. Now there was anger, the kind of anger that made one foolish and led to foolish actions, the sort of actions you would regret later if only you survived.

"And she could stop it anytime she likes," Pen said. "He's made of fire but she's made of ice. She could bank his fires, stop the burning, but she won't. She could have stopped him burning my brothers alive, the way she wouldn't let me die when I cut my own throat. But she won't give him the attention he wants, and now my brothers are dead. And *he* takes everything he can, bit by bit, and still she pretends not to notice him doing it. Soon he'll set the whole forest alight, scorch all the ground right up to the door of her castle, and then she'll have to take note of him or burn herself."

"Why?" Alice asked, and there were so many questions in that "why." She didn't understand all the details, but she understood enough to know that somehow she'd gotten snagged in a struggle between Magicians, just as she had done in the City.

"She's scared of him," Pen said, and there was a great deal of relish in his voice. "She thought she could make him a toy in her playroom, like everyone and everything else. Only he wouldn't play the way she liked, and she tried to throw him away when she found him tiresome. But he wouldn't be thrown, that one."

Alice found she had quite a lot of sympathy for this man, despite his habit of burning everything in his path. Someone had called her a toy once, too, and expected little of her.

And the men of the City want him too, Alice thought, remembering the strange flying machines chasing through the air, and the light in the desert that could only be fire. Those machines had never returned.

Then, too, she remembered Pipkin and the girls they'd saved from the Walrus, blackened husks under a merciless sun, and her compassion receded. However much the White Queen had wronged this man, the innocent should not have to pay the price.

"But, Miss Alice, how is it that you are here at all? I thought . . ." He trailed off, his face a mixture of guilt and relief.

"You thought I should be dead, or taken by the goblin—is that it?" Alice asked.

"It wasn't . . ." Pen began.

"I've no doubt you were forced to take me to that cottage," Alice said, holding up her hand to stop his protestations.

Pen hung his head. "When she orders me, I must obey."

"Yes, I understand," Alice said, though she really didn't.

"She sent a crow while you were asleep, and told me to leave you in that place."

"So you never really did search for Hatcher, did you?" Alice asked. He could still be somewhere out there in the forest, looking for her.

"No," Pen said. "But I didn't need to look for him."

There was something in his voice that made her look up at him sharply. "You know where Hatcher is? Where?"

Pen shook his head. "I don't know where, exactly, but I know what happened to him."

He paused, like he wasn't sure he wanted to tell Alice, like he was afraid of how she would respond.

"What happened?" Alice demanded.

"Well," Pen said. "Remember as how I told you I followed his scent to a clearing and then it just stopped? And I pretended to be sort of bewildered by that?"

"Yes," Alice said, restraining the urge to shout at the giant so he would hurry up and tell her what she wanted to know.

"Well, his scent stopped because your man changed. And it's a certainty that she changed him."

"Changed him?" Alice said. "Changed him into what?"

For a terrible moment she thought, *Not a giant. Not a hideous monster like you.* It was cruel, she knew, to think this, for Pen was only hideous to look upon. His nature, when given free rein, seemed sweet and human enough. But she did not want her

Hatcher to become like the cursed creature before her. She simply did not.

"She changed him into a wolf," Pen said.

A wolf. Not human anymore, not even close. An animal that would run and bite and howl, all the wildness in Hatcher's heart finally given its freedom.

Alice might have adjusted to that, might have concluded that perhaps it was better for Hatcher to run in the woods than pretend to be something he was not, even if her heart ached and wept that she lost him. Then Pen spoke once more.

"Your man is her creature now, and he'll never belong to himself again."

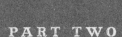

PART TWO
. . .

The Mountain

Alice and Pen stopped just as the village came into view. It was a real village this time, Pen assured her, no more tricks or traps.

She nodded wearily. Alice would stay here one or two nights, and sleep in a regular bed, and eat something besides stale bread and cold mushrooms and hard sour berries. It had been fortunate, she supposed, to have those things at all. If not for the giant's presence she would have swallowed something poisonous and died choking in the woods, for he had warned her away from plants that would kill.

Yes, the giant had been helpful. But he was also alternately furious (with the Queen) and anxious (for Alice) and the constant swing of to-and-fro emotion was exhausting. She ought to be grateful, and somewhere deep down she was. But mostly she was tired and heartsick.

Hatcher was a wolf, under the spell of the Queen. It was entirely possible that the barking and growling Alice heard during the night she passed in the cottage had come from Hatcher, no longer himself.

Alice had a scream lodged in her throat, and if she gave vent to it she would never stop. So she didn't scream or weep or tear her hair or pound with her fists until they were bloody, though she wanted to do all those things. Instead she grabbed on to one thought and wouldn't let it go—*every spell can be undone.* She had to believe this, though she had no evidence of its truth. She had to believe that she could get Hatcher back.

Pen hovered beside Alice, who'd stopped walking and stared at nothing. He spoke, his voice hesitant. "I'll see you in a day or two, Miss Alice."

"Yes," she replied.

"At the other side of the village."

"Yes."

"And then we'll go on to the castle and take vengeance for my brothers and your man."

"Yes."

She said yes, though how this was to happen, Alice did not know. Somehow, though she had tried her hardest, everything had gone wrong. Through all of the horror and sadness, Alice had had just one certainty—that Hatcher would always be with her. And then suddenly he wasn't. Hatcher wasn't even Hatcher any longer.

And you are a Magician who can't even change sand into bread. How will you change a wolf into a man?

"All spells can be undone," Alice muttered.

She must believe that. She must. But this wasn't a problem that could be remedied by courage or love or determination or even by wishing. It could only be solved by magic, real magic.

Alice came to herself again and realized Pen lingered there, waiting for some sign from her.

"It's all right, Pen," Alice said. "I remember what to do."

"If you say so, Miss Alice," the giant said doubtfully.

"I do."

He looked as though he would like to say something else, but thought better of it and turned away from her.

And then Alice was alone again. No giant lurking over her or goblin lurking behind her. No Hatcher talking through the mouse hole, no Cheshire talking in her head. She was alone, at least for the length of time it would take her to walk from here to the outbuildings of the village. The night before, being alone had seemed a frightening prospect. Now it was relaxing. She could stop pretending to her companion that she was fine when she was most decidedly not.

The village was about a quarter mile from where Alice stood. The forest ended in an abrupt line, as if someone had come along and told the trees where to stop. Between the forest and the village was a field of tall grass, yellow-gold in the slanting rays of the afternoon sun and Alice-waist-high.

Wood smoke rose from the chimneys of the little houses, and the wind caught the heavy scent of pig and cow and attendant slop. There was also meat cooking on someone's fire, and the pleasant smell of sun-warmed vegetation and turned earth.

Alice tipped her face toward the sun, reflecting for a moment on the loveliness of just seeing the sun properly for the first time in—how many days had she walked in that terrible wood? It seemed a lifetime.

And if you do not wish to spend another night out of doors, you must move yourself along, Miss Alice.

So she trudged forward, for there was nothing else to do and nowhere else to go.

The village had been built at the point where the open field ended and the mountain sloped upward, so that one end of the main street was lower than the other. It seemed an odd choice to Alice, to deliberately choose to make your home in a place that tilted sideways. How was one to have tea when all the tea things constantly slid off the table?

She giggled a little, and recognized both this and her silly thoughts as signs of increasing hysteria. She needed time to collect herself, to gather her strength for the ordeal ahead, and for the possibility that she might fail.

Perhaps she would not be able to free Hatcher from the curse. She could, at least, free him from the Queen. They could roam the countryside together, and folk would tell stories of the tall girl and the grey-eyed wolf who seemed to love her.

When they found Jenny (which might be much easier, Alice

thought, if Hatcher were a wolf, for he would be able to track her with his nose) Alice would simply explain that her father was under a spell, but could Jenny come away with them anyhow, please?

"Hysterical," Alice said to herself. Her thoughts were getting sillier by the moment.

She passed the edge of the settlement, her mind only half on her surroundings so the goose she startled had flown in her face, squawking and scattering feathers about, before she really noticed its presence.

"Come away with you, stupid bird!" a boy's voice rang out.

Alice backed away from the furious creature, waving her hands to keeps its snapping beak from her face but to little avail. She felt the snip and snap of it at her hands and in her hair, and she cried out.

A moment later was the sound of pounding feet, and then a pair of dirty hands grasped the goose around the middle.

"Sorry about that, miss!" the boy said. He was all arm and leg and bone and freckles, with a thatch of messy brown hair on top. "She's nesting right now and is very particular about who comes near."

Nesting? Alice thought. *Isn't that something birds do in the spring? Does that mean it's spring?*

She realized she had no idea of the season, or even how much time had passed since she and Hatcher had left the hospital.

"Eigar, you come away, now!" a woman's voice called.

Alice touched her head, felt a wet stickiness there. She looked from her bloody hand to the direction of the calling voice. A woman aged by care and worry stood on the stoop of one of the small stone houses, her hair covered by a cloth and her blue eyes angry and suspicious and glaring at Alice.

"Sorry, miss," the boy said, and gave her a kind of half bow before running home, still wrestling with the angry goose.

Alice watched him go, watched his (*mother? grandmother? aunt?*) gather the boy and the bird inside and firmly shut the door.

So much for the kindness of strangers, Alice thought. The woman could have at least offered Alice a wet cloth for her head. It was their bird that had caused the injury, after all.

Alice tore a strip from the end of her shirt and tried dabbing at the cuts. She looked a fright, that was certain, and that even before her face was bloodied. It was no small wonder the woman on the stoop had looked at Alice askance.

Perhaps there was a public well or trough in the village where Alice could wash her face. She trudged along, her mind half on her messy appearance (*the blood plus my scar hardly equal an appealing figure*) and half on her surroundings.

Most of the houses were closed up tight, the shutters pulled on the windows, the doors decidedly closed. If anyone was about, they would only glance at Alice before quickly looking away, almost as if they thought she would disappear if they ignored her.

Alice, walking slowly and trying not to feel too conscious of the way she looked, wondered if it would be best to buy some food and move on. It didn't seem that this would be a pleasant place to spend the night.

Then she noticed there was a symbol burned into some of the doors, blackened and charred in the wood. She paused, peering closer, and something shifted in her memory.

Hatcher, caught in a fever of Seeing, carving shapes into the sand. A large pointed star surrounded by seven smaller ones.

"The Lost Ones," Alice said.

Her path, then, would have inevitably come here, for her fate—and Hatcher's—were somehow tied up with these Lost Ones. There could be no passing through this village for Alice. She must find out more about the Lost Ones.

The thought of a purpose made her feel stronger, less despairing than she had felt a moment before. Hatcher and Alice were meant to be here. And that, Alice hoped, also meant that there was a future for Hatcher yet.

Her chin lifted and she coolly met the gaze of two middle-aged men—farmers, from the look of them—who gave her suspicious stares as she passed. Hatcher's voice echoed in her head (*Don't scurry like a mouse*).

He was right, of course. Alice might not be much of a Magician, but she was a Magician. She had survived things that would surely have broken others. She was not helpless. Believing this made it so, and stiffened her spine.

The center of the village was arranged much in the same manner as the false settlement at the edge of the plain. An assortment of shops—baker and butcher and so on—framed an open square. Of course, this place was perched on the upward slope of the mountain, so everything was oddly tilted.

At the center was a well, but unlike the other village's, this water appeared safe to drink. A small knot of people were collected around, filling buckets to carry home. Alice noted that while all were polite, there was none of the friendly camaraderie one might expect from a small town.

There were no calls of familiarity, no jokes, no laughter. Above all, there were no children, and there ought to be. There ought to be children running and squealing and being scolded by partly attentive mothers, but the only child Alice had seen was the boy with the goose.

She fell in with the group of people around the well, hoping to refill her waterskin and wash her face without attracting too much notice. As soon as she joined the few people waiting their turn, however, what little conversation there was immediately ceased.

All eyes turned to stare at her—cold and suspicious. Alice put what she hoped was a friendly smile on her face and held up her waterskin. Perhaps the fading light would disguise the blood on her face as dirt or shadows. "I wonder if I might share in some of your water. I've walked a very long way today and I'm awfully thirsty."

"Here, now, where did you come from?" an old man barked. He was withered as a dried apple and just as brown, with gnarled hands that spoke of a lifetime of work.

Alice was about to say "the City" and then thought perhaps these folk might not believe that. The City seemed very far away from here, both in miles and in mind.

"The forest," she said, pointing behind her and down the mountain.

Several mutterings began at this, and Alice definitely heard the word "liar" more than once.

"No one comes from the forest," the man said.

"Well, I did," Alice said.

She hadn't expected a warm welcome, but neither had she anticipated total disbelief. Where else would she have come from? She hadn't fallen from the sky, though their expressions indicated she might as well have.

"Then you must belong to the White Queen, and that means you are not welcome here," the old man said.

"Hush, Asgar," a younger man said, his eyes frightened as he glanced at Alice. "Don't insult the Queen."

"I'll do as I wish, Gunnar," Asgar cried. "She's taken enough from us, and more than enough. If this creature would punish me in the Queen's stead, then so be it, but I would not willingly give one drop of water nor anything else to her."

Some of the people backed away during this speech, as if fearful Asgar's words might taint them.

"He doesn't mean anything by it, miss," Gunnar said, his expression pleading for mercy, for understanding. "It's only his granddaughter was—"

"Don't you talk about my Asta!" Asgar bellowed, his face

purpling. He stepped toward Alice, shaking his fist. "That witch—That witch—"

He crumpled suddenly, his shoulders shaking, his face covered by his hands.

"I am not from the White Queen," Alice said. "And I have as much reason to dislike her as you. She took the man I loved and turned him into a wolf, and she set her goblin upon me as I passed the night in the woods."

Gunnar narrowed his eyes at her. "If you are not her creature, then how did you survive the goblin's assault?"

Alice explained how she had spent the night in the cottage, and how the goblin tried to trick her into coming out. Several villagers frowned, and one woman asked hesitantly, "But why would the goblin not enter the cottage?"

Alice sighed. It was quite unfair that they were suspicious of her simply because she hadn't been killed in the woods. "I do not know. There are many things I don't know and don't understand."

"How are we to believe you, that you are what you say you are?" Gunnar asked.

"I have no way to prove it," Alice said. This too was new territory for her. In every encounter in the Old City she had been instantly recognized because of the scar on her face. Here in this little village, though, no one had heard of Alice or the Rabbit. "But I assure you I mean no harm. I wish to rest here, and eat and drink if you will allow me to do so, for I must go to the top of the mountain to find the one I love, and try to save him and bring him back again."

"No one returns from the mountain," Asgar said. "She takes them away there, but they never return."

"Who?" Alice asked, though she thought she knew.

"Our children. The Lost Ones."

A few of the women in the group covered their faces at these words, and more than one stifled a noisy sob.

"Why does she take them?" Alice asked. If she could understand this, then maybe she could also understand why she was here, why Hatcher had been taken from her.

"Who can comprehend the reasoning of a witch?" Asgar said, some of his spirit returning. "Once a season, on the third full moon, we are to send one of our own to the great oak and leave the child there. Always, some of the men will stay and try to capture the Queen before she takes the child away. Always, they fail. They fall asleep and when they wake the child is gone and there is no way to follow, for there is a barrier closer to the castle that none can penetrate. So you see—you can't reach her, or your man. None goes to the top of the mountain unless she wishes it, and if she wishes it you'll wish she hadn't."

"You can't save the children who have been taken, and you can't prevent the taking of the others," Alice said. "Why do you not leave here?"

"And go where?" Gunnar said. "To one side is the Queen's mountain; to the other side is the Queen's forest. If you truly passed through the forest, then you know that monsters live there, giants that eat the flesh of men."

Alice shifted uncomfortably, thinking of Pen waiting for her at the other end of the village. "Yes, I know of them. But I also know that two of those giants are dead, burned by a fire far from here, at the edge of the plain."

"Did you set this fire?" Gunnar asked.

"No," Alice said. "It was another who has been wronged by the Queen."

"The Black King," one of the women muttered, and another woman hushed her.

"The Black King?" Alice asked. "Is that how he is known?"

"We don't speak of him," Gunnar said, giving the woman who'd spoken a quelling look. "But if he is indeed the one who killed those giants, then it would be far more dangerous for us to cross the forest. Besides, there is hardly a family here not related by blood or hand-fasting. Who would leave their kin behind, if there was even the smallest possibility that our children might come home?"

"If they leave the castle we must be here," the woman who'd spoken of the Black King said. "How their hearts would break if they returned to us and we were gone."

And how your hearts do break every day, Alice thought. The grief of all suffused the air around her. How many of these people sat by their windows nightly, staring out at the shadows on the mountain, hoping against hope that one of those shadows would morph into a missing child? And how each mother, each father would dream that they would run to their darling one and hold them and never, ever let them go again.

Instead of reunions would come more grief, as another child was sent away, and still another, and another, with no hope of escape and no hope of the end until all the children were gone.

And if the villagers went away through the woods, if they chose to save the remaining children, where then would they go? The plains were scorched by the man they called the Black King, and beyond was the City, and Alice knew well enough that there was no hope to be found there. So they would stay and wait for their inevitable fate, to waste away here until their future had completely disappeared.

"When is the third full moon of this season?" Alice asked, for she had no sense of time or the season.

"Three days hence," Gunnar said. "The lot is drawn tomorrow eve."

"The lot?" Alice asked.

"The child is chosen at random, by a lottery," Asgar said. "It was the only way we could consider it fair, though I suppose it does not matter which order they are taken in. She won't be happy until she has them all."

"There is no need to draw another name," Alice said. "I will go in the next child's stead."

Silence fell completely then, no mutterings or shiftings or intakes of breath. All the villagers seemed astonished. The old man was the first to regain his speech.

"Why would you do that?" Asgar said. "You owe nothing to us."

"It is not for you," Alice said. "It is for myself. I need to reach the castle, and only those left under the oak are able to cross the Queen's barrier. If I save one of your own children in the bargain, then so be it."

"It will never work," Gunnar said. "The Queen will not take you instead of one of our young ones. And then she will bring her vengeance upon us."

"What vengeance could be worse than that which you already suffer?" Alice asked. "Besides, I think that she will take me. She wanted me in the woods and she didn't get me—or, at least, her goblin wanted me."

As she said this Alice felt again the whisper of long fingers against the back of her neck, and she shuddered.

"We should let her try," the woman who'd spoken earlier said. "She is right. Nothing can be more terrible than what we suffer now."

"And if she fails, Brynja? If the Queen sends her goblin or some other creature here to destroy us all?" Gunnar asked.

"Then it will, at least, be over," Brynja said. "If I had courage enough I would have taken a dagger to my own heart long ago."

"That is not courage," Alice said. "It takes more courage to go on living, to keep in hope."

"What do you know of it?" Gunnar asked, his face harsh. "Have you lost a child?"

"Not in the way you think," Alice said, thinking of the girl she once was, the girl who had been swallowed up by the Rabbit. "But I understand suffering and loss, and I can't go forward without trying to get back my Hatcher."

"Hatcher? Is that your man?" Brynja asked.

"Yes, that is his name," Alice said, and something passed between the two women, some understanding.

"And what will you do when you get there?" Gunnar asked.

Wish, Alice thought. She did not say this, for she thought these people might be suspicious of her if they knew she had magic, even though her magic was a poor thing when compared with the White Queen.

"I will confront the Queen," Alice said.

"You'll die," Asgar said.

"You don't know that for certain," Alice said. *I was supposed to die when I met the Jabberwock, and I didn't.* "If I fail, nothing has changed for you. If I succeed, perhaps I can break the curse on this place. Perhaps she will return your children to me."

If they are alive. No one said this, but the thought seemed to run around the circle of faces.

"We must meet on this," Asgar said. "Gunnar, call the others to the hall."

Gunnar nodded and ran off. The other folk gathered at the well collected their water and hurried toward their homes.

"You may stay here at least this night," Asgar said. "While we decide on your proposal."

"Thank you," Alice said.

She assumed some collection of village elders would decide

whether or not they should let Alice go in place of the child. But no matter what they decided, Alice knew she would go anyway, with or without their approval. She must reach the castle. She must see the Queen and speak to her and try to get Hatcher back, and the Lost Ones. Alice had no real notion of how these things might be achieved, but she must try all the same.

"You may stay with me," Brynja said, and gestured for Alice to follow.

Alice trailed along beside the silent woman. She noticed Gunnar knocking on the doors of certain houses and speaking with certain men. If those men caught sight of Alice as she passed with Brynja, they stared, and Alice felt the weight of their suspicion.

Brynja led Alice to a small and neat little cottage with a clean stoop and the brand of the Lost Ones scorched on the door. The other woman lit the candle that stood on a small table just inside. The faint, flickering glow revealed a single room with a large fireplace on one side. In one corner stood a small round table with three chairs around it, and at the other side a large straw mattress with a brightly colored quilt spread across it. A very small wooden trunk stood at the foot of the bed, and beside the trunk was a pair of children's leather slippers.

Brynja followed Alice's eyes to the slippers. Brynja herself had very pale blue eyes and very light blond hair, almost white. "They belong to my daughter, Eira. She was one of the first to be taken. She was only five. My husband went mad after that. He could not accept that he could not cross the barrier to the castle. He spent all of his time hunting for a way to reach the Queen, to get Eira back. He did not succeed; nor did he ever come home again."

Brynja told this story with no emotion, like it was something that had happened to another woman, one whom she did not know very well.

"I am sorry," Alice said. She was certain no phrase had ever been so useless or inadequate. "How long has Eira been gone?"

"More than two years," Brynja said.

Two years? Alice thought. The child is dead, or damaged beyond repair.

Brynja smiled an unhappy smile. "Yes, I know what you are thinking, for I have thought it too, that she is lost to me forever. I have nothing left but hope, and so I wait here for her. My man is gone, and he is probably dead, fallen from a cliff or killed by the Queen or perhaps even eaten by one of those giants. But my Eira might come home again. She might. Nobody knows what happens to them once the Queen takes them away."

They scream, Alice thought, remembering the nightmare she'd had in the woods. *They scream all day and all night, and their cries are terrible to behold.*

"I have some soup for you once the fire is high again," Brynja said, and she bustled about the cottage in a way that told Alice she was keeping busy so as not to think too hard about Eira.

Brynja gave Alice some of the water collected from the well so Alice could wash her face and hands. Alice surveyed the state of her shirt and pants and wondered if she might be able to wash them the next day. She had spent many years in the hospital wearing the same dirty shift day after day but now she was sick of the smell of herself. She longed to be able to change into fresh clothes daily, and take a bath if she wished it. She never realized, when she was young and lived in the New City, that these things could be taken away by circumstance.

Brynja put out soup and bread and glasses of warm milk ("fresh from our goat," she said with a note of pride). Alice had to force herself to eat slowly so as not to burn her mouth on the soup, and also so she would not offend her hostess with her manners. The worst thing, Alice thought, besides not being clean was being hungry all the time.

"It's been long since you've eaten a decent meal," Brynja observed.

"Yes," Alice said. She had not done a very good job of hiding it, then, for she'd wolfed down her meal while Brynja sat picking at hers. "Food is hard to come by, in the forest."

"And how is it that you came to be in the forest?" Brynja asked.

Alice considered how best to answer this question. She did not wish to lie to someone who had been kind to her; nor did she wish to tell Brynja all that had happened to lead Alice to this moment.

Finally she said, "Hatcher's daughter, Jenny, was taken from him a long time ago. We were following a rumor of her, a rumor that she had been taken far to the East."

"We have heard of girls being taken to the East, even here," Brynja said, her face troubled. "Their fate is not a pleasant one."

"Neither is their fate pleasant in the City, which was where we came from before the forest," Alice said. "But how is it that you and your people came to settle here?"

"Our ancestors came from the north, where everything is covered always with snow and ice. Our people kept to the old ways, but there were some who no longer approved of the old ways. They said that our gods were dead, and they burned our trees and our altars and our homes. We rebuilt our houses, and moved our altars to the forest, and replanted our trees. But they came again, always saying that our ways were wrong, even though some of those who said so had believed in those same ways not so long before. And they burned our homes again and told us we needed to obey or else things would not go so well for us the next time.

"Some of the men tried to fight, to convince others who did not love the new ways to rebel. But there were more of the new ones, always more, and if you did not do as they wanted, you could lose everything. Even those who agreed with us were afraid, afraid that their houses and farms would be burned, afraid that their children would be harmed if they tried to fight. So they went along with the new ways, and condemned us with the rest.

"Finally one of our elders had a dream, a dream that said we must cross the great ice and then over several mountains until we found one mountain on the edge of a forest, and that we would find a safe place to live there. So we who would not give up the old ways left our country and all we knew. We traveled across a great sheet of ice, so thick that it could hold up an entire city, but dangerous, for the ice is not a settled thing. It shifts and cracks and moans under the surface, always changing, never constant. And so some of us fell when the ice shifted, but we knew this was the sacrifice the gods demanded of us, and we kept our faith and went on.

"We passed into the mountains, and the winds howled there and the rocks fell, and we were hungry and thirsty and a few more were lost, but we kept on, for our elder's vision was true and we knew we must follow it.

"Finally, after many months of peril and hardship we reached this place. It seemed a good place to us, for there was a field to plant and the soil was rich and black. In the forest ran many animals to hunt, and there was a vein of water under the ground for the well. Yes, it seemed a good place, and a happy place, and we built our houses and planted seeds and lived in hope, for a time."

"But the Queen?" Alice asked, thinking of the story Pen had told her. The Queen had cursed Pen and his brothers long ago, long before these people could have settled here.

"She was a different queen then," Brynja said. "This queen, the new queen, is far crueler than the old queen was."

"There was another woman as queen before?" Alice asked.

That didn't tally with what Pen said. He seemed to believe it was the same queen. If there were two different queens, then the old one was just as horrible as the new, for she had capriciously cursed three boys and kept them as her playthings for many years.

"This queen came from the East, and took the old queen's power into her body. I think, though I do not know for certain, that the taking made her mad."

"How do you know any of this at all?" Alice wondered aloud.

"The Black King told us some, before he was the Black King," Brynja said, and she looked away.

"Who is the Black King?" Alice asked.

"We are not to speak of him," Brynja said, but her eyes told another story. She wished to speak of him. "He was one of us once."

Alice waited, but Brynja did not say anything further on the subject. She stood and cleared the dishes, and Alice silently helped her wash and dry and put everything away neatly in a small cupboard. All the while Alice wondered about the Black King and the White Queen and the people who had come to this place searching for a safe home but found a nightmare worse than any they left behind.

She wondered, too, what the village leaders might be deciding at this moment. If they did not decide in her favor, then she must find some way to take the child's place, anyway, for her magic would not be sufficient to break any barrier the Queen had made.

Really, Alice thought, *my magic doesn't seem to be good for much at all. And there is no one who can help me learn, for all the Magicians I have met have been mad or cruel or both. I was mad once too, but it doesn't seem to have taken properly. I didn't come out of the hospital with any powerful powers.*

Brynja did not seem inclined to speak anymore, neither to make polite conversation nor to tell Alice more of the Black King or the White Queen. The other woman sat silently at the table, staring out the window (*hoping against hope that one of those shadows would turn into Eira,* Alice thought) and hardly seemed to notice Alice's presence now that the meal was over.

Alice pulled her blanket from her pack and arranged it before the fire. She stared into the flames, the hard floor making her shift uncomfortably, and thought that this was all very familiar. Soon she would fall asleep, and the fire would go out, and then someone would knock on the door and call her name.

Far away outside, perhaps from the very top of the mountain, a wolf howled. The sound was so faint that Alice thought she might have imagined it, except that Brynja started a little.

"A wolf," the other woman said.

"It's only Hatcher," Alice said sleepily. Her eyes closed but the orange flames still danced before her eyes. "Hatcher won't hurt anyone."

Not the innocent, not on purpose, anyway.

The cry of the wolf sounded again, but it seemed closer. That was impossible, though. If the wolf was far away at the top of the mountain, it couldn't possibly be so close already, even if he ran very fast.

What if he had wings?

Stop being silly, Alice; wolves can't fly.

But neither can men have ears like rabbits or women have tails like fish, but you have seen both of those things and more.

Alice drifted in an almost-asleep place, strange nonsense thoughts running through her brain, listening as Brynja gave up her watch and settled into bed. The wolf sounded once more, and Alice felt a comforting warmth in her chest, knowing that Hatcher was out there.

Brynja rolled over on the mattress, the straw rustling as she moved. The fire shrank down and down, and darkness covered the little cottage, and both Alice and Brynja slept.

Alice awoke some time later, when there was nothing left of the fire but a few orange embers, and she shivered with cold. She sat up, groping for her pack in the darkness, looking for another shirt to wear even if it was dirty.

There was a large grey-eyed wolf in the window, its front paws perched on the sill and its tongue hanging from its open mouth.

"Hatcher," Alice said, and threw the blanket aside.

A fur cloak hung on the chair where Alice had sat for dinner and she threw it over her shoulders, grateful for the warmth. She opened the door to Brynja's cottage and walked out into the night, a night where silence had fallen so completely that Alice thought she could hear the ringing of the stars above.

Her feet were clad only in stockings, for she had left her boots inside and wasn't inclined to go back for them. The wolf trotted around the corner of the house and stopped a few feet from Alice.

"Hatcher," Alice said again, and stretched out her hand toward the wolf.

She expected him to approach her, but instead he turned and

trotted away. After a moment he glanced back at her expectantly. Alice followed him through the village, where nothing stirred except her and the wolf.

Soon enough they left the buildings behind, and the moon rose, revealing a stark landscape of tumbled boulders. High above, almost impossibly so, was the gleam of the Queen's castle.

I'd have to be a bird to reach that, thought Alice. Even if she could pass this barrier everyone spoke of, it would be no easy task to get to the castle.

The wolf continued ahead of her, and Alice climbed after him, wondering that she was not clumsy and breathless as usual. She could only credit the quality of the air, which was so clear and pure that it seemed to penetrate into her blood and bones and fill her with an energy and vitality she had never known before. She felt strong, and quick, and she even felt like she might be able to do magic, proper magic, not just the wishing kind of magic.

Alice bounded after Hatcher, the fur cape streaming behind her. She lost her stockings somewhere along the way but her bare feet gripped better on the rock and it was easier for her to follow the sure-footed wolf. They came at last to a tree, and Alice thought this must be the great oak the villagers spoke of.

The wolf came and stood beside her and they waited. Along came a woman, her face and form covered by a white hooded cloak, yet still she somehow gave the impression of great beauty. Alice saw just a glimpse of her pale, luminescent skin and the fine bones of her face before they were covered again.

The woman stopped beneath the great oak, and a man appeared from the shadows. No, Alice thought, he was *made* of shadow, shadow and smoke, and when he took the woman in his arms her white cloak gleamed like the surface of the moon, like she was lit from within.

Alice turned her head away as they embraced, and when she looked again the two seemed to be arguing. The man tilted his head to one side, flashed a smile with so much charm even Alice could feel it, though it was not directed at her. But the woman shook her head and left him, and her stiff back told Alice she was angry.

Alice shifted, thinking to follow the woman (who was surely the White Queen), but the wolf nudged her leg with his nose, telling her to stay. The man slipped into the shadows again, moving not like a man at all, and Alice knew that he must be the Black King.

After a time the White Queen and the Black King appeared again, and Alice understood that this was a different evening she watched, that it was not the present she saw but the past. It was not a single past, either, but several pasts flowing through this space, like the memories of the tree. This time there was no tender embrace, no attempt at charm.

The man demanded; the woman refused. The Black King's shadow seemed to grow, to reach the height of the great oak, to smother the pale woman in the pale cloak. Her white hands emerged from the folds of cloth and the shadow shrank away, frosted with ice.

The shadow burst into angry flame, swiping at her, but she was no longer there. She dissolved into the moonlight. The Black King shot upward into the sky, howling his rage, and far away there was an answering scream, a woman's scream of heartbreak and betrayal.

"She loved him," Alice told the wolf. "She loved him, but he didn't love her, or perhaps just not as much as her. He wanted something from her, though, something she would not give. I wonder what it was."

The wolf banged his nose against Alice's leg again. Alice knelt and buried her face in his ruff and smelled the wild forest smell of his fur. Then the wolf pulled away from her and ran away, up the mountain where Alice could not follow.

She descended slowly back to the village, for the burst of strength had disappeared and now her breath came in painful gasps and her feet bled where they were cut by sharp rocks.

When she reached the well in the village, Alice pulled up a bucket of water and drank until her stomach pressed against her shirt. She was so thirsty.

Alice wiped her mouth and cleaned her sweaty face and hoped she would be able to find Brynja's cottage again. All the little homes appeared the same in the darkness and Alice had not observed very carefully their direction when Brynja had brought her home.

The brand of the Lost Ones seemed to glow like the coals of a dying fire on every door. *She takes the children as vengeance for the love he denied her,* Alice thought. Brynja said the Black King had once been one of them, and so the White Queen must have thought to hurt him this way. In return, he burned everything he could, for she denied him something he wanted.

And all the villagers here, and the people who once lived on the burned plains, and Pipkin and the Walrus' girls, Cod and Gil, Hatcher, all of us, we are caught in the web of their anger and desire and suffer in their stead. And both would rather keep on trying to hurt than to yield.

There was a glow at one of the windows, and as Alice approached she saw her footprints in the starlight, interspersed with the pads of a wolf. She carefully opened the door to the cottage, expecting her hostess to be waiting to scold her.

Instead she found Brynja in conference with a man at the table, a candle guttering between them. The man looked up as Alice entered, and she gasped when she saw his eyes, for they were made of red flame.

She covered her face, afraid of the fire, and when her eyes opened again, it was morning. She had curled into a tiny ball on the floor, and her body felt stiff and frozen in place. Her fingers clenched the blanket to her neck and her bare feet stuck out at the bottom.

A dream, she thought, but when she rose the soles of her feet were sore, and she noticed that they were cut and dirty. The window was open and Alice heard Brynja behind the cottage, milking the bleating goat.

Alice rubbed her face. Had the Black King really sat at the

table with Brynja? Had Alice really walked into the night with a wolf and seen a vision of the past? There was no sign of the fur cape, and no dirty footmarks on Brynja's well-washed floor.

The other woman reentered and gave Alice a brief smile. "A message came from Asgar this morning. You are to meet with the elders at noontime. I have some spare clothing you can wear, and I thought perhaps you might like a wash. I can bring the tub in, though the water will be cold."

This, Alice thought, was a very tactful way of saying she needed a wash. She doubted if she would fit in any of Brynja's clothes, as the other woman was much shorter than Alice, but the offer was kindly meant and Alice took it in that spirit.

She felt troubled, though, as she ate the bread and butter and milk that Brynja put out for breakfast, and those troubled thoughts followed her as she washed in the icy bath. When Alice was done Brynja brought out a pair of woolen pants and a home-spun shirt and thick grey sweater, and Alice realized she was given the clothes of Brynja's husband.

"Thank you," Alice said, and tried to make Brynja understand that Alice knew that she had given her more than clothing.

"He won't come back and use them again," Brynja said, strok-ing the sweater. "I made this for him in our first year together, and though I did a better job on others, he always preferred this, because it was the first."

Alice dressed, and Brynja looked her over, saying, "You look like a boy."

"I suppose I do," Alice said, feeling her hair. It was perhaps the length of three fingers now, and could not be braided like Brynja's beautiful pale locks. Alice hardly thought of her appearance, most days, for it did not seem important anymore. She remembered party dresses and combing her long, long hair but those things were far away in the past.

"May I ask—how your face . . ." Brynja trailed off, indicating the long scar on Alice's cheek.

The scar was something else Alice hardly ever thought of anymore, now that the Rabbit was gone. He had marked her, and now he was dead, and his mark meant nothing. Nothing except that Alice wasn't pretty anymore, and it wasn't just the scar. There was the cut on her head that had been stitched by Bess, and the little pinch marks from the bites of the goose. Alice could feel the hollowness in her cheeks, the fullness of youth and good feeding disappeared long ago. No, she was not pretty, but pretty was not going to save her life, or Hatcher's, or anyone else's.

Brynja shifted uncomfortably, and Alice realized she had gotten lost in her thoughts and that the other woman might be thinking she had offended by asking about the scar.

"It happened many years ago, when I escaped a bad man," Alice said.

Brynja nodded, and did not ask any more questions. Alice was glad, for telling a small part of the story would necessitate telling all of it, and there was so much she did not wish to speak of, things she wished that she didn't remember—

(like girls stacked like firewood, their faces eaten away)

Whatever the White Queen did to those children—could it possibly be worse than the Walrus? Alice thought that nothing was worse than the Walrus.

"Brynja," Alice said, for she had been thinking on what she had seen in the night. "Is the Black King related to you?"

Brynja lowered her eyes. "Why would you believe such a thing?"

Because I saw you with him, Alice thought. Instead she said, "Is he?"

Brynja nodded, a short, sharp nod. "He is—or was—my brother. I don't know what he is now."

"Are you—" Alice paused, not certain how to ask the question. Brynja might be offended.

"A witch?" Brynja offered.

"I was going to say Magician," Alice said. "For the Black King is certainly so, and it seems to run in families."

She resolutely pushed away the thought of her own mother, who was also a Magician, but who had hidden that power from herself and from Alice.

"There is no magic in my blood," Brynja said. "We have had those among us who could see visions of the future, and sometimes perform small spells, but nothing like the White Queen. And nothing like what my brother became. Magic does not run strong among us."

"Then how did he gain this power?" Alice asked.

"I believe he stole it," Brynja said. "Though the story he told me was somewhat different, and showed him in a better light.

"My brother was called Bjarke, and that name in our language means 'little bear,' and that was what he was to us, a little roly-poly bear that we all adored. He was younger than me by many years, my only sibling, but the apple of my parents' eye, and mine too. He could charm you, charm the birds right down from the trees if he so wished. We all spoiled him, for we couldn't help it, and none of us could bear to see him sad for even a moment. It is likely, then, that what followed was our own fault, for he never learned to suffer or to wait.

"When Bjarke was sixteen, he went out hunting in the woods for the first time on his own. Our father was ailing then from a sickness in the lungs and could not accompany him. My mother worried that Bjarke would not be safe without my father, though many boys his own age hunted alone. It was a sign of how we babied him, you see, a sign that we did not think him mature enough.

"Bjarke went out in the early morning, carrying his bow and assuring us all that he would return in the evening with a deer or a lovely fat turkey. As the sun fell my mother watched anxiously at the door and my father coughed anxiously in his bed and I paced anxiously before the fire, but Bjarke did not come home.

"My mother wished to raise the alarm and send the men of the village out for him, but my father said that the boy had likely only lost track of time and would be home tomorrow, none the worse for wear after spending the night in the woods.

"We did not know then of the giants that lurked on the far side of the forest. If we did I am sure my mother would have gone off into the woods herself to find Bjarke. As it was, we all three passed the night pretending to sleep and getting no rest, and when the sun emerged over the mountain, my mother went once again to the door to wait.

"An hour or two later Bjarke appeared. He did not carry a deer or a turkey, and he did not seem harmed at all by his night in the woods. He grinned from ear to ear and told my mother not to fuss and allowed her to make him a very large meal. He said he had come upon a sick traveler in the wood and stopped to help the man, and that had delayed him past sundown. We all accepted this story, for it pleased us to think well of Bjarke and to believe he would help someone in need.

"I, too, was relieved that my little brother was home safe, and did not think more on the story of the sick traveler. We had always been a close family, and enjoyed our company together, playing games and telling stories. But after that night in the woods Bjarke would often sneak off on his own, and he seemed not to enjoy the pursuits we all had once liked. He grew thin, though my mother gave him extra helpings of everything at the dinner table and he gladly spooned it up. It was as if he were being eaten from within by some sickness, and the worry my mother carried grew tenfold, for my father was going very bad. Every day he coughed out more blood, and the healer could do nothing to help him. I could see in my mother's eyes that she feared the same illness had fallen on Bjarke, and that soon he too would cough and we would lose both of them. The next full moon after Bjarke's hunting trip my father was gone, and we burned him in the old way.

"The morning after we burned my father's body, Bjarke disappeared for sixteen days. My mother was deep in her grief at the loss of my father and now Bjarke was gone. I was no comfort to her, and she too fell ill with fever, and then suddenly she was gone too, so quickly I could hardly believe it.

"Now I was alone in the house, waiting for Bjarke to return, though many in the village told me that something must have befallen him, else he would surely have come home. But I believed—I had to believe—that he would not abandon us. I thought that he was so hurt by the loss of our father that it made him wild like the bear we called him, and that when he was done rampaging he would find his way home again, and be sorry.

"On the seventeenth day Bjarke returned. I wanted to scold him for being gone so long, but his face was pale as death and his bones showed through his shirt. *He is dying,* I thought, and everything inside me crumpled in grief, for all of my family was slipping away from me.

"Bjarke took to his bed, and the healer came and spoke over him and gave him many foul-smelling potions, but nothing seemed to change. I spent all my time sitting in a chair beside him and listening to Bjarke ramble in his fever. Some of the things he said in that fever made me think this was no ordinary illness, and that he had been fooling with things he did not understand.

"A week passed, and then suddenly one morning Bjarke bounded from his bed as though the illness had never been. When I asked him where he had been and what he had been doing he dismissed me, and when I told him of our mother's death he showed no grief. A short time later he tried to slip away from the cottage without my noticing, but I saw him leave and followed him.

"He went deep into the woods, striding with a strength that seemed astonishing given his week in bed, and I had trouble keeping up with him. I managed not to lose the trail, though, and came upon a small tumbledown place in the wood, a place so miserable that I could hardly believe it still stood. And when I peeked into the window my astonishment was even greater, for the inside seemed completely at odds with the outside."

My little cottage in the woods, Alice thought, though she did not interrupt Brynja's story. There was magic in that house, layers and layers of magic, though Alice had been too silly to notice it at the time. Perhaps some of it was put there by Bjarke, or perhaps it was there in place already and the boy was merely drawn to it. In any case, it would explain why the goblin had been unable to enter and instead had been forced to try to draw Alice out.

"Through the window I saw my brother, and what I saw him doing chilled my heart to the bone. There was an old man lying on a bed there, and the old man looked so shriveled as to scarcely be alive. Bjarke knelt beside the man, and made a long cut in the man's arm. I saw that there were many other cuts there, on both the man's arms and legs, and most of them looked recent. Then Bjarke put his mouth to the blood that welled from the cut. I covered my face in shock and shame, for what he was doing was terrible beyond comprehension. When I peeked through my hands again I saw the old man shuddering in his final throes, and the look upon my brother's face was horrible to behold. It was no longer Bjarke, my little brother-bear, but a monster made of shadows and flame.

"His eyes met mine then through the window, and I turned and ran, ran back toward the village, hoping against hope that he would not follow me, for I did not want to pretend that this monster was my brother any longer, and I did not want to hear the lies I knew he would tell me. I do not know how I even reached home, for my eyes were blind with tears and I could not see the way.

"When I returned to the cottage he was there already, and I saw at once that he would try to pretend it had never happened, that he would say it was not him out there in the woods. I gave this tale short shrift, and told him to leave and never return, that my brother no longer existed. Then he told me a tale that I would have been a fool to believe, and however much I loved him I could not believe, though I wanted to and my heart broke with the wanting of it.

"He said that the man in the cottage in the woods was the sick traveler he had encountered the night of his hunting trip. He had helped the man to that cottage and the man told Bjarke that he was a sorcerer, and that he was dying and wished to pass his power along to a worthy child, so that his legacy would live on. He told Bjarke the secret way to take the magic into my brother's own body. Bjarke said he was naturally repulsed by this, but I saw the way his eyes gleamed, and I do not think he was bothered in the least by this. In fact, I think he enjoyed it.

"As Bjarke told it, the old man spent the night convincing him that he was dying and it was very important that his magic not repose in his dying body, for it could be stolen by other sorcerers with evil intent. Since Bjarke was pure of heart, this man strongly wished to pass on his power to him, and finally Bjarke relented."

"But you do not believe that the power was passed willingly," Alice said.

"No, I do not." Brynja sighed. "I think it far more likely that Bjarke saw the sorcerer working magic in the woods, and that he harmed the man to weaken him. Once weakened, he would only have needed to torture the man to find out how to take his magic, or perhaps Bjarke simply solved this difficulty on his own. In any case, the moment I saw through the window was the last moment of the old sorcerer, and all of his magic had now passed into my brother."

"What did he do then?" Alice asked.

"He tried to stay in the village at first, though I would not have him live with me. I could not accept that the same creature who would willingly drink the blood of another was also my brother. He showed the others his newfound power, and tried to tell them that he could use it for the good of all. But as I said, that kind of magic does not run through our people, and most were frightened of it, and of the new cruelty they saw in Bjarke. Soon enough he went away, back to the forest. Now and then one of us would see him there, a creature of shadow, and some who went into the woods and encountered him there would find later that they were burned in strange places on their bodies, and that the burns would never heal properly.

"Later, much later, some claimed that they saw him walking hand in hand with a woman in a white cloak, and that the ground was scorched where they had walked and that nothing would ever grow there again."

"They were in love, your brother and the Queen," Alice said. "Or at least she loved him. I think that he wanted something from her, and she would not give it."

"And that is why Eira was taken, and the others," Brynja said, the light dawning in her eyes. "She is punishing him by punishing us."

"Yes, I think so," Alice said. "You must let me go in the next child's stead. This will not end unless someone confronts the Queen."

"But what can you do?" Brynja said. "You have no power that I can see. If you did she would not have been able to take your man from you. And it is pointless, pointless for her to take our children. Bjarke doesn't care for them. It did not hurt him to see his niece stolen from me, or to see my husband go mad. We are nothing to him now, for we feared his magic instead of embracing it."

Alice did not correct Brynja's impression of her as powerless. It tallied, mostly, with the way that she felt herself. But the difference between Alice and the villagers was that Alice was not willing to let Hatcher go without a fight. She didn't understand how they could let their children go so easily and thought that Brynja's husband, though he had gone mad, at least had shown some spirit.

There was not much to do except wait until the time for Alice's meeting with the elders. At the appointed time Alice hoisted her pack over her shoulder, though why she kept it she did not know, really. There was naught in it except a blanket and dirty clothing and something she ought to forget, a jar with something that should be dead by now. The knife was gone and the rose charm that Bess had given her was gone (it had fallen with the knife, she supposed, when she'd been turned upside down by Cod) and all of her food was gone too. She might want the blanket, Alice supposed, especially on the mountain.

Brynja brought Alice to the town meeting place, which was called a hall but was nothing so grand. The room was not very large, with low ceilings and a table at the front, where five old men, including Asgar, sat with forbidding expressions. Still, the entire population of the village could probably fit inside this space with room to spare. Alice felt very alone and strangely small when Brynja left her.

"What is your name, girl?" Asgar said.

"It's Alice."

"Well, Alice, I can't say that any of us believe you can make a difference, but our village Seer has told us that you must go to the oak tomorrow in the place of one of our children, and so you shall."

Alice didn't know what to say to this bald statement, so she simply nodded. She had expected, somehow, something like a trial, that there would be arguments presented or that she might have to convince them to agree to her plan.

"You may go," Asgar said, and the other men nodded.

Why on earth all the formality? Alice thought, as she left the hall. They could have just sent a message to Brynja.

They wanted to get a look at you, to see if they could see what you were made of, a voice whispered, and it was not Alice's voice. She brushed at her ear like she was brushing away a fly. Really, she didn't know how Cheshire had managed it, but he had clearly managed to make some sort of connection with Alice again. That connection was inconsistent and not as powerful as before, else he would constantly be providing her with unwanted advice.

Why was he following her about, anyway? Alice was far from the City, far from Cheshire and the influence he had gained through Alice's actions. She had not meant to help him, but she

and Hatcher had killed the Rabbit and the Walrus and the Caterpillar and so Cheshire now controlled a large part of the City.
What did he need Alice for, except to amuse himself?

And really, Alice thought, *if he must watch me and interfere,
then why not do something useful, like warn me before Hatcher
went running off into the woods?*

The odd experience with the elders and the reminder of
Cheshire left Alice feeling very grumbly, so when Brynja looked
at her hopefully Alice just said, "They're letting me go," in a short,
angry voice.

A moment later she said, in a more subdued tone, "I'm sorry."

Brynja shook her head, dismissing Alice's apology. "It's all
right. You have much on your mind now."

"Yes," Alice said, coming to a decision. "I think I should
leave now, and go to the oak tonight."

Brynja stared. "But the full moon is tomorrow eve."

"Yes," Alice said. "And if the White Queen does not collect
me tonight, then she will surely do so tomorrow, so long as you
all stay in the village and do not send any child forth."

"But why leave tonight?" Brynja asked.

"I . . . have a feeling that I ought to," Alice said. She did not
say that she was worried about Pen lurking about at the far end
of the village, even though she was. She didn't wish the villagers
to catch sight of the giant, or for anything to happen to him.
Alice hadn't forgotten that the Black King had burned Pen's
brothers without reason or mercy.

"Well," Brynja said as they reentered the cottage. "I have some things for you to take with you, if you will accept them."

She had made Alice a little pile of supplies—fresh clothes to replace Alice's old ones, and some bread and cheese wrapped in a cloth. And hanging on the chair was a heavy fur cloak, one that seemed very familiar to Alice.

Alice emptied out her pack, carefully switching the bottle with the thing-to-be-forgotten from her old pants to the bottom of the sack. She didn't even look at the bottle as she made the switch, but kept it carefully covered with her hand. Brynja wrinkled her nose at Alice's dirty clothes and blanket and carried them outdoors without a word. A short time later the pack was refilled. Alice fastened the cloak around her neck.

"I have one more gift for you," Brynja said, and she opened the trunk that stood at the foot of the bed.

She drew out a large knife, very much like one of the knives that Hatcher carried, and Alice knew this was her husband's hunting knife. Alice held up her hands in protest.

"I can't," she began, but Brynja cut her off.

"It's of no use to me," she said. "And you do not know the dangers ahead of you. Please take it."

Alice did. It was much heavier than the little knife that Bess had given her, the one that she had lost in the woods, and it seemed more obviously a weapon, somehow. The little knife had been a last resort to defend herself. This was the blade of an aggressor, of something Alice was not.

But something you might have to be, she thought.

She slid the knife inside her pack. Then she stood before Brynja, and wondered what to say to this woman who had lost so much.

Brynja put her hands on Alice's shoulders and tugged her down so that she could kiss Alice's forehead. "May all the gods watch over you, and bring you courage when you need it."

"I will do my best for you," Alice said. "For Eira."

Brynja nodded, and Alice left. As she walked through the village, the people she met bowed their heads. Some kissed the tips of their fingers and then placed their fists over their hearts, a gesture that Alice hoped meant good luck and not that they were already mourning her loss.

The village ended as abruptly as it began, though at a slightly higher elevation due to the odd nature of its planning. Alice wondered once more why the people had chosen to build it that way, and then shook her head and decided that their Seer must have told them so.

The ground immediately before Alice was covered in scrubby grass and small rocks. Farther up she could see the tumbled boulders of her dream, a field of rock that looked like it would be difficult to climb. There was no sign of the great oak, but since there were not many trees, it should be easy enough to find.

The day was bright and clear, and the sun shone down and made the fur cloak Alice wore heavy. She took off the cloak and carried it over her arm, but this soon became awkward as the slope of the mountain grew more extreme. She wished to leave the heavy thing behind but knew this was a foolish thought. It would be cold at the top of the mountain.

After a couple of hours passed, she glanced behind her and saw that she had not come as far as she hoped. How was it that the villagers could walk with their children to the great oak so easily? Did they begin earlier in the day than Alice had? She stopped and ate a little and drank some water and wondered where Pen might be hiding. There were no obvious places for a giant here where everything was exposed.

Alice continued on until night fell and she reached the start of the boulder field. As the sun set, the air quickly grew chilly and she was grateful for the cloak again. She was very tired, and looked for a crevice that might comfortably hold her for the night while protecting her from the wind.

Once she settled into a place, Alice closed her eyes and tried not to notice how very silent it was, much more silent than the forest had ever been. She closed her eyes and hoped she would not dream.

"Miss Alice."

A very large voice. A very polite voice.

"Miss Alice," the voice repeated.

Alice opened her eyes and found it was still dark out, and Pen loomed over her, a shadow blotting out the stars.

"It's a good thing I found you, Miss Alice," Pen said. "I heard a wolf howling, up on the top of the mountain."

"It's only Hatcher," Alice murmured, drifting in and out of sleep. The exertions of the day had made Alice sleep very hard, and she wished to close her eyes again until morning came.

"No, I don't think it is," Pen said.

"You can't know that," Alice said, pulling the fur cloak tighter around her and settling in again.

"Neither can you," Pen pointed out. "I've lived in this place longer than you have, and I tell you that I don't think this wolf is safe. The goblin keeps a wild pack of his own, and the White Queen has a white wolf that does her bidding."

"Oh, very well," Alice grumbled, rising to her feet. "Where shall we go, then? If there is trouble from the castle, then we would only go toward it, for that is where our path should lead us. And a wolf can track us no matter how we try to hide."

"I don't wish to hide," Pen said. "I only wish for you to be awake, in the event that something happens."

"Yes, yes," Alice said. "As long as I am awake, let us continue to the great oak."

Pen gave her a quizzical look, and Alice told him of the tree where the villagers left their sacrifices to the Queen.

"I did not know of this," Pen said. "Is it not enough that she fools all travelers entering the wood?"

"And another thing," Alice said. "One of the women in the village told me that this queen is not the queen that cursed you and your brothers."

Alice could not read the giant's expression in the dark, but she thought she felt him start.

"It is not?" Pen asked. "How could that be? It *feels* like the same queen when she speaks to me."

"I was told that this queen stole the powers of the old queen, and that the stealing made her mad," Alice said.

How funny, Alice thought, *that both the White Queen and the Black King are false Magicians, thieves who took the magic of another. And how very not funny the way that they ruin everything between them.*

"Pen," Alice asked. "When was the last time you actually *saw* the White Queen?"

"The night that she cursed me and my brothers," Pen said. "Though Cod said that he saw her many times in the woods."

"And she speaks to you in your mind?" Alice asked.

Pen nodded. "Yes. Though she has not since the night that I left you in the cottage in the wood, and my brothers were killed."

There was something Alice was missing here, she felt. It was important that this was not the same queen as before, though if her magic had passed to another, perhaps it should not be so. Magic was magic, no matter who wielded it. If that were not true, then why had the Walrus wanted to eat her?

And the vision she'd had, the one of the Black King trying to cozen something from the Queen—what did that mean? What did the Queen have that the King wanted?

And the children—what was the Queen doing with the children? It was all fitted together like a jigsaw puzzle, Alice thought, only the pattern didn't make sense to her. The White Queen was not the same queen as before. The Black King stole his powers from another Magician, as she had. The Black King burned everything in anger, but he did not burn down the Queen's castle. The Queen stole the children of the village, but the Black King did not seem to care.

Alice had not heard the crying of the wolves before, but now she did. There was very definitely a pack, barking and howling and running their way down the mountain, directly toward Alice and Pen.

"We must move away from here," the giant said.

Alice didn't really see the point in running about trying to avoid the wolves. If the animals wanted to find them, then there was nothing Alice or Pen could do about it, as she had told him. But the giant seemed very anxious to get away from the animals, and Alice was willing to cooperate for the moment.

Pen moved downhill, toward the village. In just a few short steps he was far enough away from Alice that she had to shout to stop him.

"Not that way," Alice said. "You don't want to lead them into the village."

"Of course, Miss Alice," Pen said, looking abashed.

Alice stood for a moment, listening to the movement of the pack. It was difficult to determine exactly where they were, given the way sound echoed so oddly down the side of the mountain. First it seemed as though the wolves were directly above them, then almost beside them. Alice decided to ignore the noise and move directly up, which was the direction she ultimately wanted to go in any case.

Alice climbed, and Pen climbed with her, often getting far ahead and having to wait for her to catch up. He had offered to carry Alice again, as he had in the woods, but she wished to move under her own power.

A very small part of her still mistrusted the giant, and did not wish to be trapped in his hand. If the White Queen spoke to him, would he still obey her? He said not, that the death of his brothers had him seeking vengeance against her. But how could Alice be certain? Pen had served the White Queen—in one form or another—for a very long time. He said he hadn't wanted to leave her in the woods, but he had anyway. What if he was leading Alice into a trap?

While Alice was thinking these thoughts, the sound of the wolves abruptly stopped. She didn't notice at first, until she caught up with Pen and found him looking around in confusion.

"What is it?" Alice asked, and then the silence registered. "Where have they gone?"

"Maybe they were never there in the first place," Pen said.

A trick, Alice thought, *like the one the goblin played on me at the cottage.* She very much hoped that did not mean the goblin was about.

Then suddenly there was a barking and howling and growling and snarling such that they had not heard before, and it seemed to be only a short distance behind them. Alice peered into the darkness below and thought she saw shadows moving very quickly toward them, and the gleam of white teeth in the moonlight.

"Hurry, Miss Alice, hurry, hurry," Pen said. "You go ahead and I will hold them here."

Alice hurried, clambering over the rocks and going higher and higher, until she lost sight of Pen in the dark. The sound of wolves kept approaching, and Alice wondered if the animals had avoided the giant altogether.

Then she felt what seemed to be the shifting of the very earth beneath her feet, accompanied by a loud scraping sound. She realized that Pen had picked up a boulder or two and was about to throw them on the wolves below.

And one of those wolves could be Hatcher. Alice felt a spurt of panic as there was a crashing, rending noise and the yelping of panicked animals.

"Hatcher," she breathed, and then heard the smashing of rocks into bones again. The whole mountainside seemed to tremble.

The wolf pack was silent now, whether because they had scattered and run away or because they were all dead, Alice did not know. She squinted into the shadows, expecting to see Pen coming toward her, but there was nothing. She couldn't even see the outline of the giant.

"Pen?" Alice called.

There was nothing, no sound of giant footsteps, no clatter of falling rocks as Pen climbed.

She called the giant's name again, and the word echoed in the night air.

Now what? Alice thought. The giant had disappeared, a fact that Alice didn't think was even possible. Her stomach jittered nervously. Whatever could remove Pen could remove her without taking half a breath. The giant had seemed unbreakable, and Alice knew she was very breakable indeed.

The wolves seemed to be gone as well, at least for now. Should she investigate? Perhaps Pen had been injured by one of the wolves.

But if so, why didn't he respond when I called? Alice hesitated. Even if Pen were hurt, he would answer if he was able. If he was not able, then Alice didn't think there was anything she could do for him. It seemed very cruel to leave him to possibly bleed to death, but there it was. Hatcher had taught her not to worry on those who could not be saved.

And truth be told, Alice thought, a little guiltily, *I'm relieved not to have to pretend that I trusted him.*

Still, Pen may have saved her life, if the wolves were truly out to get them. If so, then she was grateful. If not, if he had disappeared along with the animals as part of some spell of the Queen's or the goblin's—well, then Alice was wise not to look back.

She continued on, worried that she might pass the great oak in the darkness. The anxious feeling was growing in her belly, a feeling of urgency. She must reach the tree before the sacrifice was to be taken by the Queen. The first purple and orange fingers of dawn were emerging when she finally caught sight of the tree. She wondered that she thought she could pass it accidentally, even in the dark.

The oak was much, much larger than it had been in her dream. The trunk was so big around that Pen could have just touched his fingers if he wrapped his giant's arms around it. What seemed like hundreds of branches reached into the sky.

The whole position of the tree was so strange that Alice didn't wonder that the villagers thought its presence was magical. There wasn't another tree anywhere for miles, and hardly even any plants taller than Alice's knee. Had the White Queen—the first White Queen—planted this tree? Or had it appeared from some other magic?

Alice had heard no more of Pen or the wolves in the night, though she had twice stopped because she thought she'd heard the scrape of a footstep behind her. Each time she had turned, heart pounding, afraid that she would see the grasping fingers of the goblin. Each time there had been nothing except empty air and her own fears.

Now that the sun was rising and she had reached the tree, Alice suddenly felt the exhaustion she'd been denying. The worry and the fear and the uncertainty washed over her until she staggered, falling to her knees. She had only a moment to think that perhaps it was not safe just because it was daylight, and then her head smashed against a large protruding tree root and she thought no more.

Alice opened her eyes and found she was nestled in the roots of the trees like in the arms of her mother. The ground beneath her body was warm, warm and rich and pulsing, like a vein with ripe red blood running inside it. She touched the roots on either side and they shivered beneath her fingers, like a cat seeking affection from its owner.

There was something different about the tree, Alice thought as she drifted in a sort of dreamy half-awake state. The branches were different. Then she noticed that there were leaves on the branches, lovely green leaves as bright as jewels. There had been no leaves when Alice arrived, which made sense if it was spring and the branches hadn't started budding yet.

(The only reason you think it is spring is because of that boy and his goose, the goose that was supposed to be nesting. You don't really know what time of year it is. In fact, Miss Alice, if anything is clear from this trip it's that you don't know very much at all. You've been stumbling about in Hatcher's footsteps ever since you left the hospital, and when his footsteps were not there anymore, you stumbled around in circles. There's not much to you, Alice, though Cheshire seems to think there could be.)

The ground beneath her pulsed again, and she began to get a funny feeling. A funny feeling that there was something underneath that was trying to get out.

If there is something underneath, you probably don't want to be lying just there, a voice said, a voice that sounded more like Cheshire's than like Alice's.

Alice would normally be very cross at Cheshire's interference, but what he said was sensible. She *ought* to move before something terrible happened, like this pulsing earth opening up to swallow her.

She rose, but very slowly. Somehow even the thought of being eaten by the mountain couldn't seem to work up any urgency. Thick knots of pollen drifted from the tree above, landing softly on her face. She swiped at her cheeks and found she was entranced by the glittering stuff on her fingers.

Move along, move along.

"Oh, very well," Alice said.

She didn't particularly want to move along, but the ground was acting very funny. Waves rolled along beneath her feet, lifting her up momentarily and then setting her down again.

"This is really all very strange," Alice murmured. "One of the strangest things I've seen, and I have seen lots that is strange. More than my fair share, as a matter of fact."

A shadow fell over Alice, and she looked up to see Pen standing there. The giant shrunk down to a normal-sized person while Alice watched in amazement. Quite a handsome person, in fact, with somber green eyes and thick brown curls and the ropy muscles of a farmer.

"Pen," Alice said. "What happened to you?"

"She crushed my heart," Pen said, very matter-of-factly. "I was fighting off those wolves and thinking it was nothing to crush them with the rocks, and then suddenly I heard her voice in my head again. So angry, she was, calling me a traitor and saying I was her creature. I said I didn't belong to her anymore, not after what happened to my brothers. And she said, 'Well, if you're going to be like that about it.' Then I felt something horrible in my chest, like her hand was wrapped around my heart, squeezing it tight. Then I was all gone. Now I'm here, and, Miss Alice, I'm awfully sorry I left you alone."

"That's all right," Alice said, feeling terribly guilty that she had suspected Pen wasn't trustworthy. "Thank you for saving me from the wolves."

"Of course," Pen said. He gestured at something behind Alice. "You'd best move along. I think it's going to open up now."

Alice turned, and saw a split form in the trunk of the tree, just as if it had been sliced open with an axe. Thick red sap oozed from the cut, and the ground beneath made a wet sucking sound. The roots gurgled as they pumped (*whatever it was*) into the tree.

The crack in the tree deepened and lengthened. Alice shuddered as the bark broke apart, blood (*for of course that was what it was, not sap at all*) spewing from the body of the tree.

The cut seemed to shape itself into two doors, and each door opened out from the tree. Alice felt drawn there, as though some inexplicable (*magical*) force pulled her as the tree slowly opened and revealed what was hidden beneath.

A woman lay there, her skin white and waxy in death and hair as black as a raven's wing and wearing a dress the color of the blood that ran all around her. The trunk held her like a coffin.

"The Red Queen," Pen said behind Alice. "There hasn't been a Red Queen in a long time."

Alice noticed that there was a slender silver circlet nestled in the Red Queen's dark curls, a crown that looked like woven tree branches. In the center was a small red jewel.

"The Red Queen is supposed to balance the White, and the White to balance the Red," Pen said. "But the White Queen did not want anyone to check her. She killed her red sister long ago, before she turned me and my brothers into giants, back when there was no City but only a village on the side of a river. The White Queen buried her here and planted a tree over her, so no one could steal the Red Queen's magic and she would be forgotten."

"You seem to know an awful lot about it," Alice said absently.

She wished to touch the crown, to take it from the Red Queen's head and place it on her own.

"I know a lot more now that I'm dead," Pen said. "Don't wait until you're dead to learn all that you need to know."

"What do I need to know?" Alice asked.

Her fingers reached for the crown, brushed against the Red Queen's black hair. It was downy soft, like the glittering pollen that fell from the tree.

"The way to the White Queen's castle," Pen said.

His words arrested Alice's motion, broke the fever that was upon her. Was she really about to steal a crown from a corpse? She drew her hand back, repulsed.

No, you need that, Cheshire said. *It will be harder to get later.*

Alice ignored Cheshire and turned to Pen, resolutely putting her back to the Red Queen and the bleeding tree and the gleaming silver crown with its shining jewel.

"What is the way to the White Queen's castle?" Alice asked.

Pen pointed behind her. "Through the tree, of course. You

must leave a little something for the Red Queen, though I think you have already done so."

Alice touched her head, just under her fringe. The place where she had smashed against the tree root was sticky.

"I must go on now, Miss Alice," Pen said. "My brothers are calling me."

She felt a sudden affection toward the former giant, and a little bit of fear. She didn't want to be alone again. "Don't go."

Pen smiled gently. "I must, and you must go on, for it is not yet time for you to rest."

"I want to rest," Alice said, and she meant it with all her heart. "Once I lived in a cage, and before that a different kind of cage. I tried to break free from the first one and they put me in one that was much, much worse. All I want is to find the place I have dreamed of, a little cottage in a green field by a lake."

"That cottage is far from you still," Pen said. "You have a long way to go, but you will never get there unless you go through the door."

"Of course," Alice said, and tried very hard not to cry. Crying would do no good. Crying never fixed anything.

"My brothers are calling me," Pen said again.

Alice opened her eyes.

She was flat on her back beneath the giant oak, and the tree branches above her were bare, with not even a hint of bud. Slowly she sat up, rubbing the new sore spot under her hair and reflecting that she needed to stop leading with her head, for it had taken much abuse these past weeks.

She faced the trunk of the tree and her pack lay on the ground beside her. There were a few drops of blood on the tree root where Alice's head had lain. The droplets seemed to melt into the root, and a split appeared in the bark of the tree.

Alice gasped a little and rose to her feet, drawing the fur cloak around her as a sudden chill took her. She expected the bark to shape itself into doors, and it did. Then she expected to see the white waxen face of the Red Queen and the winking silver crown, and she did not know if she could resist it a second time.

But when the doors of the tree opened wide, the Red Queen was not there. There was, however, an impossible tunnel, impossible because there should not be tunnels inside of trees. There certainly should not be tunnels that went past the back of the tree and on into the distance.

"You'd better start believing in the impossible, Alice, for the impossible will keep happening," she said, and she had a vague memory of saying this once before, except that it hadn't stuck that time.

Alice didn't really want to go into the tunnel, for she was a little anxious of small spaces, and while the tunnel was long, it looked like it would be close. But there was nothing for it. Pen had told her that she must go on, and she knew herself that she must go on, for the children and Hatcher and the White Queen—

(and the goblin)

—were waiting. Alice knew that surprise was not on her side. The White Queen had killed Pen, and she surely knew that Alice was not a child from the village.

So why, Alice thought as she stepped inside the tree, *does she not simply crush my heart as she did Pen's? Is it because her goblin wants me and she indulges him, or is it because she can't hurt me without a connection, like she had with the giants?*

There was so much Alice did not understand, and truthfully, she did not really wish to understand it. She only wished to finish what she must finish so she could go home. It had been a very long time since she'd had a home.

Your power would be wasted in a little cottage, Cheshire said. *And what would you do with your pet murderer? Tame him and make him play husband and father to a litter of little Alices?*

"That's enough, Cheshire," Alice said, and the voice quieted.

She did not know for certain if Cheshire could actually hear her thoughts or if the voice in her head was just her imagination. It would make a strange kind of sense that she had a bossy voice that pretended to be Cheshire.

He could see her actions, that seemed certain, and there was still some kind of connection between them, though Alice had thought she'd broken it. He still wanted something from her. Alice, however, had quite enough to get on with. She didn't need Cheshire hounding her.

The doors closed behind her, swiftly and silently, and the tunnel was very dark. Alice reflected for a moment that perhaps it would be better to stay in the dark, for then she would not be so conscious of the ceiling looming just above her head and the walls squeezing in on her.

Then she thought that darkness was a good place for a goblin to lurk. There was an itching between her shoulder blades, that horrid feeling of someone sneaking up behind whether they were actually there or not.

She needed a light, and of course now that she wished for some help from Cheshire, he had gone away—

(*sent away by you,* she thought in her own annoyed voice)

—for she had no notion of how to make a light out of magic.

"Stop thinking about it," Alice said. Her voice echoed weirdly in the tunnel, so that it sounded like she was whispering in her own ear. "You made the firewood out of the ashes, didn't you?"

That was different. You were only changing something back to its original shape.

She shuffled forward, tapping her hands on the side of the tunnel. "Don't be afraid, Alice. If you're not going to try magic, then you must not be afraid."

But she was afraid, and her shoulders itched, and she felt that any moment something would loom out of the darkness and lunge at her. She stopped walking, and sighed.

I wish for some light, she thought, squeezing her eyes shut very tight like a little girl wishing on her birthday candle.

I don't think you're trying very hard, Cheshire said.

Of course I am trying, Alice snapped back. *Do you really think I wish to walk about blind in this horrid tunnel?*

You must, because you aren't trying. And it's not nearly so horrid as it will be, yet.

Alice opened her eyes. The shadows seemed to move ahead of her, to make monster shapes that had not been there before. She wished she could pull the covers over her head as she had when she was small and the shadows had made monsters and tried to come for her in the night.

"That's quite enough of this nonsense, Alice," she said. "Either you are a Magician or you are not. If you are and you don't wish to walk in the dark, then make some light."

And just like that Alice understood that magic wasn't about wishing, but about her will. The tunnel glowed softly as a line of torches set in the wall lit with fire, one after another.

Much more satisfactory, Cheshire said, and Alice's voice said it too, so that she really *wasn't* certain if Cheshire was in her head or if it was just the part of her that got impatient with her dithering.

Now that the tunnel was lit, Alice could see that the floor was paved with smooth stones joined together. The walls were rough, like the bark of a tree, and there appeared to be nothing ahead save more tunnel.

Alice thought of Cheshire's maze and the passage that connected the Caterpillar's lair with the Rabbit's and the Walrus'. Finally she remembered the long walk from under the City until they reached the burned remnants of the plains.

She sighed. "Soon enough you'll be known as Alice the Tun-neler, for you spend so much time underground, or Alice the Traveler, for you've walked all over creation and back and still have far to go."

Very far to your little cottage and your fair green field, she thought, and walked.

Alice walked, and walked. When she was tired she rested, and when she was hungry she ate. Without the sun she had no sense of the passage of time. When it seemed she had walked a very long way, she came to a large room.

That is, she thought she arrived at it but it really appeared out of nowhere, like it hadn't been there a moment before and popped in especially for her.

Which was entirely possible, and even probable, Alice thought. Why should a magical tunnel that ran through a tree just be a tunnel? Especially as Alice was starting to suspect that the White Queen needed to trick her somehow, to get Alice to break some unknown rule, in order to harm her. It was the only possible explanation for why the Queen hadn't simply used her power to toss Alice off the side of the mountain.

I've simply got to be very, very careful and she won't be able to hurt me, Alice thought, and then, as she surveyed the room, *This is not going to be easy.*

Nothing ever was easy, not for her, she reflected. The room was round, but slightly uneven, like the pattern of bark around the trunk of a tree. There were four doors set approximately at the points of a compass. Four perfectly ordinary-looking doors that Alice was quite certain were not ordinary at all.

"One leads to the White Queen," she murmured. "And one leads to certain death."

And the other two? Perhaps they also led to certain death, or perhaps they all did. Then Alice thought that would not be playing fair. The White Queen did seem to at least offer the hope of a sporting chance, else there would have been no escape for Alice and Hatcher from the false village at the end of the plains.

"The best way to avoid finding out what's behind the bad doors is to go through the right one the first time," Alice said.

She stared at each one in turn, hoping to gather some useful hint.

Each door was made of heavy dark wood and polished to a high gloss. Alice wondered who came to polish the doors every day.

The floor and walls were black and white tiles laid out like a chessboard, and looking at them for too long made Alice dizzy. She closed her eyes so she would not get sick.

Did the children of the village go through these doors? If so, Alice imagined that they must be led directly to the correct one.

"You're delaying," Alice said to herself. "And being quite foolish about it too."

If she was honest, Alice would admit that she was terrified that she would open one of the doors and find the goblin standing there, waiting to close his arms around her and pull her away into darkness.

Stop dithering. She half expected it to be Cheshire's voice, but it was her own. There was an empty place where Cheshire had been, as if he'd only been able to go to the entry of the room and no farther.

Alice didn't know if she was pleased about this or not. It was lonely to be here in this strange place and Cheshire was at least a kind of company.

"Just choose," Alice said, and the words echoed in the small space.

Choose, choose, choose.

Eeny, meeny, miny, mo, Alice thought. She closed her eyes and spun in a circle. When she opened them again the tunnel that had led her to the room was gone, and all that remained were the four doors.

"Very well," she said, and pulled open the door in front of her.

She stood in the doorway for a moment, bewildered. The room looked like an exact copy of the room she presently stood in. The polished doors, the black-and-white checkerboard, everything was precisely the same.

Alice glanced over her shoulder to make sure she hadn't somehow ended up back in the tunnel where she'd started. She hesitated, uncertain if she should continue through and try a door in the next room, or if she should step back and give this room another go.

Before she could decide, something shoved her directly between her shoulders, like a great gust of wind or a giant hand. Alice stumbled into the room, falling to her face.

"Are you all right, miss?" a voice asked.

Alice raised her head, and blinked. She was not in the round room with all the doors. The sun was shining very brightly overhead and someone was leaning over her, a male someone who was just a dark silhouette against the blue, blue sky. Beneath her was soft green grass and the smell of earth.

The man held out his hand and Alice let him help her to her feet. She was several inches taller than the man, who had a round brown hat and a bushy grey mustache and very kind blue eyes. She dusted the dirt from her skirts and readjusted her white kid gloves. There was a green stain on the left one, and she thought vaguely that Mother would be annoyed when she saw that.

"Thank you, sir," she said, unable to keep the confusion out of her voice. "I'm not certain what happened."

"Boys," the man said grimly as he stooped to pick up Alice's dropped parasol. "They're only having fun, to be sure, but they run through these crowds with no regard for the rest of us. Can I help you to a bench, miss?"

"No," Alice said, looking around her, still unsure. She seemed to have forgotten where she was and where she was going, but she didn't want this nice man to know that. "I'm . . . waiting for someone. Thank you very kindly, sir, for your assistance."

"Good day, miss," the man said, lifting his hat, and he continued on his way, leaving Alice in a bewildered puddle.

All about her were well-dressed folk walking arm in arm, laughing and talking. Children ran in small mad mobs, giggling wildly, faces covered in the remnants of flavored ices. Music from a carousel drifted in the air, as did the smell of smoke and grilled meat from a food cart.

Alice wore a beautiful white day dress with satin ribbons on the skirt and sleeves. Her hat had been knocked askew in the fall and she straightened it as she looked about. She was in an open park, there was some kind of party or festival or fair occurring, and she had no notion what she was doing there. She was supposed to meet someone, she felt sure, but she wasn't certain who.

Well, she thought, *I'll just wait on that bench over there until I remember.*

There was a bench tucked between two large lilac bushes and she wandered in that general direction, hoping her memory would return.

She paused when a familiar voice called her name. "Alice! Alice!"

She turned, and a tall handsome man with grey eyes pushed through the crowd toward her.

"Nicholas!" she called, hurrying to meet him.

Part of her knew it was very wicked to meet like this without a chaperone, but Dor had gone off with her own man, winking at Alice as she went.

That's right, Alice thought, trying to make sense of the jumble in her head. Her mother had given Alice permission to go on an outing with Dor, not knowing the girls intended to meet their young men while they were out. *Not that Hatcher is exactly young,* Alice thought, noting the flecks of grey in his dark hair.

Then everything in her seemed to stutter to a halt. *Hatcher? Why did I think of him as Hatcher?*

"Alice? Are you in there?" Nicholas rapped his knuckles on the side of her head, very gently, and grinned.

She shook away the strange thought and smiled at him. "Some boys knocked me down while they were playing. It seems my brains have gotten rattled a bit."

"Are you hurt?" he asked. His eyes inspected her all over, in a way that was just concerned about her well-being but made Alice flush all the same.

"Of course not," Alice said, and smiled, and slid her arm into his. She always liked being close to him, so that she could smell his shaving soap and the wool of his coat and the cigars he sometimes smoked.

"Let me get you a lemonade," he said.

"I'm quite fine," Alice protested. "There's no need to make a fuss."

"Well, perhaps I would like a lemonade. Did you ever consider that?" Nicholas asked.

Alice laughed at this, for she had never seen Nicholas drink anything tamer than wine at her father's table. She sighed, resting her head on his shoulder, thinking it was a lovely miracle that she had met Nicholas at that garden party. They had laughed and talked and danced all the afternoon, while her parents smiled approvingly. He had asked her father for permission to court, and her father agreed, for Nicholas had just been named a junior partner in his firm and his prospects were excellent.

Of course, they were not, strictly speaking, supposed to meet on their own even if they were courting but Alice was certain Nicholas would ask her father permission to wed any day now. *So really it is quite all right,* Alice thought. They were nearly betrothed, and in the meantime it was just a little bit thrilling to be so naughty.

Nicholas gently disengaged his arm so he could buy a cup of lemonade from a cart. Alice fanned her face with her hand. The sun seemed suddenly unrelenting (*like the burned plains*) and she was very hot.

What plains? she thought, and then there was a strange sensation in her fingertips, like she was running her hand through silky ash.

"Here you are, Alice," Nicholas said, holding the cup toward her.

She reached for it, but as she lifted it to her lips she realized it was filled not with lemonade but with blood. The cup slipped from her nerveless hand, splashing all over the grass and the hem of her skirt, nothing but harmless lemonade after all.

"Oh, that was foolish," Alice cried. "It just slipped out of my hand."

"That's all right," Nicholas said, but his eyes didn't match his easy tone. He seemed annoyed. "I'll just get you another."

"No," Alice said hurriedly. She didn't think she could drink anything now without gagging.

"What about an ice, then?" Nicholas said. "Something cool

to take the edge off the sun? Or perhaps a lovely bit of cake? We could have tea in one of the shops and sit in the shade."

"You seem awfully eager to feed me up all of a sudden," Alice said.

(like the Rabbit)

(like the Walrus)

Who on earth is the Walrus? White gloves, she thought staring at the white gloves on her own hands.

White gloves pressing a plate of yellow cake toward her, pushing forkfuls into her mouth. And he wanted her to eat and eat so he could eat her.

"Alice?" Nicholas asked. "What's wrong? You're white as death."

Death, Alice thought. *Yes, death, that's what you will bring me.*

Why had she never noticed before how cold his eyes were, grey and frozen like a winter morning? And why had she never noticed how hard his hands gripped her, how they pushed and bruised?

But Hatcher would never hurt her, not on purpose.

"Who's Hatcher?" Alice gasped. "Who is he? He's not you?"

Nicholas stared at her. "Alice, I do believe you're right and your brain was rattled by that fall. What are you babbling about?"

Alice rubbed her forehead. There was something not right here, but she couldn't put her finger on it. Perhaps Nicholas was correct. Perhaps she was more shaken from her fall than she thought.

"Let's just sit on the bench over there," Alice said. "I'm certain I'll feel better after a little rest."

Nicholas took her arm again, but it wasn't comforting any longer. His arm seemed to be holding her in place rather than holding her like a lover, as if he wanted to ensure she didn't get away from him.

But that's silly, Alice, she thought. She shook her head, trying to shake away anything that didn't make sense. She loved Nicholas, and he loved her, and they were to be married soon. Nicholas wouldn't hurt her.

(But the other did, oh, yes, he did, and she put a knife in his blue-green eye and marked him forever, but he marked her too, so anyone who saw her would say, "You belong to the Rabbit, so off you go, my girl, back to him what owns you.")

Alice placed a hand on her left cheek, her fingers feeling for a hard ridge of tissue, a scar that ran from her ear to her mouth. The skin there was perfectly smooth and untouched, a fact apparent even through her glove.

"I don't belong to anybody but myself," she whispered.

Nicholas settled her on the bench and then sat beside her, saying, "Eh?"

"Nothing," Alice said. "I feel very strange today, not at all like myself."

"I still believe you should have something cool to drink," Nicholas said doubtfully. "It is quite hot out today."

Alice glanced at him, and whatever it was that she'd thought had been in his eyes was no longer there.

Of course not. It's only some strange fancy of yours. The sun is too hot. This is Nicholas and he loves you.

"I just need to rest," Alice repeated, and closed her eyes for a few moments. The warm breeze blew on her face, and the smells of the trees and grass and smoke and Nicholas filled her nose.

Nearby a man guffawed loudly, followed by the polite twitter of a woman with an irritating high-pitched voice. A (*mother? governess?*) scolded a wailing boy for hitting his sister, who was also wailing. The two seemed to be in competition to decide who could make the most noise. Underneath it all there was something else, something out of place.

Alice cocked her head to one side, trying to catch it. It was almost like a *tick-tick-tick*. A watch? But Nicholas didn't carry a pocket watch. She strained to listen. There it was again.

No it wasn't a *tick*. It was a *drip-drip-drip*, like droplets falling in a lonely pool of water.

(*In a cave*) she thought, and opened her eyes. The whole scene melted away for a moment, like chalk paintings in an afternoon rain, and beneath the streaks of paint there was wet stone, like a cavern in the heart of a rocky mountain.

Then Nicholas grasped her hand, and the paint slid back into place, and everyone around her was having a lovely time on a lovely summer's day again.

"Alice," Nicholas said, and his tone made her look at him. His gaze was very earnest now and he was slightly pink around the ears. "You know that I wish to marry you, and I believe you wish it also."

She said, "Yes," and smiled a little at his blushing ears (*like the insides of a furry white rabbit's ears*).

The thought made her smile fade, but Nicholas did not seem to notice, intent as he was. "I know it's terribly forward, especially as we are not formally betrothed yet, but would you allow me to kiss you, Alice?"

She felt her own face warm. No one had ever kissed her before. No one would have had a chance to do so. She was always watched over carefully, except when she was out with Dor. She and Dor always had such adventures, not really dangerous, but they *felt* dangerous.

Like this. Nicholas was asking to kiss her, in full view of everyone in the park. It was a little scandalous, she reflected, but really very safe. It wasn't as though he would ravish her out here in the open—not that she knew in the least what it meant to be ravished. She only knew it made the housemaids giggle, so perhaps it was nice.

(Except it wasn't nice; he would lay on you and hit you and make the insides of your legs bleed.)

Alice's breath drew in sharply. Nicholas, who'd inched closer to her, hesitated.

"Are you unwilling?" he asked, unable to keep the disappointment out of his voice.

"No," Alice said, unable to explain. "I just . . . I don't really know what's going on in my head today."

"Then close your eyes," he said, and smiled.

Alice did so, but she immediately felt fidgety and restless and wanted to open them again. She peeked under her lashes, but all she could see was Nicholas' chin getting closer.

Her eyes opened wider, and she saw Nicholas' were also open, and when his lips were a hairsbreadth from hers she saw the flare of triumph and that his eyes were not grey at all. They were black and pupilless and endless.

Alice's hand flew out in panic to push his face away. She expected to feel the hard resistance of muscle and bone, but instead her hand sank into Nicholas' face as if it were made of mud. The skin peeled away and folded around her hand, holding her fast.

She screamed and screamed and tried to escape, for the face beneath the mask was that of the goblin and he was so close to her, too close, and his long fingers were wrapped tightly around her own. All around them the park melted away, the people and the food and the sunshine and the carousel and the grass, running in rivulets down the wall of the cavern Alice had walked into, all unknowing.

She screamed again, or maybe she had never stopped screaming, and tugged to get her hands free but they wouldn't come. Her face was wet with tears and she couldn't break loose, he had such a hold on her. His face, that long, horrible, stretched-out, *wrong* face was right there, too close, and her heart slammed in her chest so hard she was sure it would burst through her rib cage.

"Alice," the goblin said, and the voice was wrong too, a sibilant hiss such that a snake might make if snakes could talk.

That voice slithered up her spine and crawled over her scalp and tried to slide under her eyelids, but she shook her head from side to side in a panic and kicked out at him.

Her boot made contact with his body, but like her hand it sank into him, as if the goblin were not made of flesh at all. Alice couldn't think, couldn't plan. Her mind repeated only one thought over and over—*get away, get away, get away.*

"Alice," the goblin crooned, and his free hand stroked her cheek. "Lovely Alice of the golden hair. Don't deny me, my lovely Alice. Don't push my love away."

Her skin shuddered where he touched it and her eyes were almost blind with tears and now she thought, *Love? Love? This monster thinks he loves me?*

The screaming panic in her brain didn't quite go away but it subsided enough that she could try to think, to plan, to escape. She must escape.

The goblin had tried to trick her (again), tried to force her compliance through an illusion as he had in the cottage in the woods. This was a theme in the White Queen's doings. Why? Because he couldn't claim her, couldn't harm her unless she agreed or broke some rule. She'd figured out that much at least, but oh, she needed to get away; she needed him to stop touching her.

"Alice, Alice," the goblin said, petting her hair like she was a truculent cat. "As soon as I saw you I knew you must be part of my collection. That hair. That beautiful golden hair. Though it is very short. It would be more beautiful if it were long, long, long, and I could wrap it around my hands."

That would be too terrible, if the goblin could grab her and hold her by her hair (*as the Rabbit had*) and Alice vowed never to let her hair grow past her chin again, if only she could get away from here.

She glanced around the cavern, searching for a way out, a weapon. Her pack and cloak lay a few feet away. She had no doubt dropped them when she'd stumbled into the room (*when you thought you dropped your parasol*).

Her eyes drifted from the things on the floor to the things on the wall and she screamed again, because it was the only defense she had.

"Yes, yes," the goblin said, "aren't they lovely, my lovelies? All of my lovelies."

Alice screamed and struggled and tried not to see, for the walls of the cavern were lined with heads. Heads of women (and some girls, and Alice's heart wept), perfectly preserved, like a lepidopterist's collection of pinned butterflies.

Yellow-haired and dark-haired and red-haired, lined up by the color of their dead hair, their eyes wide-open and glossy and all of them smiling. Row after row after row of white smiling teeth in smiling mouths, like every one of them had died happy, knowing they would be placed on that wall.

Alice fought and kicked but the more she fought, the more she sank into the sticky miasma of the goblin, but it just couldn't be. He had a body and it was solid; he was stroking her hair with his terrible hands and they didn't sink into her, so why did she sink into him?

Then stop fighting, you nit, a voice sounded in her head. She'd expected Cheshire, but this one sounded like Hatcher.

I'm going mad for good now, she thought hysterically. *They're all living inside my head, talking to me, and everyone knows voices are a sign of madness, and you really ought to know; you've been mad before.*

Whatever form the voice took, it *was* right. Struggling wasn't helping. Alice stilled, and the goblin's eyes widened in pleasure.

"What's this?" he asked, his hands still stroking all over her head. "What's this? Will you stop denying me, my Alice? Will you be a part of my collection?"

Alice drew in her breath, drew up everything she knew about magic.

"Never," she said, and put all the force of her terror and anger behind it. "I will never belong to you and I will never yield to you."

It wasn't a wish, more like a promise, a magical promise. *I want to be over there,* Alice thought, looking at a far corner of the cavern. And suddenly, she was. Her hands and feet were no longer submerged in the goblin's treacherous body.

Her limbs felt strangely light, like they weren't attached to the rest of her, but they were and she was free and part of her just couldn't believe it.

You must believe it, and it was her own voice for a change. *You must believe it because if you don't you will never escape.*

Alice had surprised the goblin, but he was still dangerous and she didn't understand all the rules yet and she must somehow avoid breaking them.

The goblin rose up from the cavern floor where he had crouched over Alice, his black eyes narrowed.

"Oh, no no no no, my Alice. That is not playing fair at all. Nobody said that you were a Magician. You came from the City and all the Magicians are gone from there long ago so you should not be; you should not have magic even in your little finger. *She* didn't tell me you were a Magician, and *she* ought to know. *She* knows everything that goes on in her kingdom."

"Perhaps," Alice said, her eyes moving around looking for a weapon, for an escape, "she knew and she didn't tell you."

The goblin moved toward her, his stride strangely fluid, almost as if he slid across the floor instead of walked. He hissed at Alice and black spittle flew from his mouth.

"*She* always tells me everything. *She* knows I am her very best and most loyal servant, for I am the only one who came to her by choice."

"Choice?" Alice said, her voice rich with contempt. *Perhaps I can throw him off balance, make him angry and take him by surprise again.* "Who else would have you? No respectable society would allow a creature like you among them."

"What do you know of it?" the goblin spat. "I can do things for the Queen that no other can."

"What, illusions?" Alice said. "I haven't met a Magician yet that couldn't make illusions."

Except yourself, but never mind that.

"You can't have met any other Magicians," the goblin insisted. "You came from the City and there are none there."

"Did your Queen tell you that?" Alice asked. And if she had

told the goblin that, was it because she believed it herself or because she wanted him to believe it?

The goblin looked hesitant, just for a moment. "*She* knows everything. I am loyal to my Queen and you cannot fool me. If you're a Magician you can't have come from the City, and if you're from the City you're not a Magician."

"Unless your Queen lied to you," Alice said.

"*She* does not lie to me," the goblin said. "She does not; she would not; she will not. I serve her and in return she lets me have my lovelies, oh, yes, my lovelies."

The goblin rubbed his hideous hands together. "As soon as I saw you, I knew I must have you for my collection. *She* wanted that man for her own too, and so we each took one, you for me and him for her."

"She seems to have done a faster job of it," Alice said bitterly, thinking of the way Hatcher had disappeared into the forest and never returned to her.

The goblin grinned, and it was a horrible mockery of a smile, one that showed the blackened remains of his teeth and no joy. "He was weak and my Queen is powerful. You are much more difficult to catch, my Alice, and that makes the prize all the sweeter."

"I am not a prize," Alice said. Really, why did she feel like she had to say this over and over? Why did every man she encountered want to put her in a box and keep her there? Her eyes lighted on her pack, and she remembered what was in there. The knife. The huge hunter's knife that Brynja had given her. It was in the pack.

But the pack was closer to the goblin than Alice. Even if she grabbed it, would she have time to open the bag and take out the knife?

"You say you are not a prize. You say you do not belong to me, and yet you are here," the goblin said. "This is where I keep all the things that are mine."

"Why not kill me, then, and take my head?" Alice asked.

"So eager, so eager," the goblin said. "But that is not how we play the game here. You must accept my love before you become part of my collection."

It was as Alice had thought, then. She must capitulate, or break a rule; otherwise they could not touch her.

"And all of these women accepted you?" Alice said.

She slid her foot a few scant inches in the direction of the pack and waited to see if the goblin would notice. He did not appear to. He gazed around the room at his collection of heads, and his look of bliss repulsed her.

"Yes, yes, they all said yes in the end."

"Though not always to you," Alice said, thinking of the false Nicholas/Hatcher.

"What is a mask?" the goblin said, his sibilant voice dreamy and full of remembrance. "What lover does not wear a mask when he is courting? What lover does not lie and say sweet words when what he wants from his beloved is not sweet at all?"

Alice slid closer to the pack while the goblin spoke. It was just possible, she thought, to dive for it and yank out the knife before the goblin caught on. She drew in a steadying breath.

Now that she had a plan, even a not-very-good one, she felt calmer. She was at least attempting to master her own fate.

"I shouldn't bother if I were you," the goblin said.

"Shouldn't bother what?" Alice asked, all innocence.

"Shouldn't bother leaping about and looking for the knife," the goblin said, and Brynja's gift appeared in his hand.

Alice wondered if the goblin could read her thoughts like the Caterpillar. She imagined a field of clouds in front of her mind, a trick she'd used to disguise her thoughts from that other Magician.

"Oh, I can't look into your mind," the goblin said, and sounded richly amused. "But your face shows your intentions plain as day. And I have already swum among your thoughts and wishes, Alice, and your man's too. He dreams of blood, that one."

Tell me something I don't know, Alice thought, and that thought was so incongruous that it startled a laugh from her. The goblin looked at her oddly, and Alice remembered where she was and what he wanted to do to her.

"How can you see our dreams if you can't read our minds?" Alice asked.

"You slept in the Queen's village, and in the Queen's forest. Your dreams go walking in the night and she knows how to walk with them. This is how she can see into your heart, how she lures you with your fondest desire." The goblin frowned at Alice, tapping the flat side of the knife in the opposite hand. "I thought you wanted a normal life and garden parties and a respectable man. But I seem to have made a mistake. You do not wish for a quiet respectable life. You had one of those and you ran from it, ran to a life of blood and death. So that must be—it has to be—what you really want. Your man dreams of blood, of the wet slice of blade in flesh, and you curl yourself about him in the night, so you must dream the same dream, or wish you did. And once I give that to you, then you will love me."

The cavern walls slid away then, melting like wax in a fire. All the heads on the wall slipped and screamed, their smiling mouths shaped instead in matching Os of despair, their eyes wide and fearful.

Get out, get away, before you become one of us, they called to Alice. *Get out, get away!*

The floor shifted beneath her, no longer the hard rock of the cavern but something wet and sticky and soft, like muscle flayed open by a sharp, sharp knife.

All around her the walls ran red and the air was filled with the cries of lost girls. The goblin stalked toward her, the knife that was supposed to defend her in his hand, and it wasn't his hand but Hatcher's.

It wasn't the goblin's face either but Hatcher's face, the stretched-out nose and chin morphed into Hatcher's beautiful, wild planes of angle and bone, the black doll's eyes turned into Hatcher's grey ones.

"Alice, come to me," he said in Hatcher's voice.

This was somehow more terrible than anything the goblin

had done thus far. He was her Hatcher, the madman who loved her. This was not some false, idealized dream of what Hatcher might have been. The goblin took the face of the man she knew, the man she loved, the man she was trying to save.

"Alice, come to me; let me kiss you and love you and tear you to pieces," he said with Hatcher's voice and Hatcher's mouth and Hatcher's hands holding that long, wicked blade.

She could run. Yes, she could run, and the goblin would likely enjoy that. He would chase her and croon at her and laugh all the while. It would not, however, change her circumstances. Alice could see no obvious exit out of the cave, so she was trapped until she had time to pick through the goblin's illusions. The goblin with Hatcher's face held her knife.

But what if he didn't? What if I just . . . wished?

It could work. She would have to be very careful and very patient and take him by surprise, just like with the Jabberwocky.

Alice stood motionless and tried to look scared. It wasn't difficult. She *was* scared. She was terrified deep in her bones that she would not escape.

There had been worse in Alice's life to be sure, but this was a cage of a different kind. In the Rabbit's warren there had been no illusions, only her will to live free against the Rabbit's will to keep her there.

Here the goblin could change himself over and over until Alice was too exhausted to remember who she was and why she was here, and then she would be lost. So she must stand and find courage she did not have.

Alice blinked and the false Hatcher was before her, only a few inches separating their faces.

"Alice," he cooed, "let me love you; let me rip you."

He reached for her face with the knife, the edge aiming for her unscarred cheek. She saw the blade move in slow motion, watched it until it was almost nothing but a winking flash out of the corner of her eye.

Then she thought, *Right, I'll take that.*

The incredible thing about magic was how easy it was once you more or less knew what you were doing, Alice considered. The handle was in her grip and she slashed right across the false Hatcher's neck with all the force she could muster and all the anger and fear in her heart.

The neck separated like a smiling mouth and the Hatcher mask broke apart. The bloodstained walls shivered all over and the goblin clutched both his hands, his grotesquely long monster's hands, at his throat but there was no stopping the flow of black liquid that oozed out. Dark clots of blood clustered at his mouth and nose and dripped out of his eyes, and all around them the headless girls made a noise that sounded like a strange kind of joyful singing.

The goblin gurgled, his mouth working like he was trying to talk, trying to call out for help. *Trying to call his Queen*, Alice thought, *but I don't think she will trouble about him now. She doesn't seem the sort to dwell on a lost soldier, even one as loyal as this.*

His eyes were fearful now, staring at Alice, and mixed with

the fear was a kind of patent disbelief that she found she could easily read.

"How could this girl, this nothing, this lovely for my wall defeat me? And why is my Queen not here now punishing her for this? And why did SHE not tell me that this one was a Magician?"

The goblin staggered away from her, and Alice was reminded of something Hatcher had told her once, about finishing them off so they didn't come back for you later.

She was loath to touch the goblin again, loath to use the knife that cut so easily. Alice feared all the blood on her hands was turning her into a monster, but she must do this.

Pretend you're Hatcher, she thought, and strangely that did make it seem easier, for Hatcher was a virtuoso musician and his instrument was a sharp edge. When he moved to murder, his body would arc and spin like a dancer, always knowing exactly what end would occur.

Alice stepped nearer, almost into the goblin's arms, and put that knife where the thing's heart ought to be.

He cried out then, and all the heads on the shelves joined in, a horrible high-pitched screaming that made Alice cover her ears. She backed away, trying to escape the sound that seemed to drive deep inside her ear like a long shiny needle, but there was no escape from it, for it filled up all the empty space in the air.

The cavern shook and rumbled like there was an earthquake deep in the mountain, and the walls peeled downward, taking the heads with them. The girls, all the goblin's lovelies, rolled right up inside the cavern like they were rolling up inside a carpet prepared for moving.

A circular chasm opened up at the goblin's feet and he fell inside, his face still set in that rigor of disbelief. Alice could hardly believe that was it, that the nightmare who'd haunted her almost since they entered the wood had simply fallen away into a dark hole.

The cave was falling into the chasm now too, everything swirling like the water at the bottom of a bathtub. Alice glanced around helplessly for a sign, for anything that would show her how to get out before she too was sucked into the swirling vortex at the center of the room.

The door, the door. I came in through a door so I must be able to go out again.

As the cave walls disappeared they revealed exposed beams and brick, the way a house might look when it is not finished yet. The wall behind Alice bumped into her legs as it rolled up toward the hole that sucked in the goblin.

For a terrible moment she felt the momentum of the rolling cavern move her toward the abyss, that endless fall where she would be trapped with the goblin forever.

Then she was knocked backward over the tube just as one would fall over a spinning log. Her body slammed into a dirt floor and clouds of dust puffed up all around her, making her cough. Alice sat up just in time to see the remains of the goblin's lair pulled into the hole. Then the hole closed, followed by an audible "pop," almost like the sound Alice heard when she'd broken the string that connected her to Cheshire.

Or thought I'd broken it, at any rate, Alice thought. The little Magician did seem to cling to her somehow, like a cobweb tangled in her hair.

It was interesting, she reflected, that the goblin's cave had collapsed the way the Caterpillar's crazed Butterflies had when Alice killed him. Was it Alice, or was it that Magicians were tied so closely to the place they lived? And if so, what did that make her?

A Magician without a home, she thought, one that wouldn't cause a ripple in the world if she died. Who would even miss her? Her parents, no doubt, thought she'd died in the hospital fire and were likely relieved in that knowledge. After Alice returned from the Old City, she'd never been anything but an unwanted burden to them.

Hatcher was a wolf who'd probably forgotten he'd ever been human, tied now to the White Queen. If the goblin had added Alice to his collection, no one would know and no one would care. That was a disheartening thought, one that made Alice wonder why she bothered to move forward and fight at all.

Because you must live, Alice.

It didn't feel like living. She'd just killed a horrible nightmare and she'd done it all on her own, without any help from Cheshire or Hatcher or anyone.

"I won," Alice said to the empty room.

It didn't feel like winning either. It felt like surviving. Alice was tired of surviving, tired of magic and quests and blood. She wanted to live, really live, the way ordinary people did.

Like Brynja and the other folk of that village at that bottom of the mountain? Is that living, to have your children stolen because of the caprice of a witch?

"I'm alive," she said, as if that should be a comfort.

Then she cried. She cried because she was frightened and alone. She cried because she'd been terrified of the goblin, because she so narrowly escaped becoming one of his victims. She cried because she still had far to go, because there were lost children to find and Hatcher to save. She cried because she still had to face the White Queen and because her hands were black with the goblin's blood.

When she was done crying (and it took a long time to be done, for her heart had carried many unshed tears), she stood up, dusted herself off and then stopped.

Her pack and cloak were gone.

It was logical, of course, that they would have been rolled up with the rest of the room and sucked into the hole. All she had now was the knife in her hand and the clothes on her back. That might not be a problem, but there was something more in the bottom of the pack.

There was a small glass jar with a pretty purple butterfly. That butterfly had fallen into a magical abyss and was now, she hoped, gone forever. Part of her felt an immense relief at that thought, a weight lifted that she'd been dragging around ever since the day she'd tricked the Magician into it.

Another part of her, that niggling, nagging little voice that lived in the back of one's mind, was worried. What if the magic that had destroyed the goblin's lair somehow brought that little purple butterfly (from now on she wouldn't say his name, wouldn't even think it) back to life?

"You can't trouble yourself about it now, Alice," she told herself firmly. "You have plenty of troubles in front of you without taking on more."

But what if . . . ?

No, there would be no "what if." The butterfly was gone now, and she certainly wouldn't reopen that hole and dive after it to make sure it was really dead, even if she knew how. There was only the path forward for Alice, always.

She glanced around the remnants of the room, looking for a door and finding none.

There must be a way out. If there is a way in, then there is a way out.

The goblin could come and go, and he had lured her inside here, so she just needed to examine the room very carefully.

It was terribly slow going, and more than once Alice wanted to just sit down and hope that someone would come to free her instead. Of course, anyone who came to free her would likely be an agent of the Queen, and that wouldn't end well for Alice, so she kept looking.

She ran her hand over every brick within reach, every beam of wood. She peered into every cobwebby corner, disturbing more than one spider, some of which were large enough to give her angry looks before scuttling away.

Finally, when she was far past the end of her rope and starting to despair, she found it. It was a very thin seam in the brick, camouflaged perfectly and shaped like a rectangular door. She pushed at it, and though it had no hinges, it swung open ever so slowly.

As she waited for the entrance Alice thought, *This had best not be one of those rooms of many doors again. I'm not choosing another door after the last one. If that's the case I will sit right down in the middle of the floor and let the Queen's soldiers find me.*

Alice didn't know why she thought the Queen had soldiers, except that queens always had soldiers, or ought to. Weren't the pawns on a chessboard nothing but soldiers for the royalty in the back row?

This is rather like a game of chess, isn't it? A White Queen and a Black King and all the little pieces—me and Hatcher and the children from the village—moving in between, trying not to get swiped.

But the brick door revealed yet another tunnel, this time made of ice. Alice felt that this must mean she was finally close to her destination, that the White Queen would be at the end of this. She stepped into the passage and shivered despite the thick knitted sweater she wore. Alice thought longingly of the fur cloak that had disappeared along with her pack.

"Walk faster, Alice; you'll stay warmer," she said, wrapping her arms around her elbows, careful not to drop the knife she still gripped, the last thing she had to defend herself.

Besides magic, she thought, but she also thought that she was quite out of her class here, magic-wise. The White Queen had old magic, magic she had taken from someone else, magic that had endured for hundreds of years.

But magic that is also somehow . . . unstable? Alice wondered. There was something there she could almost grasp, but not quite. It was important that the Queen's magic didn't belong to her. It implied that perhaps it could be taken away. Alice shook her head. She wasn't certain, and it would have been helpful to have a few hints from Cheshire now, but he had gone away again.

The cold soon made it difficult to think, to see, to even breathe. Every inhalation seemed to spread ice inside her from her chest outward. The passage was slippery and the upward slope of it inhibited fast progress. She shook with cold, the knife falling from her hand many times. On each occasion she spent several minutes picking it up again, only to have it slip from her numb fingers.

She remembered as she walked in a daze of cold, thinking of her dream of the castle made of ice at the top of the mountain. She wondered, too, what she would find when she arrived there.

In her dream all the children screamed, screamed all day and all the time, and she thought she could hear just the faintest echo of those screams, as if they had seeped into the ice and came forth again in the cold steam that rose when Alice passed.

Her teeth chattered. Her ribs shook so violently that her back seemed to seize up and freeze, all the muscles locked painfully against her spine. Her hands were blue and rimed with frost. When she blinked, crystals of ice fell from her lashes, burning her frozen cheeks. The upward slope of passage and the constant need to struggle for purchase made Alice tired and angry.

Upward because the Queen must have her castle at the top of a bloody mountain. She paused for a moment in her thoughts there, for Alice was fairly certain she had never even thought such a curse word—a "low word," her mother would have said— and despite the cold her cheeks flushed.

Why not a valley? she continued, deciding that after having slashed someone's throat she should hardly worry about her language. *Then one could simply roll down the icy path until one turned into a giant snowball.*

Alice imagined rolling and rolling in her great ball of snow, getting larger and larger and larger until you could not even see her hands or feet. The ball would roll and roll and gather speed until she was spinning so fast it would make her feel sick and dizzy but full of joy too, the way that she felt when she was on a carousel or riding a horse that galloped too fast.

The enormous snowball would crash through the gates of the Queen's palace and would break apart to reveal Alice inside, like a pudding with a prize in it. Then the Queen would think it all so funny that she would laugh and laugh, and she would set the children free and Hatcher free and they would all have tea and cake together in their best party clothes.

Alice recognized that her thoughts were getting very silly indeed. It was the cold, the cold that made her eyes want to close. Her brain twisted into knots, going this way and that, and she felt she might never be warm again, never again.

If someone touched me right now I would shatter into a million pieces. A million million million shards of ice would Alice be. Little Alice bits all over the floor and no one to clean them up.

And then, like so many other occasions in Alice's life since the hospital, the tunnel ended and there was a door.

The door appeared so abruptly she was certain it was a figment of her fevered brain. She stopped, staring at it, trying to decide whether it was real or not.

Her hands reached for it of their own accord, a smooth perfect door made of ice, and she hoped there would be no trick necessary to open it. Alice was really and truly tired of tricks and trials and illusions and things never quite working out the way they ought to.

The door opened at the slightest pressure of her hands, and then Alice was inside the castle.

She didn't know what she might find—knights in shiny white armor that would come running at the sign of an intruder. Or perhaps courtiers made of snow, bejeweled and bevelveted, dancing to music played on instruments carved from ice. The ballroom would be all black and white like a chessboard, of course, and the Queen would sit imperiously at one end of the room, watching the dancers twirl with mad eyes.

At the very least there would be servants, carrying trays of food or feather dusters, servants who would stop and stare in astonishment at the frozen girl emerging from the wall.

But there was nobody and nothing but a blast of warmth that melted all of the frost from her body. She shook all over now as the heat seeped back into her fingers and nose and stomach and legs and down into her bones, and warming up was nearly as painful as the freezing had been. Alice fell to her knees, the short locks of her hair clinging to her head now as the ice melted, water flowing over her face like tears. Her teeth clattered together so violently, she feared she might bite off her own tongue.

After a while she was done shaking and shivering and felt that she could get up. The knife had fallen from her grip during these seizures and she rooted around in the dirt for a while before she found it. Once it was secure in her hand again, she felt she could look about safely, and that thought was another troubling one, that she would not go forward without a blade, like Hatcher and his axe.

There was nothing here that required her vigilance, though, for Alice appeared to be in some kind of cellar. It was like no cellar she had seen before. The cellar at her parents' home had bins of potatoes and turnips (she wrinkled her nose at this memory, as she had never been fond of turnips) and jars of pickled vegetables and strawberry jam and also some nice wine that her father saved for special parties.

This place was completely empty, no shelves or jars or bins, though it had some of the same musty, earthy smells of a root cellar. At the far end was a staircase lit by a series of candles set in the wall. There was no noise at all.

Alice tried to breathe more quietly, so as not to disturb the stillness. She waited, letting her eyes search the shadows, making certain there was nothing lurking in the corners. She hoped very fervently that by stepping farther into the room she would not trigger a falling gate, or signal some monster to emerge from the stairs.

These things seemed absurd until you'd been in a maze with roses that tried to kill you or in a house where you had to drink a shrinking potion to go through a tiny door. When those things had happened, you began to expect the most absurd and horrible outcome to any situation, and Alice would not have been in the least surprised if a dragon slithered down those stairs in a moment and set her on fire.

No dragon appeared, nor any goblin or soldier or queen. Alice slid her boot an inch across the dirt floor, trying not to make a sound, though she thought the shifting of earth beneath her foot clattered like a rockfall on the side of a mountain. No cry went up, no creature appeared, and she slid forward again.

She reached the halfway point of the room slowly, like a snail moseying along in search of a nice green leaf (*and not knowing that a bird was about to swoop down upon it,* Alice thought, still waiting for something bad to happen as it always seemed to). She'd just about decided that her overcaution was unwarranted when she heard something.

Alice tilted her head to one side. The sound was so faint she hadn't even identified what it was. She took a firmer grip on the knife and held it out in front of her, heart racing.

What was it? She turned slowly in a circle, listening, listening. *There. There it was again.*

She strained, trying to locate the source. It seemed to come from inside the wall to her right.

A snarling tiger breaking free, the scared-little-girl part of her thought, but she dismissed that almost immediately. There was no tiger inside that wall, nor a bear or a unicorn or anything else. It was nothing but rough wood planks, sloppily nailed together.

There. Again. A sound that went *thump-thump.*

There was no animal inside there (she was almost sure of this), but something wanted her attention. She pressed her ear against the wood and listened.

Thump-thump.

Alice drew her head back and stared at the place where her ear had been a moment before. A heartbeat. *Was* there something alive in there? Or worse . . . perhaps the castle itself was alive.

She stared around the room, half expecting the wood and dirt to melt into muscle and bone, to contract into a hand that would squeeze her tight until all her blood ran into the floor to feed the castle. But this was not the goblin's illusion room, and the castle was not alive. If it were, the heartbeat would be so much louder, she was sure. It would be so loud it would drown out her own heart, which was beating against her ribs like a butterfly's wings in a glass jar.

Curiosity was a dangerous thing, Alice knew, and this was no time to be curious. Hatcher was waiting for her. The sound was probably a trap, meant to lure Alice into some design the Queen had for her. She should go away; she should ignore it.

Thump-thump.

Curious, Alice thought, *it's almost as if it is calling me, just me, and nobody else would be able to hear it.*

She felt drawn irresistibly to the sound. She would not be able to leave this place without finding its source, without knowing what called to her and made her blood sing so.

There was a place where the boards were loose near the floor. Alice curled her fingers under the board and pulled it up with all her strength. The wood was brittle and old and it cracked immediately, coming away much more easily than she expected.

She fell back on her bottom as several boards (poorly nailed together, as she'd thought) clattered to the floor. Her blood rushed in her ears as she sent a panicked glance toward the stairs, expecting booted feet followed by flashing swords, thinking that noise was surely loud enough to draw the attention of the inhabitants of the castle.

Again, there was nothing; there was nobody. Alice thought this was very odd, but then, it was not her castle, and of course, it was much better not to be taken prisoner. Especially as she had not yet found whatever heart thrummed inside the walls of this cellar, playing its music only for her.

Once the boards were removed, the thumping was much louder, or perhaps it was more insistent now that it felt Alice's approach. She could not see what made the noise, as the wall behind the board was crumbled dark earth like the floor.

She pushed her fingers into the dirt, felt it give way, but there was still no sign of the heartbeat's source. Her hand went farther, until it disappeared up to the wrist.

Curious, she thought again. *I must know what is inside this wall. I don't think I can leave here until I find it.*

Her arm sank deeper, up to her elbow. Worms and spiders and other things fled from her grasping hand and fell out of the wall. They climbed over her hair and face and fell to her boots, and Alice hardly noticed.

The dirt encased her arm up to her shoulder now. And she thought that in a moment the rest of her would follow, that she would seep into the wall and swim through the earth like a mole until she found the thing that she searched for.

Then she touched it.

Her fingers went around it and she felt a surge of triumph. It was warm, so warm, like it ran with blood inside. She knew what it was as soon as her hand closed about it, for she had longed for it once before.

Alice drew it from its hiding place, her arm pulling free of the dirt that encased it and dropping several more small, crawling things to the floor. Those crawling things made a terrific din (or so it seemed to Alice) scurrying away, like a crowded room of people emptying out. Or maybe it was the thrumming of her own heart and the thing in her hand, the two of them twining together and beating in time.

The Red Queen's crown, removed from its hiding place, the gleaming wrought silver and winking red jewel unaffected by the dirt they'd been buried in, shimmering even though there was almost no light in the cellar.

Alice had been certain she'd never see this crown again after she'd turned from it in her dream, and yet here it was again. She recalled Cheshire's voice in that vision urging her to take it then because she needed it, saying it would be harder later.

"But getting it wasn't so very difficult," Alice said, unable to keep the smugness out of her voice as she examined the crown. It was too beautiful for words, and the heat inside the metal seeped into her skin, making her feel as though she were lit from within. "All I had to do was take it from the wall."

There was a very, very, very faraway whisper in reply, irritated and possibly not even really there. *If you had taken it when I said, you could have avoided all that bother with the goblin.*

"Bother?" Alice hissed in reply. "Bother? I was nearly killed."

And you could have avoided it, for the crown is much stronger than any hob of the White Queen's. This was even fainter than the last comment, as if it were too difficult for Cheshire to break through the Queen's barrier, as if he were straining from a very long distance to speak to Alice.

She thought about arguing more, but the idea that Cheshire might be right (and he did usually seem to be) arrested her. Could she have escaped that final encounter with the goblin she so feared if she'd only taken the crown earlier? She did not know, and could never know for certain. Cheshire was always certain, but she thought that was part of his magic.

Perhaps if Alice, too, were certain instead of scared and unsure, maybe she would be a powerful Magician. Or maybe she would still be Alice, because no matter what happened to her or around her, she always seemed to still be Alice; no amount of changing could change who she essentially was, the Alice that she had always been as a curious girl with Dor or mad in the hospital or on the run with Hatcher. Underneath all of it there was some essential Alice-ness.

There was some wisdom in that, she thought as she stared into the jewel set in the crown, the jewel that seemed to want something from her. If only she stayed Alice, if she did not let Cheshire or Hatcher or the White Queen change her, then she would be all right.

As she thought this the warmth in the crown waned a little. It was not a bad feeling—rather, it seemed Alice had done something correct, something that the crown liked.

That the crown liked? she thought, shaking her head. *No, not the crown. The Red Queen. The Queen's magic lives on in this object, and if I take it and use it against the White Queen, then the Red Queen will help me.*

And not, Alice hoped, turn her into somebody who was not herself. She didn't think this Queen would, somehow. It wasn't that the Red Queen's magic was necessarily good and that the

White Queen's was bad. It was that the power that coursed through the crown was softer, perhaps kinder—though no less strong for all of that.

She turned toward the stairs now, those strangely silent stairs with the rows of flickering candles. The knife that had belonged to Brynja's husband was in her right hand and the crown that had belonged to the Red Queen was in her left, and in between there was just scruffy, dirty Alice. She didn't have to be Cheshire's ideal of a Magician or Hatcher's ideal of a lover or her parents' ideal of a daughter. She could be Alice.

And whoooo . . . ?

The whisper was so light and delicate now, hardly there at all.

And whooo . . . are . . . you?

"We shall see, won't we?" Alice said, and climbed the stairs.

She'd expected another long climb, perhaps with twists and turns and perils, but the stairwell was terribly ordinary and bare and comparatively short. At the top of the stair was a little alcove, and from the alcove Alice entered a large kitchen.

There was no fire in the huge brick fireplace, nor any cook stirring soup and shouting orders at those who were to wait at table. There were no stable boys hanging about searching for scraps or bits of cake to steal, nor dogs that weren't supposed to be indoors anyway. There were no harried maids carrying tea trays or valets trying to cozen those maids into a walk before bedtime.

There was nobody and nothing, and Alice should have expected this. When she and Hatcher emerged from the tunnel to the plains, they'd thought there would be green fields and farms and pleasant travelers, and there was nothing. When they entered the village at the end of the forest, there were no people, only the doll's game set there by the White Queen. Even the forest itself had been strangely barren. Alice had not seen a fox or squirrel or deer in all the time she'd spent trudging through that crouching, creeping wood.

The only place that had been real and alive was the village at the foot of the mountain, and it was dying slowly. Everything the White Queen touched was wiped clean and barren and cold.

Where are the children? Alice wondered. And what did the Queen do with them? Would Alice even find any of them alive?

She had to face, for the first time, the possibility that none of them were. The Queen might take the children and kill them as a sacrifice to her magic. Or they might not survive her presence simply because everything around her died. It was only the dream Alice had, the dream of the children's screams echoing through the castle, that made her think they were still alive. But her dream might not be true, after all.

Alice crossed through the kitchen, passing the rusted pans hanging from hooks and the dusty tables where no bread had been rolled out for a long, long time. She passed from the kitchen into another corridor, and thought she knew this time where she was going, for the dining room was usually a short walk from the kitchen. Important people who lived in palaces such as this liked their food to be the temperature it was meant to be—hot food should be hot, and cold food cold.

The dining room was where it ought to be, with a magnificent long table carved of dark heavy wood and matching chairs. The chair seats had velvet covers in bright jewel tones faded by dust and age. The walls were covered in intricately threaded tapestries. Alice glanced over this disinterestedly; then something caught her eye and she stopped, staring.

The first scene showed a girl with long blond hair and a pretty party dress, walking hand in hand with another girl into the mouth of a rabbit hole. The next scene showed the same blond girl, all alone now and covered with blood. Next the girl was in a white room staring through the bars at the moon.

On and on it went, every detail of Alice's adventures with Hatcher and beyond. There she was sitting in the palm of Pen's hand, and climbing the mountain, and killing the goblin. There she was pulling the crown from the wall, and passing through the empty kitchen. She reached the end of the tapestry and her eyes widened.

In the carefully embroidered picture, Alice looked at a tapestry. She could see herself there, tall and thin and dirty, with the crown in one hand and the knife in the other, and behind her there was a shadow deeper than any night she'd ever known.

Alice whirled around, the knife coming up to slash, but the shadow had already moved back and away, and now she could see that it was not a shadow at all. It was a person, a person cloaked in black so pervasive that his face and hands seemed to be made of nothing but the shifting darkness.

"I know you," she said. "You're Brynja's brother. Bjarke."

The darkness shuddered, as if the name Alice spoke hurt him.

"That boy is dead," the shadow said. His voice ground out, as if with a great effort, like he'd forgotten how to speak. "I am called the Black King now."

"No," Alice said with great certainty, and she walked toward him as if she were not afraid. "Your name is Bjarke, and you have a sister named Brynja who loves you despite all you have done."

Despite all you have done. Yes, Alice thought, *I love Hatcher despite all he has done. And when I see him again I will not be a child trailing his coattails. I will be a woman, and I can love him with clear eyes.*

It was a strange time for such a realization, when her life was probably in danger from this boy who called himself a king. She'd had a lot of realizations on this journey, and she was learning to take them when and how they came to her.

The Black King turned his head from Alice, or seemed to, at any rate. It was difficult to tell exactly where the head was, or the shoulders. The size of it seemed to change, to grow and shrink and move even when it was standing still, just like the way a shadow will in the corner when you think something is there but it really isn't.

"The person who was once my sister is a fool if she still loves me, for I do not love her. I love no one," he said.

"I know very well that is not true," Alice said. "You love the one who lives in this castle, and you have burned the plains and killed many innocents, only to make her take note of you."

The shape of him grew again, threatening, tendrils of him seeping around the room like he would close around Alice and pull her into his darkness. But she was not afraid, and she wondered why.

"I can destroy you with a thought," the Black King said. "My power is stronger than anyone's, even hers whose crown you hold."

Alice could not see any eyes inside the shifting mass of darkness. Nonetheless she felt the hungry gaze of the Black King upon the Red Queen's crown, and the way the crown throbbed in warning.

"You can, or say you can," Alice said. She had felt this calm only once before, when she faced the one she'd defeated in the streets of the Old City and put him in a little glass jar. "But if you can defeat me so easily, why have you not already? Why do you hesitate when you are so powerful?"

"I am!" he cried, and his voice was no longer the sound of darkness. It was the cry of a boy, a boy who wanted something and couldn't have it and didn't understand why, because he wanted it so badly, and when you want something so badly, then someone ought to give it to you.

The darkness covered the room now, everywhere except where Alice stood, and it was as though she were a clear prism lit by the sun. He could not touch her.

"No," Alice said. "You are not a Magician. You took something that did not belong to you, all because you felt you should have it. And now it is eating you, eating you inside and you don't know why and it's making you weaker every moment that you try to hold on to it, Bjarke."

"Stop calling me THAT NAME!" he cried, and the room shook, and plaster fell from the ceiling.

"Bjarke," Alice said again, wondering that the Queen did not come running at this display. Could she not feel his presence inside her castle? Hadn't she built barriers around it to keep him out?

The thoughts were idle ones, and did not trouble Alice. If the Queen wanted to suddenly appear, there was nothing Alice could do about it.

"Stop calling me that!" the boy shouted.

"Bjarke," Alice said again, calm and assured.

A thin coil of darkness snaked around the crown in Alice's hand and pulled at it, trying to take it from her. The crown blazed with heat, though Alice did not need the warning. Alice didn't struggle, didn't fight or tug at the crown or try to prove she was in any way stronger than the Black King.

She said, very quietly, "That doesn't belong to you, Bjarke."

He seemed to wither then under the relentless assault of Alice's steady assurance. The shadow shrank back into itself, until it looked almost like a man with a black cloak, a young man with a haggard face and eyes like his sister's, a very pale blue. His body seemed drained of blood, the skin so white it almost glowed, and the bones of his face were sharp against the skin. He might have been a handsome boy once, but now he was a used-up thing, used by the magic that he should never have taken.

"I don't know how," he began, and stopped, for there seemed to be a mighty struggle within him. The muscles of his throat jumped in an odd and distorted way, like there was something alive in there trying to get out.

"I don't know how," he repeated, swallowing several times, "to let it go. I needed it, to get her and keep her."

"The White Queen," Alice said.

"Yes," Bjarke said. "But I couldn't keep her. And then she took away the only thing I wanted in the world, out of spite."

"What did she take?" Alice asked.

The question hung in the still room for a long moment, and then everything shattered.

Bjarke howled, howled the cry of a bear with a thorn buried in his heart, and Alice realized she'd read her vision all wrong. She'd seen the Black King try to take something from the White Queen, and thought that he hadn't loved her as much as the Queen loved him, and that the Queen felt betrayed by this. But it was the other way around. The Queen did not love him as he'd loved her, and when the Queen's cry echoed from the mountain it was a cry of spite and hatred, not the cry of a woman betrayed.

He howled, and the magic that was eating him alive poured from his mouth like a cloud of tiny dark bugs, something terrible and amorphous that must be caught before it found someone else.

Oh, no, you don't, Alice thought, and then her own magic was there easily in a way it had never been before.

A little glass ball surrounded the swarm of bugs and encased them, just as Alice had done with the butterfly. Only this time there was no killing what was inside. It wasn't a Magician but magic that had been set free by Bjarke's actions, and now it was dangerous. Dangerous because it could not be destroyed by the simple expedient of killing the Magician that housed it. It was wild magic now, magic that ate and burned, and all Alice could do was hold it.

And make sure no one else uses it, she thought, as the glass ball grew smaller and smaller until it was the size of a child's marble. She pushed the crown back on her wrist like a bracelet and plucked the marble out of the air and put it in her pocket.

The Black King, now just Bjarke, was nothing but a huddled clump of cloak and bone, his eyes red from weeping.

"I'll never get her back now," he said. "Never, never."

Alice knelt before him. "I do not think you really want her; do you? She has been cruel to you, and to the people of your village."

Bjarke looked at Alice in astonishment, as if she had lost her mind. For a moment she thought she had, for his look was so scathing.

"Her? You think I want the Queen back?" Bjarke said, and then his voice broke. "She took our *daughter*."

"Daughter?" Alice said, and she was certain her face showed her shock. "Yours and the White Queen's?"

Now she understood the scene at the tree in her dream. The Black King and the White Queen had been lovers, and the

White Queen bore a child, and she would not give that child to the King.

"Why did she keep your child?" Alice asked.

"I told you, because she is a spiteful witch," the Black King said. "She saw how much I wanted the child and she was jealous, for nothing can be more important than the White Queen. The stars and the sun and the moon must spin around her and her alone, and nothing can take her place in your heart. She took my child, and then she took Brynja's child, and when it wasn't enough that I was bleeding from my eyes and nose and ears from the pain, she took my cousins' children too. And I could not reach them. I could not break through the barrier she set, for my magic was not strong enough."

"How did you get here now, then?" Alice asked.

"I followed you," he said. "You went through the tree, and you broke something, just a tiny crack. I've no notion of how you managed it, but you did. Your passing made enough space for my magic to seep through, and I think one other as well. I thought I heard a laughing whisper as I traced your footsteps."

"I'm sure you did," Alice said drily. This explained how Cheshire's voice was able to follow her, though it was clearly difficult for him. "But how did you follow me so far without my knowing?"

Bjarke coughed, a wet, sickly cough, and a little blood showed in the hand he used to cover his mouth. "I wasn't directly behind you. It took me some time to widen the crack in the barrier.

And then you disappeared into a room and I couldn't follow, so I found another way through."

"Be glad you could not follow," Alice said. "That room was the lair of the goblin."

Bjarke sniffed dismissively. It was an odd gesture coming from a man who looked like a half-dead corpse. "Him. There was nothing to be afraid of from him. He was all smoke and illusion."

Alice remembered the shelves of heads, lined up neat and smiling on the wall. "No, he wasn't. Though perhaps he was no danger to you, and you felt that. When did the White Queen bear your child?"

"Six months past," Bjarke said. "She showed me only my daughter's face, enough to let me fall in love, and then the Queen hid the girl away in the castle here."

"And you went mad," Alice said, thinking of Brynja's husband beating against the barriers day after day, begging for the White Queen to give back their Eira.

"Not at first," he said. "But then the rage in me grew and grew, as time after time she would meet me and laugh when I said I wanted my girl, my own child. The White Queen didn't want her, only to keep her from me. She doesn't love that baby. The Queen told me I could have my daughter when I could come and take her. And here I am, and these months of madness have spent me. I am finally on my daughter's doorstep, and I am dying."

"Bjarke," Alice asked, remembering something. "Did men from the City come to try and take you? Men on flying machines?"

Bjarke nodded. "Special soldiers, I gathered, on the ministers' mission. They tell everyone in the City that there are no Magicians left, you know. But there are."

"I know," Alice said, thinking of the Rabbit and Cheshire and the Caterpillar and, yes, her mother, the mother who'd taught her to hide her magic deep down where no one could see it. The mother who'd been afraid, once upon a time, that someone would take Alice away. And then someone did take Alice away, and her mother decided she didn't like the daughter she'd gotten back. It was hard, Alice decided, not to be bitter about this.

"They keep the magic for themselves," Bjarke went on as if Alice had not spoken. His voice was dreamy and faraway. "They use it for things that would shock the folk of the New City if they knew. And they hunt down and root out every Magician they can find, every child with potential. They take them and hide them and wring every last drop of magic out of their veins, until they are twisted and broken things to be tossed into the Old City."

Twisted and broken and used by someone else, for if you can't defend yourself, the Old City will gobble you up in an instant, Alice thought

"The ministers aren't afraid of magic. They're afraid of anyone having it but them," Bjarke said.

These things Alice had already suspected. That Cheshire was able to stay in Rose Way with his obviously magical cottage meant that someone knew, and someone approved.

"How do you know all this?" Alice asked.

"I looked inside the mind of one of the men who came to take me away. Then I burned him until he was nothing but ash," Bjarke said.

It did not seem as though this action troubled him at all, that burning people (evil or good) was of very little consequence. Alice did not care if he burned agents of the Ministry, for they did nothing to save the lost folk of the Old City. But she cared about those who'd strayed into the Black King's path, and therefore punished for nothing.

"And the plain too," Alice said, thinking of Pipkin and the lost girls he'd tried to save. "And the village and the giants who lived in it."

"Those giants," Bjarke said, coughing more blood into his hand as he spoke. "They were nothing but the Queen's lapdogs. They ate people who passed through there, the ones that fell into her trap."

Alice considered telling him of the innocents he'd killed in his rage, of how Pen and his brothers had been victims of the White Queen, as Bjarke was. Telling it could not change the past, though, and Bjarke had been more than punished for stolen magic. And there was more to do and no more time to tarry here while the Queen perhaps marshaled her magic against them.

"Are you coming?" Alice asked, standing up and holding out her hand.

Bjarke looked at her outstretched hand, hesitating as though he were afraid it would transform into a biting mouth. After a very long pause he took it. His hand felt as delicate as a moth's wing in

Alice's, the bones of the fingers long and somehow brittle, like she could crush them if only she exerted a little pressure.

"I want to see my daughter," Bjarke said.

"I want to see my Hatcher," Alice said. "Let's find them."

They exited the dining room, found another corridor, passed through several unused sitting rooms and finally found the ballroom. It was almost exactly as Alice had pictured it when she was hallucinating in the tunnel. The floor was made up of alternating black and white tiles, like a chessboard. Tall floor-to-ceiling windows draped in white velvet curtains framed the ocean of ice and snow outside. The only thing missing was the courtiers. As before, as always, there was no sign of life but herself and Bjarke.

At the far end of the ballroom was a grand staircase, just the kind that beautiful ladies in long dresses used to make an entrance at a party. Alice could almost see them there, hair piled high and silk skirts swishing and their hands placed ever so delicately in their escorts'.

There was movement on the stairs, a quick, dark flash that went from the top to the bottom in an instant, and then there was a wolf sitting at the foot of the steps.

A grey-eyed wolf, hackles raised, ready to hunt.

"Hatcher," Alice said.

She felt frozen, unable to believe he was finally before her and not simply another dream or vision or illusion of the Queen's. She had not seen him since he left her in the wood, and then he had been a person, so she supposed that she wasn't really seeing him again, but the thing he'd become under the Queen.

You're getting silly again, Alice. She took one step toward him, thinking only that if she could touch him, say his name as she had said Bjarke's, the spell would be broken and he would be her Hatcher again.

"What are you doing?" Bjarke asked, grabbing at her shoulder. He seemed hardly able to hold himself upright, much less hold Alice back with his waning strength. "If you had any sense you wouldn't walk straight for a wolf that's growling at you."

"That's not a wolf," Alice said, and her voice came from somewhere faraway. "That's Hatcher."

"Who's Hatcher?" Bjarke asked.

His eyes, Hatcher's grey eyes, no longer mad but wild. That wildness had always been there, the desire to run free and unhindered, but Alice hadn't wanted to see it. She wanted him to be with her, to stay with her. She'd thought he wanted that too.

Yet he'd run from her, run at the first opportunity. He'd run to the madwoman who ruled all she surveyed from the top of an ice-covered mountain.

She could hardly see him now, for her vision was blurry with tears. Alice shrugged easily out of Bjarke's grasp, moving toward the wolf who growled, who sat like a coiled spring ready to strike.

Bjarke followed her, grabbing her arms with more determination and strength than she would have suspected.

"For the love of . . . Stop, would you?" Bjarke said. "I don't even know your name, but you saved me, and I'm not going to let you walk into the teeth of a wolf."

"I'm Alice," she said. She couldn't tear her eyes from the animal at the bottom of the stairs. "He's Hatcher."

Bjarke shook her a little. "Whoever he was before, he's not that anymore. He'll tear out your throat if you take another step, and he might do it anyway even if you stay still."

"He won't hurt me," Alice said, but her voice shook.

She wasn't sure anymore. Hatcher wouldn't hurt her, but this was a wolf. In her dream the wolf had walked beside her, let her sink her face into his fur. This wasn't that wolf.

But you must believe, Alice. You must believe that Hatcher is somewhere in there, else you would not have come all this way to get him back.

Bjarke looked doubtfully at the wolf. "I think he will hurt you, and me. I think that we should go back."

"Back where?" Alice asked, her anger flaring. "There is no going back. You burned down the world so you could see your daughter again, and now that you are nearly there you would turn away? There is nothing behind us save dust and empty rooms. Hatcher is protecting something at the top of those stairs. Your daughter, the children from the village, perhaps the Queen herself. I passed through ice and blood and the scorched plains, and before that nightmares I can hardly describe. I will not leave here without Hatcher."

She moved forward, ready for Hatcher to leap at her, for Bjarke to try to pull her back again, ready for anything except what actually happened. Her foot stepped onto a black tile—or, rather, what she thought was a black tile—and she fell through the floor and into the earth. The last thing she saw was Bjarke's white face staring after her in astonishment as she disappeared down a long, twisting hole.

It wasn't at all a comfortable fall. Alice crashed into sides of the hole and scraped her face against tree roots. She tried to use the knife to slow her progress, digging it into the ground, but the slide was too fast and steep for her to make any difference. The Red Queen's crown jangled against her wrist, forgotten until just now. As she fell her sweater twisted up around her waist, leaving her skin exposed to rocks and other sharp things. When she finally crashed at the bottom she felt as though someone had put her in a bag of laundry and then scrubbed her on the washing board.

"I am really quite sick of this," Alice said, standing slowly and painfully.

All of her fresh bruises and cuts screamed as she did so, and she was certain she'd never longed for a bath so much as she did now. The spell that had seized her in the ballroom was broken now, and she could see that she'd been very foolish. Hatcher was not, as Bjarke said, the man she knew before. She would have to find him again, but the way to do that was decidedly not by petting him while he looked as though he was contemplating her value as a meal.

The hole had led her to a room, a round room dug into the earth, and at the far end there was another tunnel.

I have become a rabbit, Alice thought. *I spend all my life tunneling through warrens.*

She automatically crossed to the entrance at the other side, certain there would be more delay and danger, and then she stopped.

"Why should I play her game?" Alice said aloud.

Finally, Cheshire said.

"No, really, why? She wants me to march through this passage so I can experience more horrors, so that the goblin can come back to life or some such nonsense. Well, I won't do it. Do you hear me?" Alice banged one hand on the side of the earthen tunnel. It didn't make very much noise but it was satisfying all the same. "I won't do it."

Very nice, Cheshire said. Alice heard the faint sound of applause. *Now that your performance is concluded, what will you do to get yourself out of this mess?*

"You're one to talk about performance," Alice muttered.

It was all very well to talk about not staying here and not playing the Queen's game, but unfortunately Cheshire was right. Alice needed to find a way out, one that didn't involve the tunnel or attempting to climb up the steep hole she'd just fallen through.

She wondered very briefly whether she might be able to fly or float up, if she only concentrated hard enough. Part of her thought this might be possible, but another part suspected that this was absurd—or, at least, as difficult to do as making food appear out of thin air.

But you made the glass ball appear out of nothing, she thought. So while she might not be able to fly, to make herself float without any visible aid . . .

A vision of the strange flying machines that had passed over the scorched plains appeared in her mind and she dismissed it almost immediately. That machine was far too complex and difficult for her to attempt. But something like it . . . something simple . . .

A noise roared out of the tunnel, a sound like a great monster rampaging toward her. Alice deliberately turned her back to the noise and crouched on the ground, sketching out a little idea of a flying machine with her finger.

The monster roared, whatever it was, and galloped into the room, but still she would not face it, would not make it true by acknowledging it was there.

She was figuring things out now, realizing a truth she should have known all along. So much of what Alice had seen and experienced since entering the Queen's realm was false—illusion, trickery. It was up to Alice not to believe in it, and now she chose not to. She chose not to trudge through the tunnel or fight the monster that dripped hot saliva on the back of her neck. If Alice swiped at the stuff, she would find it wasn't there at all. She couldn't be bothered, though. She was getting some things sorted, and had no time for silly queens and their silly toys.

"It's not even her magic, anyway," Alice said. "She stole it."

She paused, thinking of Bjarke and how the stolen magic inside him had eaten him alive. That must be what the White Queen's magic was doing too—eating her alive, for she was only a vessel for something older and more powerful than she. It was the magic that led to the madness, to the dying kingdom.

"And to the children," Alice breathed. That was it.

That was why the Queen needed the children. She could not possibly hope to hold on to such wild and old magic without it destroying her utterly, as it almost had Bjarke. So she used the children, and their young, strong bodies, to carry the weight of her magic, keep it from sucking her dry.

But how? The Queen still needed to control it, for the children must not be able to wield her own power against her. She also needed some kind of conduit to draw the magic to her when she wanted it, and send it back into the children when she was done.

No wonder the children screamed. The magic did not belong to them but it moved inside them, came and went against their will. If the borrowed magic acted as it had in Bjarke, then it slowly drained them of life.

And that meant, Alice realized with a pang, that Brynja's daughter Eira was most certainly dead. Eira had been one of the first to be taken.

Alice stood, no longer thinking about the flying machine. She noted absently that the monster was gone, having failed in its purpose to frighten her (and also, she thought, having failed to eat her alive, which meant it certainly was not real). But this truly was madness. The Queen was slowly draining the village of its children. Soon there would be none left for her to take, and what would she do then?

Well, Alice supposed, pacing the room and swatting at the figure of the goblin that appeared out of the tunnel as the rampaging monster had a few moments before, *she would look to the City, or someplace like it.*

The goblin fell backward, breaking into wooden doll parts. Alice hardly noticed.

It would be nothing to convince traders to bring her children, especially if she offered them enough money. She could go on indefinitely that way, with a supply of bodies to sustain her.

The Walrus appeared from nowhere, seeming to walk out of the cavern wall, his mouth drenched in the blood of the girls that he devoured. Alice shouldered him aside and he dropped the plate of cakes that he carried. The cake ground into dust beneath her boots.

Surely Cheshire could do something, exert his influence? That would be the least he could do after trailing around Alice and causing trouble and (only sometimes) helping. Even if she could convince him to do so, the City wasn't the only place in the world where children were taken. Hatcher's own daughter had been taken from the City and sent to the harems of the East, and Alice was certain that girls were taken from their homes in the East just as they were in the City. There was a whole wide world of children out there, waiting for someone like the Queen (or the Rabbit, or the Caterpillar) to come and take them away and replace their dreams with tears.

No, Alice must find a way to extract the magic from the Queen as she had with Bjarke, though she did not think it would be quite so easy.

Hatcher was beside her suddenly, his grey eyes wild and his axe in his hand. In the goblin's lair this vision had nearly made her heart stop. Now she sighed. He was just another of the Queen's horrors, the fourth or perhaps fifth by Alice's count.

"Go away," she said. "You're not Hatcher."

And he did, fading like smoke.

The first problem was separating the children from the Queen. Without the vessels her power would be more unstable, and hopefully easier to extract. The Red Queen's crown warmed on Alice's wrist, as if in approval of Alice's plan. Or perhaps to remind her that it was there, and that she would need it in the end.

Alice knew that this was true, had known it almost from the moment she'd taken it from the wall. The White Queen's magic was much older than Alice, and the only one who could truly stop her was her sister. The White Queen—the first White Queen—had killed her sister and buried her so none could find and use that power.

The Red Queen was wiser than the White, even in death, Alice thought. The crown had been upon the Red Queen's head, and when Alice did not take it in the dream, it had followed her, wriggling through the dirt like an earthworm until Alice retrieved it.

If Alice put the Red Queen's crown on her own head, then the Red Queen's power would move through her, the way that this White Queen took the power of the old one. But Alice thought there was something else too—it wasn't just the power of each queen that was in the crowns. There was some of their personality, their spark and their soul, for the Red Queen longed to take vengeance on her sister. And while Alice wanted help from the Red Queen, she did not want to be possessed by her. She did not want to become like the White Queen.

Some semblance of the original White Queen still resided inside the present one, and this must contribute to her madness, for two souls should not mingle inside one body and one mind.

Alice put aside these concerns for the moment. She had to separate the children from the White Queen. Before she could do that she had to get her own self out of this place.

What if she wasn't in the rabbit hole at all? What if this was just another illusion like the monster and the Walrus and the goblin and Hatcher? What if she was actually still in the ballroom, and the black tile wasn't a hole in the floor but just a black tile?

And of course, as she realized this the dirt walls faded around her and the ballroom melted back into view. She had never fallen into a hole at all. This time, though, the veil of glamour (such as it was) over the room had fallen. The room looked much more decrepit, the walls cracked and the glass in the windows broken so that the icy cold blew in from outside.

Alice shivered. Bjarke was gone—possibly searching for his daughter or perhaps lost in his own illusion. Hatcher was gone too. Alice could hear a high, thin sound, a sound that had been disguised by the Queen's magic.

The sound of children screaming.

It was real, Alice was certain. The Queen wouldn't be able to fool Alice any longer now that she had seen through the trickery. Alice climbed the stairs of the ballroom two by two, an energy she didn't know she'd had propelling her upward. At the top of the stairs was a long passageway with several doors. Everything was painted white—the floors and ceiling and doors, even the doorknobs. The screaming filled the air up here, making it difficult to tell where the source was.

Alice opened the first door. There was a cradle in this room and a white blanket inside the cradle, but no baby. She wondered whether this was where the White Queen's child had slept, and if Bjarke had found the baby. He could be stealing away from the castle at this very moment, his child swaddled in his arms. If that was so, Alice sincerely hoped that he had the strength to carry the babe down the mountain, and to keep her safe.

The next room had nothing but a pile of grey rags on the floor, like someone had made them into a nest for sleeping.

In the third room she found the children.

There were seven of them, sitting on the floor with their backs pressed against the wall and their legs straight out in front, like automatons at rest. All had their eyes and mouths open, though the eyes were blind to anything before them. Now that Alice was in the room with them, the screaming was no longer audible. The only sound coming out of their mouths was the long, slow exhalation of their dying breaths.

The children were in various stages of starvation. All looked thin, but the ones who had been there longest appeared nothing more than skeletons with skin draped over them. Their eyes bulged; their hands were nothing but wisps of bone.

Worst of all, Alice could see nothing that obviously kept them in this state. She'd been hoping (rather childishly, she thought now) for an object to break. This always happened in stories. There was a crystal or a jewel or some such thing, and if only the hero would find it, all would be well. She thought when she found the children that there might be something that tied them to the Queen and she would be able to slash it with her knife, or that there would be something made of glass that she could shatter on the ground.

She crawled along the floor in front of the children, shaking them, waving her hand before their eyes. They did not respond, did not notice in the least that she was there.

The crown on Alice's wrist warmed again. Of course. She'd forgotten that she would need the Red Queen. This was the White Queen's magic that Alice must break, after all.

She slid the crown from her wrist and looked at it, at the red jewel that seemed to beckon to her.

"I'll still be Alice," she said, and did not know if she was trying to convince the Red Queen or herself. "No matter what we do together, I will still be Alice, won't I?"

Yes, of course you will, the crown whispered.

Alice hesitated. The Red Queen, of course, had reason to lie, reason to trick Alice, for if the crown was worn again, then the Queen could once more have a body. Strangely, though, Alice felt she believed her. The Red Queen would not try to take away her Alice-ness.

Alice slowly lifted it to her head, lowered it over the shorn boyish locks. For a moment she only felt foolish, and she imagined that she made a ridiculous appearance, with her scarred face and men's clothes. This crown did not belong on someone like Alice.

Then the circlet around her head warmed once more, and soon the heat grew painfully uncomfortable. Alice cried out and fell to the floor, writhing. She reached for the crown, wanting to tear it off, but when she tried to touch it, her fingers burned and it would not be loosed from her head.

Then there was a fire in her blood, a fire that started in her brain and sank through her body, a fire that scorched all the blood and muscle inside her. This fire did not destroy like the fire that had burned the plains. It cleansed, made everything stronger and more whole than it had been before. And it found something, something that Alice hadn't realized was inside her.

Once, long ago, she'd taken her freedom from the Rabbit. She'd taken a knife from him and stabbed out his eye, but she hadn't known that the knife was magical nor that she took the Rabbit's magic when she did it. Some of the magic in the knife had gone into Alice when she used it, and the knife's magic was partly from the Jabberwock (who'd been the knife's first victim, so very long before) and partly from the Rabbit. The knife took some power from each of them, and because Alice had grasped the knife and used it with intent, that power went into her.

This magic—not precisely stolen, but not her own either— had lodged inside her own power like a piece of dust inside an oyster. Instead of turning into a pearl, however, it had grown into an ugly black cancer pulsing at the bottom of her magic, keeping her from reaching her true potential.

The Red Queen's fire torched it out of existence. It was foreign, and there was no room inside Alice for more than her and the Queen.

Suddenly, Alice felt herself swell with magic all through her, magic that tingled in her eyelashes and the tips of her fingers and into her very teeth.

The crown's heat cooled, the fire spent. Alice's lungs seized and she rolled to one side, coughing out black ash. Her mouth and throat were parched from the grit, but her body felt cool and light. She'd carried around quite a load for a long time, it seemed, without ever knowing it.

Alice wiped her mouth with her sleeve and sat up, wishing for a nice, cool glass of water. To her intense surprise, one appeared at her elbow. She drank it down thirstily, looked at the glass and said clearly, "I'd like another, please."

Immediately the glass refilled with water. She resisted the urge to clap like a child. Magic was wonderful, *wonderful*. If only she'd been able to do this in the scorched plains, she could have saved Hatcher and herself a great deal of suffering.

"I'd like an apple, please. A lovely red, juicy, sweet one."

The apple popped onto her lap and this time Alice did laugh out loud. She felt giddy, wondering what she might do with all of this magic now that she had it.

Are you quite finished?

Alice frowned. Cheshire sounded so severe, like he was scolding a naughty child.

"I've never had magic properly before," Alice said, wrinkling her nose. "Can't you let me enjoy it for a moment?"

Not while those children are dying behind you. I, personally, do not care, but I imagine you do, and you will be tiresome if one of them dies while you could have done something about it.

The giggly, giddy feeling washed away in an instant as Alice sobered. She'd forgotten about the children, just for a moment, forgotten where she was and what she was doing and why she was wearing this crown in the first place.

Brynja's knife had fallen while Alice rolled about on the floor. She picked up the knife now, and put down the glass, and placed the apple in her pocket. Then she stood and faced the children again, and this time she knew what to do.

Alice knelt before the first child, a boy of perhaps eight or nine, putting her hands on both of his cheeks. His eyes were very dark and he had dark curly hair, unlike all the other children who were fair and blue-eyed like Brynja and most of the other villagers. This boy was the thinnest of the lot, and when Alice touched his face she was sure his bones would slice through the skin at any moment.

She sent a little of her magic inside the boy, searching for the White Queen the way the magic of the Red Queen's crown had found and destroyed the remnants of the alien magic inside herself. Alice was scared to send too much power inside the boy.

His frail body seemed to be already at the limit of what it could bear.

This magic, though, wasn't hidden like that other power had been inside Alice. It practically waved a flag at Alice and dared her to come for it.

The trick, though, was not to hurt the child. The fire should be cleansing, not killing.

Carefully, Alice touched the White Queen's magic with her own.

To her astonishment, the White Queen's magic recoiled, a living snake afraid of the mongoose. Alice chased after it, through the boy's bone and blood, until she caught it, and set it aflame. It went up like a scrap of paper to a match, gone in seconds.

Far away in the castle there echoed a scream of pain and fury.

The boy closed his eyes and gave a long, long exhalation. Alice thought, *I was too late. He was too weak; the magic was the only thing keeping him alive.*

Then he inhaled suddenly, gasping for air like a drowning man finding the shore. His eyes blinked open again, and he croaked out, "Who are you?"

"I'm Alice," she said, and handed the boy the glass of water. "And who are you?"

"I'm Ake," he said after he'd taken a long draught of water. "Have you come to take us home? Are you a queen?"

Alice touched the crown on the top of her head. "No, I am not. But a queen is helping me."

"Is she a good queen or a bad queen?" Ake said, his eyes suddenly fearful.

"A good queen," Alice said.

She did not add, *At least until she sees her sister again.* Alice had felt the anger in the magic that chased the White Queen from this boy, a suppressed rage that only waited for its proper moment to flower. She hoped that when the time came, the Red Queen would remember that Alice wished to remain Alice, and not only to be a vessel for the Queen.

The magic inside Alice flickered, as if to say, *I remember.*

Alice went down the line of children, slowly breaking each from the White Queen's enchantment. She asked each child its name, hoping against hope that one of them would be Eira, but none of them were. They did not know the fate of the other children taken from the village, but they assumed they had died.

Alice expected the White Queen to storm into the room at any moment, to stop her, but she did not. Everything here was not as she'd expected at all. Was the Queen wasted with the magic, as Bjarke had been, and unable to fight Alice? Was she waiting for Alice to come to her instead? Was she simply too frightened to face the woman who had ignored her illusions? Or was the White Queen hiding from the Red, the sister she had murdered so long ago?

With each one Alice not only freed the child but destroyed some of the White Queen's power, so that when Alice finally faced her she would be weakened.

Weakened, Alice thought, *and wounded, like a bear with a thorn in its paw. And bears are very, very dangerous when they are in pain.*

This thought came not from herself but from the consciousness inside the Red Queen's crown. Alice knew nothing of bears,
having lived her whole life in the City. She remembered seeing a
bear only once, a circus bear that danced when its master whipped
at it. Her nurserymaid—one of many, not the one who'd taken
her to the zoo nor the one who'd taken her to the docks, but some
other one, a silly girl with yellow curls and dimples, who looked
rather like a china doll and was about as useful—had taken her
for an outing somewhere and they'd stopped to see the bear turn
on its hind legs while a boy played a hurdy-gurdy.

The bear had seemed terribly sick and sad to Alice, and she
remembered wishing that it would turn on the man who hit it
so cruelly. Her nurserymaid had grown bored quickly and
tugged Alice away, and a few moments later they'd heard people
in the crowd screaming. Alice looked back over her shoulder as
they turned the corner but could not see anything.

I did that, she thought now. *I made that bear turn on its master. I did it with my wish.*

Wishes were dangerous things in the hands of Magicians,
and that was why her mother had told her to be careful, though
she hadn't bothered to tell Alice she was a Magician. Alice had
only been a little child, and hadn't known what she could do.

The voice of one of the children brought her back to herself.

"What are we going to do now?" the girl asked. She was a
very little one, perhaps five years old, called Alfhild. She
appeared relatively healthy next to some of the children who'd
been there longer, but her face was pinched into a frown that

made her look very grown-up, with all of the worries and troubles of a grown-up.

"Well," Alice said, thinking. She couldn't very well take them all along with her while she went to face the Queen. Hatcher was somewhere about too, and she wasn't going to leave without him.

"What if you stayed here for a little while longer and had a lovely picnic, until you felt stronger, and then we can all go together back to the bottom of the mountain to your parents?" Alice asked, trying to present the idea of staying in this dusty room where they'd been left for months as a wonderful treat.

"And what are you going to do?" Alfhild asked.

Her eyes were so serious it made Alice's heart break. Children should not be so sober.

"I have to find a friend here in the castle," Alice said.

"You can't leave without your friends," Alfhild said.

"That's right," Alice said. "But I don't want to put you in danger while I look for him, and I think you'll all be safer if you stay together here."

"With a picnic," Alfhild said, and glanced around the room doubtfully, as if to say that a picnic was obviously not in the offing.

"Yes." Alice smiled, and some of the giddy pleasure of magic came back to her as she waved her fingers behind her back. She stepped aside, sweeping her arm out like a stage performer. "With a picnic."

Alfhild gasped, and so did the others. It was a very nice picnic, if Alice did say so herself. There was a cold chicken and pickles and eggs and strawberry tarts and slices of thick bread with a slab of golden butter to spread on them. There were several pitchers of lemonade and neat little plates and napkins for all the children, and soon they were all sitting about laughing and eating as though they had not been possessed by the magic of a mad witch only moments before.

Adults, Alice reflected, could learn something from the way children bounced back from horror like little rubber balls. Even Ake already had a pink flush in his face, even if a shadow lingered about the eyes. She hoped—no, she wished, wished with all of the magic in her—that soon he would be home in the arms of his loving mother and father and would never think of this place again. The shadow would pass from his eyes and he would grow up straight and strong, and he would have children of his own and his cheeks and belly would grow round with happiness and love that would endure forever.

This was a powerful wish, and one that she settled on all of the children there. It used up some of her magic for good—she felt that, could feel it leaving her, for happiness and joy are hard things to come by when you have seen the monster in the dark. It was, she thought, worth any loss to her, to give these Lost Ones the thing she had never been able to have herself—peace.

She did not want to break the spell of their joy, so happily were they chattering, so she quietly pulled the door closed and placed a spell upon it that protected them from the White Queen's vengeance. They would stay in that room, eating and laughing and playing, until Alice returned for them.

Now she must find Hatcher, for Alice was certain that every victory weakened the White Queen more. If Alice could break the spell upon Hatcher, especially after killing the goblin and freeing the children, then the White Queen would surely see that she could not win. Alice wore the Red Queen's crown, but more than that—Alice was herself, and she had power of her own. She'd done so much already without the crown.

Remember that, she told herself. *Remember that you have succeeded without the crown, and that when this is over* (she had to believe it would end, and that all would end as happily as it could for her and Hatcher; she had to believe that)*, you won't need the crown any longer.*

Alice opened another door in the passageway, and another and another. There was another stair at the end of the hall, and Alice resigned herself to climbing it. She did not know why she was so certain Hatcher was up instead of down—it was a very large castle, after all, and there were many rooms Alice had not explored—except that she felt drawn there. She'd learned to trust her instincts instead of fighting them. She'd spent so much time in the hospital not trusting her own mind, not believing her own memories. Now her certainty grew with every step— Hatcher was above her, and so was the White Queen.

The stair curved about, and there were little rooms at each

bend. Alice dutifully peered in all of these, finding the usual dusty hangings and abandoned furniture. Had anyone ever lived in this castle with the White Queen? Or had she built this place in hope, hundreds of years ago, expecting a court that never arrived?

It was sad to think of a lonely queen on a lonely throne, looking out over her empty hall. A queen like that might become wild and angry. She might kill her own sister and grow to love cruelty. She might torment a boy with a white deer so she could curse him for her own pleasure. There were so many things she might do, out of loneliness and fear.

But this Queen, the one waiting for Alice at the very top of the castle at the top of the mountain, was not the same as that Queen. Not precisely. It was the same old magic that killed the Red Queen so long ago, but inside a different body.

How had this Queen stolen the magic? Had she drained the blood of the old Queen as Bjarke had done with the man in the woods, taking that blood into her own body and the power along with it? It was a repulsive act, Alice thought, and this Queen had done more than that and worse. After stealing the power for herself, she had stolen children and used them to hide it. Alice should not feel sorry for her, not feel sad for a lonely queen in a tumbledown castle, for this woman was a monster same as any other Alice had encountered.

I have seen, Alice thought, *more than my fair share of monsters. When I was a child I feared the shadows in the corners and the creaking under the bed, and my mother or my nurserymaid would always tell me not to be silly, that there was nothing really there. Of course there was nothing really there, because the monsters were out in the wild world, and nobody told me to watch out for them.*

Alice opened another door, scanned the room with the expectation of nothing and stopped.

There was a bed in the center of the room, a beautiful bed with a carved headboard and hanging draperies made of silk. Curled up in the center of the blue velvet spread, fast asleep, was a wolf.

Alice approached the bed, but the wolf did not stir. It breathed steadily, the thick fur of its back and chest expanding and contracting at a regular rate. This was the first time she'd gotten a close look at Hatcher since he'd changed.

He was exceptionally large for a wolf, or so Alice thought, having never seen a wolf before. She knew they were larger than the dogs that ran in packs in the Old City, and certainly much bigger than the toy-sized dogs that some rich ladies kept in the New City. Hatcher as a wolf seemed to be built still roughly on Hatcher scale; that was, he was larger than most people when he was a person, and Alice thought that translated into a larger wolf also. The fur was black with white peppered throughout, like Hatcher's hair, and the wolf's muzzle was grey like Hatcher's beard.

He looked peaceful, his tail curled around his body, in a way that Hatcher-the-man never looked, or almost never. Alice stopped when her legs hit the side of the bed. The mattress shifted, and the silk hangings shook a little, but the wolf did not wake.

Hatcher.

Her mouth moved, making the shape of his name, but her voice would not come to her, would not make the sound that meant her beloved.

Hatcher.

She reached for him, hands outstretched, and sank them into his fur. He did not move, did not seem to feel her there at all.

An enchanted sleep, Alice thought. *One more task set by the Queen, one more hoop to jump through, one more circle to turn while the hurdy-gurdy plays for the clapping crowd.*

Alice did not want to dance to her tune. Now that she was here, now that Hatcher was so near, all she wanted was to go to sleep. She was so tired. It had been a long time since she'd slept, and her sleep was always so full of dreams that she woke up exhausted instead of rested.

It won't hurt to put my head down, just for a little while.

But she shouldn't be sleeping now. There were things to do, stairs to climb, queens to battle.

So very tired. It's all right to rest, to be near Hatcher for a while, to rest. Queens can be battled another day.

Alice stretched across the bed until she was beside the wolf. She curled her arm around his middle just as she did when she and Hatcher slept, and tucked her legs beside his. The velvet was soft against her cheek and the wolf's body was warm. She breathed the smell of him, forest and earth and wind. Alice knew she was safe.

She closed her eyes, matching her breath to the wolf's, and

soon she was asleep. She slept, and Hatcher slept, and they dreamed together.

He was running, running like he had never run before; four legs were better than two. His nose was full of loam and flower and root, and the little things that scurried before him, little things that did not want to be eaten.

One of them was before him now, a brown rabbit leaping over the dead leaves, but it was no match for him and soon he would have it in his teeth. Saliva dripped from his open jaw, his nails dug into the ground and then he had it.

He clamped down hard on its neck and it kicked its last breath out and the blood was warm on his tongue and in his throat and it made him feel alive, so alive to make this little thing dead. He ripped out its insides and the bones crunched in his mouth and it was too delicious, but soon enough it was gone and he was still hungry, so hungry, he always felt so hungry. But the forest was full of little things, and sometimes big things, big things with antlers that could leap away much faster than a rabbit, but if you were smart and careful you could catch them anyway and oh, then you could feast and feast, so much blood and flesh.

He took off running again, but slower now, sniffing the air for something good to eat. Another little thing scampered away but it was too small to trouble with, one of those chittering little ones that barely made a mouthful. No, he wanted a big one now;

he was thinking about his face buried inside all that muscle and fat and running blood, so he could wallow in it.

Something strange up ahead now, something different, and he slowed. He did not want to meet up with a roaring one, those big ones that stood sometimes on their back legs and sometimes on all fours, and their claws were long and sharp. They would take away your kill if they came, for they were bigger than you and could hurt you, and they wouldn't go away no matter how you barked and growled.

This didn't smell like a roaring one, but it didn't exactly smell like something good to eat either. There was a scent he knew, had encountered before, but he couldn't remember what it was. Something so familiar, and maybe it was good to eat, but he had to be careful, so, so careful. Creeping now, on silent paws, his bloodied mouth closed and the taste of the rabbit lingering on his tongue and the smell in his nose getting stronger as he got closer. Something about that smell lodged deep in his brain, something he knew but couldn't quite recall, something he wanted so much.

Yes, he wanted it. He was trotting faster now, no longer quite so cautious because he wanted it so much, wanted to open it up with his teeth and his claws and crawl inside it and stay safe there forever and forever.

Then it was there, the thing he chased now and in his dreams, but it did not see him. It was stumbling along, so noisy and foolish he could leap upon it now and wrap his teeth around its neck before it even knew he was there.

It was high off the ground and walked on two legs but it was funny, not like the other animals of the wood, for you couldn't see its feet or any of the fur except on its head, and that was yellow and there was hardly any of it at all. All the rest was covered with the skin of others, the skins of plants and animals made to look like something different but he could still tell what they had been before.

Still, for all of that he could smell the smell of it through the dead skins, could smell the heat and the blood, and he wanted it, wanted it, wanted it. He wanted to kill it and eat it and something else too, something he didn't quite understand.

It stopped walking and looked around, and he could see its eyes so frightened of what hid in the woods, things like him, things that wanted to take it for their own. He could see, too, the shadow that followed this silly, noisy thing that smelled so familiar, a shadow that reached for it with long, long fingers.

He felt a growl building deep in his throat at the thing with the long fingers. It was smart; it kept the noisy, silly one from smelling it and hearing it but he could see it following and what it was going to do to that girl.

Girl. Yes. It was a girl; though it didn't look quite like a girl, he knew that it was. The shadow wanted the girl but it couldn't have her because *she belongs to me.*

Belongs to me, belongs to me, belongs to me, and her name is Alice.

Yes, Alice, and that shadow wants her and it can't have her

because she is mine now and always. I ran from her and she is look-
ing for me. I got mixed up for a while with the smells and the blood
and forgot about her, but she is mine and now I will go back to her,
because she is lost in the woods and that shadow will try to take her.
I must make the shadow go away first, the creature with the long
fingers.

He bounded through the wood, silent and swift, so the girl
called Alice would not see him, for he thought that she would
cry if she did and he did not want to see her cry; he wanted to
see her smile. He stopped for a moment, because he couldn't
remember why a smile was nice. It was strange that girls would
show all their teeth, and it was supposed to make you feel warm
instead of scared. He wasn't scared of anything, though, not this
creature in the forest who stalked his Alice nor the lady in white
who'd promised him blood, all the blood he could want if he
only stayed with her. But he couldn't stay with her—his Alice
needed him—and now he stopped again, his mind so confused,
because there was a little girl too, a little girl with grey eyes and
he was looking for her. He wasn't supposed to eat her, though
something about her was mixed up with blood on the floor,
blood all over the cottage and his own voice howling and howling
and howling to the sky. There was something in his hands, something sharp and wickeder than any claw or tooth, something that
bit and sliced and oh, the blood, it was beautiful and it was terrible and it was all around him, but there was something wrong
too because she was gone, not Alice but the other one; they took

her away and the rabbit promised he wouldn't. That was so ridiculous because rabbits couldn't take any person away. There was nothing to a rabbit. They were little scampering things that got eaten up by animals like him, and now he couldn't remember what he was doing again. He was looking for something tasty, something to eat up, something big and delicious not scrawny like that rabbit.

He trotted on, the shadow and the girl no longer there in his mind, only the smell of the earth and the wind and the sound of hooves in the distance, the sound of deer cropping plants, and he was hungry, so hungry.

Alice woke to the sound of the wolf growling, and her body was not curved around his warm one anymore but was flat with the wolf's paws on her chest and his hot breath only an inch from her nose.

She could not see his eyes, Hatcher's grey eyes, and she knew Hatcher was in there somewhere for her dream told her that he had remembered her when he was a wolf, if only for a moment. Then it had gotten confused with Jenny and all the men he'd killed the night his daughter was taken from him, and it was too much for him and so he'd gone back to being a wolf and had forgotten all about Alice again.

"But you're in there," she said softly.

The wolf growled again, snapped at her face in warning, but

it did not bite her. It could have. It could have killed her before she woke, drained her blood without her ever knowing, but instead it held her in place and snapped and growled, almost like it was trying to remember, like her scent was familiar and it didn't know why.

"Hatcher," she said, and put her arms around his ruff.

His claws dug in deep, making her shoulders bleed, the weight of him bearing down on her body and his hackles rising as she touched him.

"Hatcher," she said again.

The crown was quiet and cool, and so was Alice's own magic. This was not something that could be undone by a spell. She couldn't push against the Queen's magic with some trick of her own. She had to make him remember.

"Hatcher. Your name is Hatcher. You are not a wolf but a man."

He snapped again, and this time his teeth grazed her scarred cheek. She felt the blood rise there, and knew that the smell of her blood would make him forget, for Hatcher the man and Hatcher the wolf both dreamed of blood, and she must overcome that, must make him remember the Alice that he loved.

"You are a man," she repeated. "You run on two legs and not four, and at night you sleep beside me. My name is Alice, and for ten long years you loved me through a mouse hole and I . . ."

She hesitated, for it was a strange thing. She had thought it so many times but she had never said it, never said the words out loud. She'd been afraid to, afraid that it would mean something would change between them.

Something *would* change—she knew that now—but it was not a change to fear. She would be a woman, not a girl. She would look him in the eye, Alice to Hatcher, and stand beside him instead of crouching behind.

"I love you, Hatcher. Hatcher, come back to me," she said.

Alice still could not see his eyes for his nose was pressed to hers and he growled, his teeth right there so close to her throat. She wrapped her arms tighter, pulled him closer, dancing right along the edge with death but she wasn't afraid.

She wouldn't cower. She wouldn't be afraid anymore. There were monsters in the night but there were monsters in the day too, and monsters inside people who smiled and showed you all their teeth like they were nice.

There were monsters inside Alice, but they only had power if she gave it to them, and other things had power too, like the laughter of children enjoying a picnic together and like the love she had for this terrible, wonderful, imperfect man, this man who hid inside the body of a wolf because he thought that was where he belonged.

"Come back to me, come back to your Alice," she said, her eyes closed and her arms tight around him. "You are wild and beautiful and deadly but you are not a wolf. You are my Hatcher and I love you."

The nose that pressed against her nose was suddenly warmer, and her eyes flew open and there were Hatcher's grey eyes in front of hers, and his mouth on her mouth, hot and tasting of blood and love.

She wasn't scared anymore, wasn't scared of his need and what he wanted from her, the thing that had scared her more than anything because she only remembered that it hurt before, that he would want her to be a woman, that he would want her the way a husband wants his wife.

But he did not ask that of her now, only kissed her and cried, and she cried too and kissed him back, and he said her name over and over and that he loved her beyond reason and that he was sorry he left her alone in the woods.

She stroked his hair, shaggier than ever, seeing something of the wolf still in his face, lingering in his eyes. Alice wondered if it would always be there now, and she thought it might, and she thought too that he might just wake up some nights and run with the moon on four legs instead of two. And if this happened she wouldn't have to worry, for he would run wild and taste blood but he would return to her in the morning and be her Hatcher again.

"Alice," Hatcher said finally, and rolled away from her, sitting up and staring down with eyes so sad and serious.

She missed the weight and heat of him already, though she knew well enough that they could not stay here in this bower forever, the two of them locked away from the world. There was still a queen at the top of the tower, and the Lost Ones to return home.

"Yes," she said, and sat up, and the crown on her head felt heavy.

She wished very much to give up the weight of it. She did not understand why anyone would choose to take the magic of another. It was a terrible burden to bear, and though the Red Queen's touch was light, Alice could feel her presence just inside her consciousness, a sense of someone who did not belong.

"It's Jenny," Hatcher said.

Alice frowned. This was not what she had expected him to say. She thought he'd ask about the crown, or how Alice had gotten there in the castle, or what they were going to do about the White Queen who had cursed him. Perhaps he'd forgotten everything except their quest, the quest they'd started an age ago, the search to find his long-lost girl.

"What about her?" Alice asked, trying to feel her way cautiously through the tangle of his mind.

She'd been inside there now, knew how it felt to be Hatcher, how everything ran and melded together and then fogged up and cleared again, and how it all moved faster than a lightning bolt. She thought she would be more patient now that she'd felt all that.

"She's the Queen," Hatcher said.

Alice stared. "Jenny? Your daughter, Jenny, is the White Queen?"

Now Alice's brain was the one that fogged up. This didn't make any sense. Hatcher's daughter was far away to the East, past the great desert. She'd been sold to a slave trader and made to work in a harem, and her beauty was so legendary that they called her Sahar and whispers of her had floated all the way back to the City. She was not a mad queen made of ice at the top of a tower on top of a mountain. Hatcher was mistaken. Things had gotten knotted inside his head.

"It can't be," Alice began, intending to tell him all of this.

"It is," Hatcher said. "I know what you're going to say—that I made a mistake, that I got confused. I didn't recognize her, though I should have because her eyes are the same ones I see when I look in a mirror. Her face is not the same as it once was, and I don't mean just that she's older, a woman instead of a child. I mean that something inside her changed and it shows on her face. There's no kindness in her anymore, and she was the sweetest child there ever was."

His heart was breaking. Alice could hear it happening, see it in his face. His Jenny was gone, replaced by some creature he did not recognize.

"Did she know you?" Alice asked. "Is that how you know it's Jenny?"

Hatcher shook his head. "No. She did not know me. How could she? I am not the father who failed her anymore. I'm not Nicholas but Hatcher, and the years have done their job on me too. It wasn't any recognition between us. It was the baby."

"The baby?"

Alice had forgotten about the baby, the daughter of the Black King and the White Queen—or, she supposed, Bjarke and Jenny. Alice drew in a breath, realizing suddenly what it meant.

The child was Hatcher's granddaughter, Brynja's niece. Though she had cared that the child would survive, Alice had not devoted much thought to her. She'd assumed Bjarke would take his daughter and leave. Now the baby loomed large in her mind. Alice could not let Hatcher's granddaughter come to harm, and Bjarke had been half dead when Alice last saw him.

"The child looks just like Jenny did when she was a baby," Hatcher said. "The spitting image of her. As soon as I saw her, even though I was nothing but a wolf, I knew the Queen was Jenny and that child was my kin."

"Where is the baby now?" Alice asked.

"The Queen set me to guard the child from that one who was in the ballroom with you. I was not to let you climb the stairs. But then something happened. You disappeared and the man who was with you, the one who was sick unto death, he did something to me." Hatcher frowned, trying to remember. "He waved his fingers and I felt very tired."

"He must have had a little magic left," Alice murmured, feeling the hard weight of the little glass marble in her pocket. "Just enough."

"He went around me and I couldn't stop him, couldn't even snap at him. I followed him up the stairs but it was like swimming in water. I saw him go into the room with the baby and take her from her cradle. He didn't hurt her. He lifted her so gently and she was sleeping. He rested her head on his shoulder and wrapped his cloak around her and put his lips on her head. I thought it was all right then, though the Queen would not like it much, and I was so tired, too tired to chase after him. He walked past me again, and he didn't even notice that I was there; his eyes were on the girl and they were shining."

"He is her father," Alice said softly.

"Aye. I wasn't as worried as I ought to be that he took her away," Hatcher said. "Then I wandered away until I came to this room and the bed looked like a nice place to rest, so I did."

So it was not an enchanted sleep of the Queen's, Alice thought. It was the remains of Bjarke's last spell, just enough to keep Hatcher from going for his throat when the young man was retrieving his daughter. And it lingered enough to affect Alice too, to make her sleep when she should have woken Hatcher up.

But how would they get off the mountain? Bjarke was barely hanging on to life, and the baby was small and would need food and warmth. Alice thought of the ice and snow outside, the cliff ledges, the dangerous drop-offs. She remembered the passage of ice that branched away from the tunnels that went through the enchanted tree. That way was no safer. Yes, she was anxious now, worried about the baby. She did not know what would happen to Hatcher if the child was harmed.

"I don't know if we can save Jenny," Hatcher said, drawing Alice back to him. His face was full of grief, and Alice thought it might have been better never to find her than to see his face look like that. "I don't know who she is anymore."

"What I cannot understand is how Jenny took the White Queen's magic in the first place," Alice said. "You have some Seeing in your blood, but you are not a Magician. Nor was your wife. The White Queen's magic is strong, and old, for I have felt it. It would take a very strong and canny person to steal the magic from the original Queen. And how did she get here?"

"You stabbed the Rabbit in the eye and escaped from him," Hatcher said. "Perhaps Jenny did the same to whoever held her."

Alice knew that this was possible, but it still amazed her. Yes, she had stabbed the Rabbit in the eye and run away. But she'd run only as far as home. She hadn't escaped a foreign city and crossed a great desert and climbed a mountain after years of trauma. Jenny had a very strong heart, indeed.

But a heart that's been twisted and broken, Alice thought. When Alice and the Red Queen took the magic from Jenny's body, what then? Would there be anything left of the girl Hatcher knew?

"Hatcher," Alice said. "Where is the White Queen?"

He jerked his chin up. "At the very top of the tower, on her throne."

"We must go to her," Alice said. She stood and held out her hand to Hatcher.

He looked at it as he had never looked before—like he was afraid, like her hand might bite.

"She doesn't know who I am, Alice," he said. "And I don't know if I can kill her, or stand by and let you do it, though I know she's done evil. I know about those children."

"I don't want to kill her," Alice said.

This was perfectly true. She didn't want to kill Jenny. She wanted to help the Red Queen destroy the White Queen.

Perhaps when the White Queen was gone, Jenny would look at the face of her father and remember, remember something happy and good, the time they had together in that little house in the Old City.

"What will you do with that crown, then?" Hatcher said. He was a madman, his face seemed to say, but not a fool.

"The White Queen's magic is old and cruel, and the Red Queen's magic can drive it out," Alice said.

"What will be left of Jenny then?" Hatcher asked.

"I don't know."

There hadn't been much left of Bjarke. Just a small amount of the White Queen's power had drained the children, had wasted them away to nothing. How long had Jenny carried the White Queen's magic within her? That, Alice thought, would matter when the magic was taken away.

"We can't delay any longer," Alice said.

She felt a sense of urgency that she hadn't felt before, and knew that it was anxiety about the children that drove her. Alice wanted the children out of the castle, wanted to find Bjarke and the baby and be certain that all was well there.

Most of all she wanted the confrontation to be over, to have this chapter resolved. Alice and Hatcher had done what they'd set out to do. They'd found Jenny, though she was not where they'd expected to find her. They'd found the Lost Ones. They'd found each other again. Alice was ready to rest, to find the place where the past would not trouble her any longer.

They climbed the stairs in silence, Alice leading Hatcher for once. His step was reluctant behind her. She could almost feel how he longed to turn and leave, to not witness an act that might result in his daughter's death.

Alice noticed her knife had gone missing (had she dropped it by the bed?) and she was down to nothing but the crown. Hatcher did not have his axe or his pack. That meant the gun was gone, and all their supplies. It was only Alice and Hatcher and the Red Queen, which was still more than Alice had when she faced the Jabberwocky in the Old City.

And there is more of me now that the Red Queen has burned the remnants of the Rabbit and the Jabberwocky inside me.

They reached the top of the stair. The door was made of cracked wood that might have been polished and beautiful once, but no longer. It was damaged by water and age and had not been cared for in a very long time, like everything else in the castle.

Alice pushed open the door.

She'd expected splendor here, at least, that the White Queen would be magnificently dressed as she sat upon a magnificent throne. There was nothing of that.

The throne might have been painted gold once, but the paint was chipped and cracked, and the carvings on the arms and back were worn and faded. The draperies at the windows were torn from their hangings and sat in dusty heaps on the floor.

The Queen gripped the arms of her chair with brittle white fingers as if her hands were the only thing keeping her upright. The nails of her fingers were yellow and long and curled at the ends. Her back and neck hunched low, as if she could not unbend even if she wanted to, and they could not see her face. White hair as long as a girl's from a fairy tale covered her head and wound around her in knotted clumps. Her dress was not the royal confection of silk and velvet that Alice imagined, but a white rag with openings for the neck and arms that draped over her, covering everything but her feet and ankles. They were strangely pathetic, her bare feet, small and fine boned and wrinkled. Something about bare feet always seemed so vulnerable to Alice, as if the world could hurt you more when you did not have shoes.

Upon her head was a silver crown with a blue jewel set in it, the nearly identical twin of the one Alice wore on her head. The jewel was faded, like everything else in the room, like the White Queen herself.

Everything about her seemed dry and withered and old, and Alice heard Hatcher gasp when he saw her.

"She did not . . ." he said, his voice trailing away.

"She did not look like this when last you saw her," Alice said. "She may have put a glamour upon herself so that you would see an illusion. Or perhaps the breaking of her tie to the children aged her thus."

Alice felt again a twinge of sorrow for this woman and the power inside her that caused so much harm. This was what it had come to, all her hatred and scheming. She was not a threat any longer but a broken thing.

The crown on Alice's head grew warm, and she felt the Red

Queen's sorrow, and also her disappointment. There was not to be a great revenge, then, only the quiet hastening of something already begun.

Hatcher seemed frozen, stunned by the changes wrought in the Queen. Alice approached her, wondering if the White Queen would attempt one last spell. The figure stirred, raised her head very slowly.

The sight of her eyes took Alice's breath away. They were Hatcher's eyes exactly, the precise shade of grey, but there was nothing of Hatcher's personality. There was hate, fierce and unyielding. That hate burned with an energy the Queen's body no longer had. The hate was the only thing keeping her alive.

The White Queen opened her mouth. Her teeth were almost all gone, just a few broken stumps remaining. Her breath exhaled and Alice smelled death.

"Y-y-y-you," the White Queen said. She drew a deep lungful of air, working up to her next words. "I-it w-w-was y-y-your f-fault."

Alice's brows knit together. "What was my fault?"

The Queen gestured to her haggard appearance. She put her tongue between her teeth, closed her eyes and seemed to draw up a great effort of will. "This," she finally spat out.

Alice looked at the Queen, at the tumbledown room. "All this was my fault? You aged like this because of me?"

The Queen struggled to speak, her mouth working soundlessly before she managed to get the words out. "Cracked . . . the . . . barrier. Cracked . . . the . . . magic."

So merely by entering the enchanted tree unbidden, Alice had made all the White Queen's dominoes fall. The magic was that unstable. No wonder there had not been soldiers to attack Alice or more spells to bar her way. There might have been those things before, but Alice had destroyed them. Just by coming here she had destroyed them.

The White Queen caught a glimpse of the crown on Alice's head. Her face split in a gruesome parody of a smile. Alice shuddered inwardly. It was the smile of a dying thing, one without contentment or happiness.

"C-c-come for m-me, then?"

Alice knelt before the White Queen, wished she could see more of Jenny in that twisted face, wished that Hatcher's daughter had not come to this end.

Alice put her hand on the White Queen's hand, and a moment later she was not Alice any longer. The Red Queen came forth—

(only for a moment)

—and Alice felt her strong and true and burning in every part of her body. She burned into the White Queen and there was no need to chase the magic this time. The White Queen's power knelt before the Red Queen's, bent its head in submission.

It was strange for Alice, for she could feel the Red Queen's sorrow and rage as her own. She felt the need to punish her sister, understood the necessity of revenge. But she also felt the hollowness of the victory, that her real sister had been killed long before, and all that remained was the bit of her still in the crown.

All this mingled with Alice's own sorrow, that Hatcher and Jenny's story would come to this end, that there was no joyful reunion, no happy ending.

The Red Queen stood before her sister, the one who had killed her, and flicked her hand.

Alice thought she heard a voice, very far away, almost like an echo of a memory in the far distant past, or maybe something that was only imagined.

Off . . . with . . . her . . . head.

The White Queen's head separated from her body, clean as if Hatcher had swung his axe. It disintegrated into dust almost immediately, as did the rest of her, as if she had only been waiting for this moment to collapse. Soon there was nothing but a pile of rags and ash and a silver crown on top, the blue jewel winking at Alice.

Alice took the red crown from her head, expecting some resistance, but there was none. The Red Queen had done what she set out to do. Alice felt the Queen receding, fading now that the balance of life and death had been righted. She would not stay with Alice. She did not want to go on now that her sister was gone.

Alice placed the red crown beside the blue crown. For some it might have been painful to give up the temptation of so much magic, but for Alice it was not. She didn't want magic that was not her own. She'd seen the price, and she was not willing to pay it.

The ground beneath her feet shifted and Alice stumbled a little before righting herself.

"The tower is going to come down," Hatcher said behind her. His voice was strangely subdued, almost passive.

Alice turned to him. His face was white and waxy, and he stared at the place where Alice had left the two crowns.

"We have to go," Alice said.

She reached for him, then dropped her hand away when he turned his face to her. His eyes were dazed, but just underneath there was something else, something directed at her. Anger.

"I thought you didn't want to kill her," Hatcher said.

"I didn't," Alice said. She felt a thrum of tension, just a little tickle on the back of her neck. His face wasn't quite right, and he'd never looked at her that way before.

She felt the tower vibrating all around them, very subtly. In a few moments it would crack. They had to get out. Not for themselves, but for the children. She couldn't leave the children to perish in this dying castle.

"Then why did you?"

Each word was a blow, but a blow Alice could not feel or acknowledge right now. The castle was on the verge of collapse.

"I didn't," Alice said, inching around Hatcher toward the door. "It was the Red Queen."

"The Red Queen," Hatcher said through his teeth. "You put some crown on your head and now you're the Red Queen, so you're not responsible for what happened to my Jenny."

"Hatcher," Alice said, and her voice was steady and betrayed none of the fear she felt, or the hurt that he would have forgotten her like this. He wasn't thinking right. "We have to leave."

He hadn't moved, not yet, but she recognized the quality of stillness in him. It was the calm before the explosion. She needed to stay out of his reach, not for her own sake but for his. Hatcher was strong. If Hatcher got hold of her, he would try to hurt her.

He wasn't supposed to hurt her. Hatcher would never hurt her. But Hatcher wasn't supposed to miss with his axe, either, and he had in the woods. And he wasn't supposed to turn into a wolf and leave her, and Alice remembered the look on his face just before he darted away, the feeling she'd had then that he might gobble her up.

He wouldn't be able to hurt her, because her magic would protect her. Alice wasn't helpless anymore. But he would regret trying to harm her later, when he came back to himself, and she would regret it if her magic injured him. It wasn't supposed to be this way, and they didn't have time for this. The castle would be on their heads in a moment.

Worst of all, Alice understood why he was angry. He had only just remembered his daughter, had lived with the regret of not saving her so many years ago. Now he'd finally found her again and Alice had killed her—or so he thought.

"Hatcher," she said. She slid behind him. She saw his back now, his hunched shoulders, his hands balled into fists. "The White Queen used Jenny. She had eaten up all that Jenny was. There was nothing left of her."

"So you say," Hatcher said, and turned on her.

His eyes were mad, and Alice ran.

The tower shook in earnest now. Alice sprinted down the stairs, barely touching the steps. Hatcher roared behind her, but she heard him stumbling, barely able to keep his feet as the tower cracked and crumbled.

Please don't let him get hit by a piece of falling masonry, Alice thought. His anger would pass, and he would be Hatcher again. She believed it. She had to believe it. He was not Hatcher right now, not the Hatcher who loved her. He was a mad thing, a wild thing, an animal in the grip of his grief and lashing out at the thing he could see, the thing he thought had caused it—Alice.

In the meantime they all needed to get out of the castle. If Alice had to make him chase her to do so, then so be it. He could chase her, and she would have to run very fast.

(Scurry, little mouse; don't let the cat catch you, run, run, run.)

She reached the bottom of the stairs, ran down the passageway to the place where the children picnicked. When she threw open the door she found them all calmly lined up, waiting for her.

"We're going now?" Ake asked.

"Yes," Alice said. She didn't want to scare the children, as they'd had more than enough to scare them already. She glanced down the passageway, saw Hatcher's shadow approaching the bottom of the tower stairs. "Follow me."

The stairs were crumbling away by the time they reached them, and Alice could see a huge crack in the ballroom beyond. "Hurry, hurry, carefully, now."

She did not look back to see whether Hatcher still followed, or what state he was in if he did. Alice picked up the smallest one, Alfhild, who looked like a little blond fairy and was just as light. The other six children crowded close to Alice, each one with a small hand on her pant leg or sweater hem, as chunks of plaster fell from the ceiling and the ground rumbled beneath them.

There was a great sound above, a screech like a dying monster, and Alice knew the tower was falling away into the chasm below. She did not look left or right or behind, did not see anything except the door at the opposite end of the ballroom. Alfhild tucked her face into Alice's shoulder. Alice made a mental note of all the points of pressure on her clothes, so if one went missing she would know.

They passed through the ballroom and Alice heard the stairs collapsing.

Please, Hatcher, get through. Get through and get out and come back to me.

But she did not look back for him. Hatcher was not her responsibility now. She must take care of the children.

They hurried through the dining room with its great tapestries, and through the kitchen where the pots and pans swung and clattered in a great unmusical din. Finally they were in the cellar, the very earth around them crumbling.

"I remember this place," Ake said in wonder. "There's a tunnel made of ice on the other side of that door."

"Yes," Alice said, panting and sweating from the run. "It will be a lovely slide for you to go down now, won't it? The longest one you've ever been on, I expect."

The children all looked at her as though she'd promised them a day out at the fair. One of the older children ran for the door and threw it open.

The tunnel appeared intact still, though Alice did not know how long that would last. She also wasn't entirely certain where it would empty at the bottom. The goblin's former lair, or somewhere else? Would the enchantment inside the tree hold now that the White Queen was gone?

The children climbed into the tunnel, one after another, whooping and hollering with glee. Alice placed Alfhild down.

"Go on," she said, giving the little girl a gentle push. Alfhild gave her a luminous smile and clambered onto the ice slide.

The castle was making terrible rending noises now, thrashing in its death throes. Alice couldn't look back. They'd spent a few moments in this cellar as the children went down one by one, and Hatcher had not appeared.

Now is not the time to grieve, Alice thought. *You're not safe yet.*

She stepped into the ice tunnel and, feeling a little foolish, sat on her bottom. Straightaway she started to skid along, first slowly and then faster and faster. The walls whipped by in a blur of white, and far below the echoes of childish laughter drifted back to her.

Much sooner than she expected, she crashed into a pile of

giggling children, rolling about like little puppies, poking and tickling one another. They howled with delight as she tried to extricate herself from them, clinging to her arms like baby monkeys and climbing on her chest and stomach and making all of the air whoosh out in a gush.

They were in a little anteroom that hadn't been there earlier. There were three doors in front of them. Alice thought one of them must lead to the goblin's former lair. She had no wish to pass through that place again, though the goblin and all his dolls had fallen away. Besides, the doorway into that cavern was hidden, and Alice didn't think they had time to search for it.

The crumbling castle was impossible to hear down here, though the ground held a faint pulse that made Alice nervous. Magic made these tunnels, and that magic was fading. They needed to be out in the open air before that happened.

"All right, all right, that's enough," Alice said, though her authority was undermined somewhat by the laughter in her voice. One of the children had found a spot near Alice's ribs and was energetically tickling it, making her gasp and giggle and try to pry the child away so she could stand up and make decisions properly.

"No, really, that's enough," Alice repeated, trying and failing to make her face look very sober.

The others had joined in now, little fingers wiggling, and Alice knew they must leave but she did not want to take their joy away, not even for a moment.

"That's enough, she said," a man's voice growled.

They all stilled, twisting around to stare at the intruder. Hatcher stood just a few feet behind them, his head scraping the roof of the ice tunnel.

All the children scampered off Alice, who stood to face him. The little ones huddled behind her, glancing up at her face, unsure what to think of this new person.

"Hatcher," Alice said. She couldn't properly see his eyes. Was he still in the grip of his madness and sorrow?

He moved closer, and Alice backed up a step, the children shuffling behind her. He stopped, and she saw then that there was blood in his hair, and his eyes said he was sorry. His eyes were Hatcher's eyes, a little mad and much sadder than before, and also eyes that loved her.

A great relief washed over her then, because Alice was a little mad and much sadder than before and she loved him. They were two broken things that belonged together to make one whole, and she knew that Hatcher had only forgotten that for a moment.

"It's all right now," Alice said to the children.

Alfhild gave her a doubtful look. "He looks scraggy."

Alice choked on a laugh, and Hatcher smiled in return. "He always looks like that. He's a wolf."

Alfhild looked back at Hatcher and then at Alice, her little face twisted in a frown. "He looks like a man to me."

"But sometimes he's a wolf, and he runs through the wood at night, and when he changes back to a man he looks scraggy," Alice said.

"Because he's been playing in the dirt all night and needs a bath," Alfhild said.

"Just so," Hatcher agreed.

"Can you really change into a wolf at night?" one of the boys asked, staring at Hatcher in fascination.

"If Alice says so, then it must be true," Hatcher said. "Alice is a Magician, you know."

"You never told us you were a Magician," Ake said accusingly.

"Where do you think that picnic came from, then, you nit?" Alfhild asked. "The White Queen never left all that for us."

"Oh. Of course," Ake said, his thin cheeks flushing red.

"Now," Alice said, wanting to distract the boy from his embarrassment. "You said you remembered passing through the cellar and the ice tunnel before, right? Do you remember where to go after that?"

Ake and the other children stared hard at the three doors, obviously hoping that a clue would present itself.

"Why don't we just open them and see what's behind?" Alfhild asked.

Alice shook her head. "There could be an enchantment on them, so you would fall in as soon as you touched the door."

"Can't you tell? You are a Magician, or so the wolf says," Alfhild said.

It was hard not to laugh at her severe little face and the adult words that came out of her pink bow mouth.

"You're right," Alice said, nodding. "I'll try."

She stood before each door in turn, placing her hand on each. Two of them pulsed in warning. One did not.

"This one," Alice said, pointing at the left door.

She grasped the knob and turned it, hoping that her magic had not tricked her, hoping that if it had, Hatcher would get the children away safely.

The door opened and behind it was a passage that appeared to be a very large branch of a tree, hollowed out now. It smelled of fresh sap and wood shavings.

"That's it!" Ake cried, and pushed past Alice before she could tell him to wait.

For a moment she was frozen, expecting something to grab the boy as soon as he entered the passage. But he was fine, and the others ran after him, laughing and shouting and telling Alice and "the wolf" to come along.

Alice ran after them, not wanting to face Hatcher just yet. His anger was gone, but the consequences of Alice's actions—or the Red Queen's—were still there, impossible to undo. Whether it was by Alice's hand or some other's, Jenny was dead and it would take some time for Hatcher to accept that.

And then . . .

She'd never *really* thought about "and then." Yes, she had dreamed of a day when she had no task before her, no nightmares to chase. Somehow she'd never truly expected the day to come. What would become of Alice and Hatcher after they delivered these children to their parents? Would Hatcher want to stay with her now, or would he always see Jenny's body turning to dust whenever he looked at Alice?

She couldn't bear to know the answers now, so she chased the children as they giggled and screamed with delight. She made monster noises and scooped them up and pretended to eat them, all the while dimly aware that they could have been eaten up in truth, eaten from the inside out by a monster who was gone forever now.

The crowns had fallen with the tower. They would sink to the bottom of the chasm in the mountain. The rubble would be buried by ice and snow and no one would ever be able to find them again. Alice was certain, too, that the Red Queen would watch over the White, now that their crowns were together. The Red Queen would make certain that the White Queen did not call to another person, someone vulnerable who would want the strength that magic brought. The White Queen would not use another puppet to bring her magic to life again.

Ahead of Alice one of the girls burst through the door at the end of the tunnel. Sunlight flooded in, blindingly bright, and they all emerged blinking and shading their eyes in the little clearing before the enchanted tree.

Bjarke lay in the shade of a large boulder, his daughter cradled in his arms, his pale eyes wide and staring. The baby was fussing, not completely committed to wailing yet, but making little mews and cries of distress and kicking her feet inside the blanket swaddled around her.

Alice moved toward the child, but quick as a flash Hatcher scooped her up. He murmured in her ear, and the baby stopped making noise, looking up at Hatcher with serious grey eyes. Her hair was dark like his, and she was plump and fine and healthy.

"Do you know what they called her?" Hatcher asked Alice, but he didn't look at her. His eyes were only for the baby.

"Eira," Alice said without hesitation.

"Eira," Hatcher repeated. "Eira, my little angel."

She'd never seen him like this, never seen him so soft and melting around the edges. All the hard, mad Hatcher-ness receded and Eira was the sun that his love encircled.

The children crowded around Hatcher, all of them wanting a glimpse of the baby except Alfhild. She stuck her thumb in her mouth and stared at Bjarke's corpse.

Alice crouched beside her. "Do you know who that is?"

Alfhild nodded, speaking around her thumb. "Brynja's brother. He's dead again."

"Again?"

"My momma told me he was dead and now he's dead again," Alfhild said, as though this made perfect sense and Alice was simply too dense to understand.

Really dead this time, Alice thought. He saw his daughter, saved her from the castle, and then his body gave out.

"And so ends the tale of the White Queen and the Black King," Alice murmured.

"Is that a story?" Alfhild asked. "I like stories."

"You wouldn't like this one," Alice said hastily.

"Do you know any stories?" Alfhild asked. "I haven't heard one for ever so long."

"I do," Alice said, taking the little girl's hand.

She walked toward the edge of the clearing and started down the mountain toward the village. The others followed, Hatcher softly crooning a lullaby to the sleeping baby. She wondered if he would be able to let her go, when the time came.

"I know a story about a girl who falls in love with a great white bear, far away to the north where everything is always covered in ice and snow and there are no green things," Alice said.

"I know about that place!" Alfhild said excitedly. "My momma told me about it. She said it was the place where she came from, where everyone in the village who was old came from."

Alice covered her mouth to hide her smile. She imagined that anyone bigger than Ake seemed very old indeed to Alfhild.

"Well, do you know this story, then? Because I don't want to tell you one that you already know," Alice said.

Alfhild shook her head, eyes wide. "I don't know this one. But even if I did I would like to hear it again, because stories get better the more you tell them."

Is that true? Alice wondered.

Would someone tell the story of Alice and Hatcher one day, and how they defeated the Jabberwocky and the White Queen? Would the story grow sweeter in the telling, and the blood drained away from it, and Alice and Hatcher become heroes? Alice hoped not. That wasn't the story she'd lived. If the story wasn't to be told properly then it shouldn't be told at all.

Alfhild tugged on Alice's hand impatiently. "You were going to tell me a story."

"Yes," Alice said. "Once upon a time there was a girl who lived with her father in a village at the bottom of a mountain. The girl's mother had died and the father spent all his day with his face in a bottle."

"That means he gets drunk," Alfhild said matter-of-factly. "Old Enok in the village is drunk all day, and Momma says it's a disgrace."

"Stop interrupting, Alfhild. I want to hear the story," said one of the older girls.

"It's my story, Dagny. I asked for it," Alfhild snapped back.

They had clustered around Alice as she spoke, though there was hardly enough room for all of them on the narrow path through the rocks. The boys clambered over the boulders so they could stay close enough to hear.

"Nobody's going to hear it if you two don't stop arguing," one of the boys said.

Alfhild stuck her tongue out at him.

"At any rate," Alice said. "This girl was very sad because her mother died and her father drank and everyone in the village said that her family was unlucky, so they stayed away."

"You didn't tell us the girl's name," Alfhild said.

"Alfhild, of course," Alice said.

"I told you it was my story," the little girl said to Dagny.

"One day the girl's father went out and got lost in the snow," Alice said.

"That was a foolish thing to do," Alfhild said. "You have to be very careful in the snow."

"Yes, you do," Alice said.

"Shut *up*, Alfhild," Ake said.

Alice hurried on before another argument began. "The man couldn't find his way home, and just as he was about to give up a great white bear appeared in the blizzard. The man thought the bear was going to eat him but instead the bear spoke. It told him that it would help the man reach home but he had to give the bear something in return. The man said he would give anything at all. Now, this was a very silly thing to say, for you shouldn't say you'll give anything if you don't really mean anything. And of course the bear asked for the man's daughter to marry him."

Alfhild pulled a face. "I wouldn't want to marry a bear."

"I'm going to feed you to a bear if you don't hush," Dagny said.

"Would you want to marry a bear if it was really a prince?" Alice asked.

The girls all gasped in delight. The boys looked as though perhaps it would not be so bad to be a prince so long as you could be a bear as well.

"The prince, of course, was under a curse from a terrible troll-witch," Alice said.

"Like us," Alfhild said solemnly.

None of the children argued this time at the interruption. Their eyes were serious and sad and they all looked at Alice expectantly.

"Yes," Alice said. "Like you. But the witch who cursed you is no more."

"Did you kill her? That is what's supposed to happen to witches in stories."

Alice glanced at Hatcher. He was paying close attention.

"I didn't kill her," Alice said. "Her sister did."

"Who was her sister?" Alfhild asked.

"Another witch, but a good one, and she helped me save you."

Alice's eyes pleaded with Hatcher to understand. His face hardened for a moment, then relaxed. He nodded and looked at the baby in his arms, now sleeping. There had been more at stake than just saving Jenny. Alice hoped that someday he might understand this in his heart and not just his mind.

"Witches can be good?" Alfhild asked. This seemed a total reversal of the world she understood.

"Sometimes," Alice said.

And mad Hatchers can be gentle fathers. The world is not made of things that are black and white but shades of grey, or (thinking of the Red Queen), *shades of blood.*

"I am glad you came for us," Alfhild said. She tugged at Alice's hand, pulled her down so she could drop a kiss on Alice's cheek. "And you too, wolf man."

The children giggled when Hatcher pulled a snarling wolf face.

"Now tell the rest of the story," Alfhild ordered, and Alice obeyed.

None of the children interrupted while Alice finished the tale that had been told to her long ago by the young sailor on the docks. And when Alice finished, they all clapped and cheered when the girl had saved her prince from the troll's curse.

"Is that what you did to him?" Alfhild asked, pointing at Hatcher. "Saved him from a curse and turned him back into a man?"

"Yes," Hatcher said. "She did."

The village was still quite a distance away, but none of the children wanted to sleep overnight on the mountain. Alice magicked another picnic for them. Everyone ate hungrily and took turns cooing over the baby Eira, who woke and cried until Alice made a bottle for her. Hatcher wouldn't let anyone else hold her, though, nor feed her. Alice shushed the disappointed children and told them to let it be. She knew that Hatcher was going to have to give the baby up soon.

They walked all the day and into the night, and Alice carried each of the children in turn as they stumbled. None wished to stop, though, no matter how tired they were. They wanted to go home, and Alice could not blame them. She wanted to go home too, wherever that was.

Alice the Traveler, she thought. There were many miles to go still for her and Hatcher—if he would stay with her. She hoped he would. She was almost certain he would.

The moon rose, casting strange shadows on the landscape. None of them had any notion of just how far away the village was, especially in the dark. Alice longed suddenly for Pen. The giant could have scooped them all up and carried them home in just a few strides.

Alice and Hatcher and the children crested a rise and saw

below the burning candles in all the windows of the village, like stars leading them back to where they belonged.

The children whooped and hollered and ran and tumbled down the hill. Alfhild, who slept in Alice's arms, woke and wriggled away and chased the others.

Alice felt a momentary sense of loss, for she had shepherded the children from the castle, but they were not her children after all. They did not belong to her.

Hatcher came to her side, the baby resting her head on his shoulder. Her face was peaceful in the moonlight, her little mouth curled in a smile as she slept.

"I know where to take her," Alice said.

His hand tightened for a moment on Eira's back. Then it relaxed.

"I suppose I'm not the sort of person who could care for a baby," Hatcher said.

"I think you are very much the sort of person who could care for a baby," Alice said softly. "But there is another who needs her more. And you and I have no home for Eira."

Hatcher nodded. "It was what my mother did for me. She brought me to Bess, who tried to do her best by me. I never let her do her best, though. Wildness was in my blood."

"I think Eira will be happy here with Brynja," Alice said, thinking of the little slippers at the foot of the bed. "And Brynja will be happy with her. She needs happiness."

"Who is she, then? The boy's mother?" Hatcher asked.

Alice was confused for a moment. "You mean Bjarke. No, she is his sister. Her daughter was one of the first children taken by the White Queen, and her daughter is not coming home tonight."

She and Hatcher followed the children down the hill and into the village, where many were now awake and crying with joy at the return of their Lost Ones. Others stared into the darkness in hope and grief, looking for the ones who would stay lost forever.

Alice and Hatcher skirted the crowd, staying in the shadows, and Alice used a little magic to keep the village folk from noticing them. She saw Alfhild excitedly telling a woman who must be her mother about the Magician and the wolf who'd saved them from the White Queen. Some of the village elders peered out into the darkness, searching for Alice.

She did not wish to be thanked, nor did she wish to be questioned, and if they wandered into the thick of the crowd they would be both. Alice led Hatcher to Brynja's cottage. The woman stood in the door, her face paralyzed by fear, watching the crowd at the other end of the village. She wanted to see, Alice knew, if her Eira was there but was terrified to discover she wasn't.

Alice removed the little cloak of magic and Brynja started. Her face fell when she saw Alice and Hatcher there and her eyes welled.

"She's gone, isn't she?" Brynja swiped at the tears with an impatient hand.

Alice nodded, and then she turned to Hatcher. "Say good-bye now."

He bent his lips to Eira's ear, and whispered something there. Then he kissed her round little cheek and passed her to Alice. He did not come closer to Brynja's cottage, but turned away toward the wood as soon as the baby was out of his arms.

Alice carried the child to Brynja, who took the baby automatically.

"Who is she?" Brynja asked, her grief softening as she stroked the baby's face.

"Her name is Eira," Alice said. "And she is Bjarke's daughter."

Brynja's eyes came up and searched Alice's. Whatever she wanted to know, she saw there, for she nodded and said, "Thank you for bringing her to me. Who is the man?"

They both looked toward Hatcher, a silhouette of darker shadow against the night.

"He is her grandfather," Alice said. "Someday a wolf might come to your door, a grey-eyed wolf with a black-and-white pelt. Do not fear it if it comes, or if Eira seems to know it."

"I understand," Brynja said.

Alice thought she did. "One thing more—"

"The child was conceived in magic," Brynja said. "So I shouldn't be surprised by anything that might happen around her."

Alice smiled. "Yes, that is so."

Brynja reached for Alice and pulled her close with her free arm. The other woman smelled of wool and the cooking fire and milk, smelled like home like a mother ought. Brynja kissed both of Alice's cheeks and then let her go.

Alice turned away before Brynja closed the cottage door. She heard the other woman cooing to Eira, singing a song in a language Alice did not understand.

Hatcher had gone into the field already. Alice saw him there, standing with his face turned toward the moonlight and his hands brushing against the tall grass.

Where now? she thought. Not back to the City, nor over the mountain to the desert. Not into the forest, though it might be safe now that the Queen was gone.

There is a place, Cheshire said.

Ah, I'd wondered where you'd gone, Alice said.

I can't chase after you all the time, Cheshire said. *I am a very important man, after all, and there are things afoot in the City.*

Alice knew he wanted her to ask about those things, wanted her to be curious, so that perhaps she might go back to see. But Alice never wanted to see the City again, and she had finally learned that curiosity wasn't always a virtue.

Oh, very well, I thought you would be that way about it. There is a place to the north, though not as far north as the land of the ice bears. If you follow the range of mountains you will come to some foothills, and beyond there is a green valley.

Alice closed her eyes, for she could see it already. A green valley and a field of wildflowers, and a little white cottage by a blue lake. Someone was calling her, telling her to stop daydreaming, that it was time for tea, and she was turning and smiling at the man who waved to her from the doorway, a black-haired babe in his arms.

She opened her eyes, and a wolf stood at her feet, his grey eyes gleaming.

"North," she said. "I'll see you at sunrise."

Hatcher ran into the night, and Alice followed. She could already feel the sun on her face.

Ready to find
your next great read?

Let us help.

Visit prh.com/nextread

Penguin
Random
House